P9-CCZ-557

Robert B. Parker's
SOMEONE TO
WATCH OVER ME

ACE ATKINS

G. P. PUTNAM'S SONS
New York

PUTNAM
— EST. 1838 —

G. P. PUTNAM'S SONS
Publishers Since 1838
An imprint of Penguin Random House LLC
penguinrandomhouse.com

Library of Congress Cataloging-in-Publication Data

Names: Atkins, Ace, author.
Title: Robert B. Parker's someone to watch over me / Ace Atkins.
Other titles: Someone to watch over me
Description: New York : G. P. Putnam's Sons, 2020. | Series: The Spenser novels
Identifiers: LCCN 2020042102 (print) | LCCN 2020042103 (ebook) |
ISBN 9780525536857 (hardcover) | ISBN 9780525536871 (epub)
Subjects: GSAFD: Mystery fiction. | Suspense fiction.
Classification: LCC PS3551.T49 R65 2020 (print) | LCC PS3551.T49 (ebook) |
DDC 813/.54—dc23
LC record available at https://lccn.loc.gov/2020042102
LC ebook record available at https://lccn.loc.gov/2020042103
p.   cm.

Printed in the United States of America
1   3   5   7   9   10   8   6   4   2

BOOK DESIGN BY KATY RIEGEL

For Mel Farman:

Keeper of Bob's memory and Spenser's spirit.

A true friend.

Spenser's BOSTON

to Susan's home and office,
Linnaean Street, Cambridge

Charles River Dam Bridge

Charles River

CHARLES STREET

ESPLANADE

Massachusetts
General Hospital

Longfellow Bridge

CAMBRIDGE STREET

ESPLANADE

STORROW DRIVE

State House

to State Police,
Boston Post Road

BEACON HILL
■ The Paramount

■ Hatch Shell

BEACON STREET

Boston Common

to Fenway Park

CHARLES STREET

The Taj Boston
(formerly the Ritz-Carlton)

Public Garden

MARLBOROUGH STREET

BERKELEY STREET

ARLINGTON STREET

■ Swan Boats

Four Seasons Hotel
and Bristol Lounge

COMMONWEALTH AVENUE

Jacob Wirth ■

BOYLSTON STREET

■ Spenser's office

Boston
Public Library

Copley
Square

Davio's

Old Boston Police
Headquarters

STUART STREET

■ Grill 23

TREMONT STREET

to Boston Police Headquarters,
Roxbury

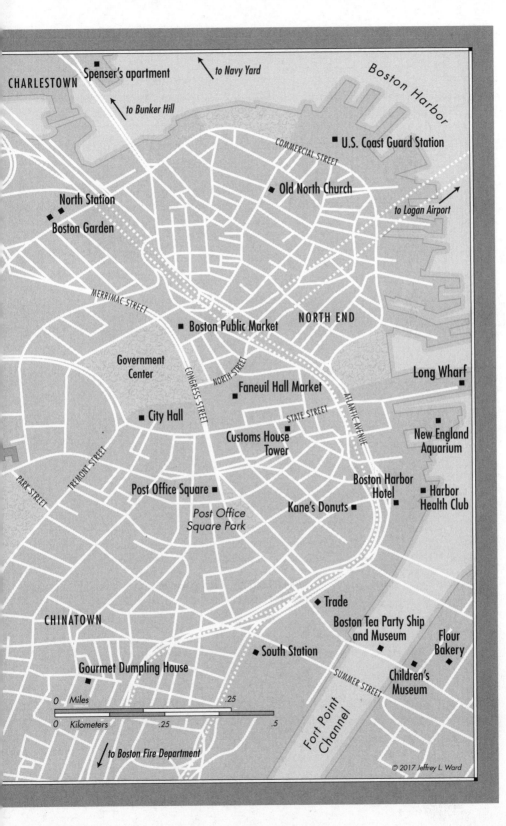

Robert B. Parker's
SOMEONE TO WATCH OVER ME

1

IT WAS EARLY evening and early summer, and my bay window was cracked open above Berkeley Street. I had a half-eaten turkey sub on my desk and the sports page from *The Globe* splayed out underneath. Dan Shaughnessy proclaimed Mookie Betts to be overrated. I'm sure many said the same thing about me. But I was pretty sure being overrated was better than being underrated. A mistake few made twice.

I contemplated Mookie's situation as I heard a knock on the anteroom door.

"Second door on your left," I said.

Mattie Sullivan entered my office.

"Still having trouble with the advertising firm?"

"Bad advertising to list their own address wrong."

"Freakin' morons," Mattie said.

Like me, Mattie suffered few fools. And as my occasional secretary, part-time assistant, and sleuthing apprentice, she didn't take kindly to the two-person agency that had rooms down the hall. Mattie leaned into the doorframe. She'd grown into a tall girl with long limbs, long red hair, and a heart-shaped Irish face full of freckles. When she smiled, she could light up a room. But Mattie rarely smiled and wasn't smiling now.

"You need anything else today?" she said.

"Nope."

"I paid the rent, deposited the checks, and talked to the painters about next week."

"What happens next week?"

"They paint," Mattie said. "This place hadn't had a touch-up since 1982."

"What do you know about 1982?"

"That's the year my mother was born."

"Ouch."

"Yeah," Mattie said. "Truth hurts, big guy."

Mattie hung in the doorway, green eyes lingering on me as I turned the page of the newspaper. I still bought a physical copy at the newsstand around the corner. I was old-fashioned that way. In fact, Susan reminded me I was old-fashioned in most ways, from my music to my movie choices. But who doesn't enjoy a little Django Reinhardt before their *Thin Man* triple feature?

"Something on your mind?" I said.

"I don't know."

I looked up from where I'd spread out the newspaper and reached for my coffee mug. Taking a sip, I realized it had grown cold. Mattie, having noted my expression, walked forward, plucked the mug from my hand, and dumped out the cold contents into the sink. She refilled the mug from the Mr. Coffee atop my file cabinet, slid it before me, and took a seat in one of my clients' chairs.

"Sugar?"

"Nope."

"So there's this girl."

"Okay."

"She's a friend, but not a great friend," she said. "Just the younger sister of a girl I know. She was a Gatey girl, too."

"Gatey girl?"

"Gates of Heaven church in Southie," Mattie said. "Christ. Keep up, Spenser."

I nodded and took a sip of coffee. Mattie demanded a keen mind and reflexes firing on all cylinders.

"So this girl, her name is Chloe Turner by the way, not that it matters to the story, but there you are," Mattie said, leaning forward from the chair. "Chloe comes to me because of the stuff I used to do in the neighborhood. You know, running favors for friends. Asking questions to the right people. Finding shit."

"Sleuthing."

"I call it finding shit out," Mattie said. "But sure. *Sleuthing.* Chloe wanted me to sleuth for her."

"And what does she wish you to sleuth?"

"Chloe lost her backpack and her laptop at some fancy-schmancy club off the Common," she said. "And she wants it back."

"Sounds simple," I said. "Why does she need to enlist your services?"

"Because they wouldn't let her back in," Mattie said. "They threatened to call the cops if she didn't leave. And Chloe had everything on that laptop, not to mention some personal shit in the bag."

"Personal shit is hard to come by."

"And so I went to the club and got the whole 'fuck off' thing from some guy working the door," Mattie said. "Not only did they say they'd never heard of Chloe Turner, they told me that if I, or anyone connected to her, came back, they'd call the cops. How do you like that?"

"Not at all," I said. "What club?"

"Place called the Blackstone Club," Mattie said. "Down toward Chinatown in some crummy brick building. No sign. Just a big door and a buzzer. What kind of freakin' club doesn't have a sign?"

"One that wishes to be elite and confidential," I said, starting to stand. "Shall we?"

"Sit down, Spenser," Mattie said. "You know the rules. When you need help, you ask. When I need help, I ask."

"So what do you need?"

"Advice."

"I am an open book of knowledge."

Mattie nodded. I nodded. I took a sip of coffee. It tasted much better hot, but I still missed the cream and sugar. Small steps.

"Here's what happened," Mattie said. "Chloe doesn't want to cause any trouble and, more than anything, doesn't want to go to the cops. Her mother would go bullshit if she knew what Chloe'd been up to."

I leaned back from the desk. Outside, down on the street, I could hear the whine of an industrial drill and planks of wood tossed against the pavement. A car without a muffler passed and headed out of earshot. A symphony of the Back Bay.

"Chloe knows a girl who knows a girl who promised her an easy five hundred bucks."

"To meet a man at the club?"

"And give him a massage," Mattie said. "Chloe says she was promised that was all there was to it."

"Had she ever met him?"

"Nope."

"Did she have any expertise as a massage therapist?"

"Christ, no," Mattie said. "She's just a kid."

"How old?"

Mattie tossed her head to the side and leveled her eyes at me. "Fifteen."

I felt the hair raise up my neck. My stomach turned a bit.

"I know," Mattie said. "But part of what I promise is confidentiality."

"This sounds like a felony."

"Hold on," Mattie said. "Only gets worse."

I listened.

"Chloe says when she first got there, a woman met her at the club and gave her an envelope stuffed with cash," Mattie said. "The woman told her the guy was some big-time executive hotshot. She didn't need to speak unless spoken to, had to wear this special outfit, pay attention to his feet."

"His feet."

"All creeps are into feet," Mattie said. "Anyway, she goes in there, the room all dim with scented candles and all that. And there's the man, laying on his back with a sheet covering the lower half of his body. Chloe says she was so nervous her hands were shaking. She starts to rub the man's feet like she'd been told. The man makes some small talk with her. *What's your name? What music do you like? Do you have a boyfriend?* All that kind of stuff. She said he was nice. And not bad-looking for an old dude. She said he was polite until things got weird."

"Massaging a grown man's feet is the definition of weird."

"Chloe said she thought the whole thing was legit until at one point the man raised up, threw off the sheet, and started going to town on himself."

I felt my face flush. I wasn't comfortable talking about such matters with Mattie. I remembered when she was fourteen, coming to see me with a collection of crumpled bills in the hope of finding her mother's killer. She was tough as old boots but would always be a lost little girl to me.

"Chloe said she just froze up," Mattie said. "She couldn't scream. She couldn't talk. She couldn't move. She just stood there as the man got finished with his business."

"Ick," I said.

"Yep," Mattie said. "That's when she bolted from the room and the club and left her clothes, her laptop inside that backpack. She doesn't want any trouble. She doesn't want to see that man again. All she wants is her stuff."

"Okay," I said. "Let me help."

"Advice," Mattie said. "I only want advice."

"I'd much rather assist."

"Maybe I shouldn't have told you."

"You made the right move."

"You want to beat the hell out of this guy," she said. "Don't you?"

"Chloe should file a complaint with the police."

"She can't."

"Why?"

"Because she took the money," Mattie said. "Don't you see?"

"That doesn't make what happened right."

"What would you do?"

I leaned back in my office chair and kicked my Nikes up onto the side of the desk. I began to mentally run through the collection of creeps I've known over the years. My go-to action would have been physical or public humiliation. Perhaps tacking his manhood to the tallest tree in the Common.

"Does Chloe know this man's name?"

"No."

"Does she know anything about him?"

"Nothing," she said. "I already asked."

"If it were me, I'd go back to this club and tell them they can either turn over the backpack or else you'll tell your story on Channel 7. Say you have Hank Phillippi Ryan on speed dial."

"But I don't."

"But I do," I said.

"And she'd show up with cameras?"

"In a heartbeat."

"Okay," Mattie said.

"I want you to have Chloe talk to someone in sex crimes," I said. "I'll call Quirk and arrange it."

"She won't," Mattie said. "But I'll try."

Mattie let herself out, the anteroom door closing with a light click. I reached for my coffee and turned to stare out the window. I spent a lot of time staring out windows.

Perhaps if I stared long enough, a sign would appear somewhere in the clouds. I peered into the sky, but there were no clouds today. So many creeps. So little time.

I turned back to my desk. Besides the sub and the newspaper, it was bare. I hadn't had a decent case since returning from Los Angeles earlier that year. Maybe it might be time for me to dig into my 401k, if only I had a 401k.

I picked up the phone and dialed Quirk.

"That sounds like one sick fuck," Quirk said.

"Kid's fifteen."

"Jesus Christ," Quirk said. "I got two granddaughters that age. What's the vic's name again?"

"I'll need to clear it with Mattie."

"Mattie Sullivan?" Quirk said. "She's a kid, too."

"Not anymore," I said. "She's twenty-two."

"She still wants to be like you?"

"Yep."

"God help her."

2

"THAT'S SEXUAL BATTERY," Susan said.

"Along with a multitude of other charges."

"Did he touch her?"

"Mattie says he didn't," I said.

"But he exposed himself?"

"Yes," I said. "Seeking solo gratification."

"Ick," Susan said.

"My sentiments exactly."

Inside my Navy Yard apartment, I continued to spoon the calamari salad I'd just picked up from Red's onto an antique china plate. A collection of scallops as large as fists waited nearby in a mix of white wine and lemon juice. I'd premade a mixed green salad with fresh tomatoes and local peppers from the Public Market. A bottle of sauvignon blanc had been opened and sat chilled in an ice bucket for Susan. I nursed a Johnnie Walker Blue in a tall glass with lots of ice.

"But Mattie doesn't want her friend Chloe to talk to the cops?"

"Mattie agrees she should talk to the cops," I said. "First the laptop. And then the creep."

"And one does not change Mattie Sullivan's mind."

"One does not," I said. "Would you like more wine?"

"I've barely started this glass."

Outside the floor-to-ceiling plate-glass window, the sun painted the shipyard, the Zakim Bridge, and downtown Boston in a lovely gold glow. The ship masts ticktocked in a slight summer wind. I refilled my glass with more ice and more Johnnie Walker. *Ellington at Newport* spun on the turntable.

As I shifted to a second plate, I dropped some squid onto the hardwood floor. A gangly creature with tall legs and droopy brown ears rushed into the kitchen to assist with the mess. The creature lapped up the squid and turned its brown eyes up to me for more, head tilted in a cheap ploy for sympathy.

I tossed down a bit more.

"You're training her to know you're a sucker," Susan said.

"Pearl has always known my weakness."

"And you still believe this Pearl and our Pearl are one and the same?"

I nodded, pouring out some olive oil into a hot copper skillet.

"Makes as much sense as anything," Susan said.

"True."

"And this system of yours, knowing when she'll be born and where to find her, is secret."

"Known only to me and Hawk."

"And what does Hawk think?"

"Hawk believes all white people are crazy."

"Hawk may have a point."

Puppy Pearl scampered away, only to return a moment later with a rope toy larger than she is, and dropped it at Susan's feet. Susan picked it up and tossed it across my apartment. The apartment was four times the size of my old place on Marlborough, and it took some time for Puppy Pearl to return. Old Pearl had passed away back in March, and the weeks after had in many ways been unbearable. Losing Pearl Two had been even tougher than losing the first.

"How about I just call her Puppy for now?" Susan said.

"Not ready for her to assume the throne yet?"

"Not yet," she said. "Give me time."

I sipped my scotch. Duke debated a tulip, a turnip, rosebud, rhubarb, fillet, or plain beef stew. The warm light across the hardwood floors and brick walls made for a pleasant early evening. I picked up the scallops and set them into a hot pan. The sizzling sound only added to the pleasantness.

"Do you know anything more about this man?"

"Mattie told me her client said he was middle-aged, handsome, and supposedly fabulously wealthy."

"No name?"

"No name."

"Did Mattie call this girl her client?"

"Not that exact word," I said. "But she believes the young woman is her client."

"Does that worry you?"

"Why would it worry me?"

"The life you lead is very interesting and very satisfying for you," Susan said. "But it doesn't come easy or without many risks and sacrifices."

"But if I hadn't been in this line of work, how else would've I met a hot Jewish shrink with incredible sexual appetites?"

"Right now, my appetites are focused on those scallops."

"But later?"

"Dessert," she said. "What do you have for dessert?"

"Where is Susan Silverman, and what have you done with her?"

Susan stared at me with a devilish little grin. I felt my heart swell in my chest and a smile creep onto my lips.

"You will help Mattie," Susan said.

"Of course."

"Even if she doesn't want help."

"Do you really have any doubts?"

I flipped the scallops, the edges turning a lovely brown color in the butter and olive oil. We were nearly ready to sit down. Pearl rambled up to my feet and looked up panting, long tongue lolling out of her little mouth as all Pearls had done before.

"Family trait," I said.

"I wonder if she'll be able to stalk squirrels in the Public Garden," she said. "Maybe track a lone french fry or candy wrapper."

"Of course," I said, reaching down to rub her long, droopy ears. "She was born to it."

3

TWO DAYS LATER, Mattie called.

I'd just finished working out at the Harbor Health Club, taken a steam and a shower, and had emerged onto Atlantic Avenue as fresh as a dozen daisies. The cell phone rang in my pocket as I opened the door to my well-worn Land Cruiser.

"I think I'm being followed," Mattie said.

"Where are you?"

"The Common," Mattie said. "Walking toward the office."

"How many?"

"Two," she said. "Late twenties. Early thirties. White dudes. One's got on a Pats cap, and the other is bald."

"Shouldn't the bald guy be wearing a cap?"

"I don't know," she said. "I'll ask 'em when they get closer."

"Have they threatened you?"

"They got out of a car over on Tremont and followed me over to the Frog Pond."

"Where are you now?"

"About to cross Charles and into the Public Garden."

"I'll be waiting at the George Washington statue," I said. "Ten minutes. Mingle with the crowd."

"I'm not scared," Mattie said. "Take your time."

"You think these guys are connected to your sleuthing?"

"I think these two fucknuts wanted to harass me after I left the Blackstone Club."

"Did you get the backpack?"

"Nope," she said. "Didn't get past the first room. A guy with a gun and a blue blazer escorted me onto the street. And then I noticed these two creeps when I passed the T station."

I drove as fast as the traffic allowed over to Park Street and then hugged the Common along Beacon, the copper dome of the State House shining with its usual early-morning luster. I parked in a loading zone by the Bull & Finch and walked across the street and into the Public Garden.

I waited in the shadow of George Washington, watching the crowds swell into a river over the Lagoon Bridge. Soon I caught sight of Mattie walking in my direction with great purpose. She had on her satin Sox pitcher jacket over a T-shirt with jeans and sneakers. Her long red hair was flying loose behind her as she spotted me.

I stood there, more still than Washington, wearing my Braves cap and Ray-Bans. I looked beyond Mattie, watching two men jostling through the crowd, half walking, half jogging, and coming up behind her. One had on a white cap with what looked to be a Pats symbol. I couldn't really tell at this distance. But the other's head was bald and shone brighter than the State House dome.

Mattie continued to walk toward me, milling in with the

crowd, taking pictures of the bridge, the swimming ducks, and tulips poking up from the manicured grounds. When she got within five yards, I motioned toward Arlington Street with my head. She winked back and continued in the same steady gait.

The men weren't far behind, walking past me, and the one in the hat elbowed the bald guy as Mattie exited through the iron gates. I turned and began to follow.

By the time I got to Arlington, Mattie was already across the street at the Old Ritz and then moving toward Marlborough where I used to live. Unfortunately, some years ago, an arsonist had decided to burn me out of my building, gutting the place and much of the two buildings on each side.

It was an unusually cool morning for June, and I wished I'd grabbed my windbreaker from my car. I watched as Mattie turned down Marlborough, Mutt and Jeff trailing, picking up the pace out of the Garden, not seeming to care if they were spotted.

My .38 dug into my hip as I began a slow jog.

As I turned the corner, the men had stopped Mattie in front of my old building. Her back pressed against the wrought-iron fence.

"How about you two go fuck yourselves," Mattie said.

"What language," I said. "If I were wearing pearls, I'd be clutching them."

"Get lost, old man," said the guy in the Pats cap.

I snatched the Pats cap off his head and tossed it into the middle of Marlborough Street. A speeding car soon appeared, smashing the hat into a pancake.

"Asshole," the bald guy said. He shoved Mattie's shoulder

and turned his attention to me. "This ain't none of your goddamn business."

"Double negative?" I said. "And you two coming from the
Blackstone Club?"

The men exchanged glances, for the first time register-
ing the distinctive height and size advantage I had on both
of them.

"Amateurs," Mattie said. "Fucking amateurs."

They were both white, pale, and pockmarked. The Pats
fan had narrow black eyes, big floppy ears, and a little scruff
of a goatee. His pal had a sloped face, like a shovel, with
wide-set eyes and the thinnest trace of a beard. They smelled
like cigarettes and BO.

"Listen, Shaggy," I said. "I'll give you two Scooby Snacks
if you guys tell me why you're following this young lady."

"None of your fucking business," he said. "Now get lost if
you don't want to go and get yourself shot."

The man opened his jacket to show an automatic tucked
into his jeans. I reached out, snatched the gun, and slapped
the man across the face.

"What the hell?" he said.

I looked to his buddy. "You have a gun, too?"

"No," he said, backing away. "I don't."

I slipped the gun into my right front pocket, opened the
bald guy's jacket, and patted him down. He was telling the
truth. Mattie eyed both of them and shook her head. "Christ,"
she said. "What a shitshow."

"Who sent you?" I said.

"Guy from the club," Shaggy said.

"Why?"

"They wanted to scare the girl," Baldy said.

I looked to Mattie. "You scared?"

"Fucking frightened," Mattie said. "My knees won't quit knocking."

"You work at the club?" I said.

They shook their heads.

"Know anything about a man who likes to get massages from kids?"

"No," the bald guy said. "That's sick."

" 'Tis."

"Why'd they want you to scare this young lady?"

They both shrugged, looking convincingly stupid and ignorant of the situation.

"My brother knows Luther who works the door for that place," Baldy said. "Sometimes they get trouble with someone getting drunk and smart. People pound on that door, piss all over that back alley. You know. We rough 'em up and get paid. That's it. That's all. I don't know jack about this girl. Okay? Can we go? Can I please have my gun back?"

"Don't tell the club what happened here."

Both men shook their heads.

"Tell them you chased this girl through the Public Garden and lost her."

They nodded. I pulled out the man's gun, a cheap little .32-cal, and ejected the magazine. I thumbed out the bullets and handed it back.

"We don't want no trouble," Shaggy said.

"Follow this girl again . . ." I said.

"And I'll kick your fucking teeth in," Mattie said.

The bald guy started to answer. But I pursed my mouth

and shook my head. He shut up and turned back toward Arlington. We watched the two men go and disappear around the corner.

"Morons," Mattie said again, shaking her head. "You really think they'll keep quiet?"

"Nope."

"How are we gonna get that backpack?"

"Let me make some calls," I said. "And perhaps change my clothes."

"You going back there?"

I shrugged. "Okay by you, boss?"

Mattie thought about it for a moment. She then nodded back and said, "Sure. Okay. But don't expect a big cut of the reward."

"Wouldn't dream of it."

4

"MR. SPENSER, WE are delighted to have you at the Blackstone Club," T. W. Shaw said, sweeping his hand into a wood-paneled lounge the size of an airplane hangar with lots of dark brown leather furniture and floor-to-ceiling shelves stuffed with old books. "You were highly recommended by two of our top members."

"I got a smoking jacket for Christmas," I said. "And no place to wear it."

A thin smile crossed his lips "Well, we do have a large smoking room with a walk-in humidor. Two saunas, a dining room, and an exercise facility."

"And the club is men only?"

"But of course."

"No women at all?"

"Except for staff," he said. "We are quite old-fashioned in our membership."

"Mother will be so pleased," I said.

Shaw looked perplexed for a moment before placing his right hand against an onyx side table that looked as if it might weigh as much as a mastodon. He was a smallish round guy with slick black hair and a thin mustache. The hair and mustache were as dark as shoe polish. His suit was navy single-breasted with a baby-blue bow tie. Few men could carry off a bow tie. Shaw wasn't one of them.

"And what is the annual membership?" I said.

He told me.

I let out a low whistle.

Shaw gave me a look as if whistling was unseemly. He then smiled at me for a moment. If he tried any harder to put a twinkle into his eye, the bow tie might start to unravel.

"Would you like to sit down?" he said. "Perhaps have an early cocktail?"

"I always like a cocktail," I said. "But perhaps you're the one who should sit down."

"Excuse me?"

"Sit down, T.W.," I said. "I want to talk to you about two lackeys you sent to pester a young woman who stopped by earlier today."

His face and the tips of his ears turned a variety of different colors. He licked his lips and pulled the hankie out from his breast pocket.

"Please don't tell me you're getting the vapors," I said.

"Who are you?"

"Two of your top members already told you."

"But you don't wish to join the club."

I shook my head. T.W. sat, forearms across his fat little thighs and hands clasped together. He looked like a child who had just been caught placing thumbtacks on his teacher's chair.

"Last week, a young woman came here under the auspices of giving a man a massage," I said. "She was paid five hundred dollars. But while she was massaging the man's feet, he stood up and performed a string rendition of 'Camp Town Ladies' on himself."

"Not here," he said. "Not at the Blackstone Club. This is an elite club, sir. For more than a century, this club has offered refuge to Boston's finest gentlemen."

"How long has the club existed?"

"Since 1883."

"Perhaps some men of lesser character have oozed through the cracks."

Shaw looked up, smoothing down his slick little mustache with his thumb and forefinger. "Are you asking me for money?" he said. "Would that make you go away?"

"Nope," I said. "I'm asking you for the girl's belongings and the name of the man who brought her here."

"Our membership is closely guarded and highly confidential."

"That's not what I asked."

"I will make inquiries into this allegation."

"It's not an allegation," I said. "You already know that. Something very bad and very icky happened here. And you're the one cleaning up the mess."

Shaw again wet his lips. His eyes wandered above my shoulder as a young black man in a waiter's uniform entered and asked what we would be drinking today. Shaw let out a long breath and flailed his hand for the waiter to go away.

"Mr. Shaw would like a double bourbon," I said. "No chaser."

"And you, sir?"

I shook my head, and he went away, silently, from the library. Shaw lifted his eyes toward me and swallowed. "Anyone who would bring a child here under those circumstances would have their membership immediately revoked."

"Of course, T.W."

Shaw swallowed, and we waited in silence. I gave a reassuring smile to T.W. He did not smile back.

The waiter returned with a short whiskey on a silver tray. It was served neat, a cocktail napkin under the crystal glass. As T.W. reached for it, I noted a slight tremble in his hand.

"The backpack contained a computer," I said. "And the girl's personal belongings."

"I will get to the bottom of it, Mr. Spenser," he said. "You have my word."

"Immediately."

He sipped at the whiskey, holding it in his hand as he tried to steady his breathing and compose his thoughts.

"I understand this man had a woman set up this massage," I said.

"We have no women here," he said. "Except for serving staff. That's against the rules."

"And what about letting in fifteen-year-old girls to massage men's feet?"

"Well, um."

"Happy to hear it." I stood up. I looked around the library at all the books, the framed oil portraits of past elite members. Many ascots and mustaches. The air smelled of tobacco, leather, and money.

"I expect to hear from you bright and early."

"Excuse me?"

"You have until ten a.m. tomorrow," I said. "And then we will alert the local media."

I laid down my business card. Simple and elegant on heavy stock with only my name, profession, address, and phone number. No need to show him the one with the skull and crossbones.

I would never be that gauche. Not at the Blackstone Club.

"Surely you don't think I can conduct an internal investigation in a day?" he said, looking down at his gold watch.

"I look forward to hearing from you."

Shaw lifted the drink and took another long sip.

5

"THERE'S A FASTER way through this shit," Hawk said.

"Do tell."

"We snatch up that man who chased Mattie off and toss him into the trunk," Hawk said. "What's his name again?"

"T.W.," I said. "T. W. Shaw."

"We take T.W. for a little joyride," Hawk said. "When we get back, I guarantee we get the laptop and the sicko who wanted his toes sucked."

"It was a foot massage," I said. "Let's not take it too far."

It was early at the Harbor Health Club, the waterfront and harbor covered in darkness and shadows. Rain fell over the moored cabin cruisers and sailboats, the ferry running from the Boston Harbor Hotel to the airport. Hawk shook his head and started back into the heavy bag. He worked out a quick delivery of body blows and head shots that sent the bag jumping up into the air and jangling from the chains.

Two young women in black yoga pants and tight white tops with spaghetti straps over shapely shoulders stopped to watch Hawk. Hawk added a bit of flair to the round, and they stayed until he'd finished. He wore a white sweatshirt with the sleeves cut off, his upper arms larger than most grown men's legs.

"Some sick puppies out there," Hawk said, wiping down his bald head.

"We've met many of them."

"Man need to be taught a lesson," Hawk said. "You don't mess with kids."

"Agreed."

"But Mattie won't let you?" Hawk said.

"Mattie says I'm there only to assist," I said. "And told me not to fuck it up."

"Damn," Hawk said. "Now she knows how I feel."

"But if the club doesn't deliver the goods," I said. "I'll do as I say."

"You always deliver, babe," Hawk said. He held out his mitt, and I met him with mine. "Many black folks members at the Blackstone Club?"

"Besides the help?" I said.

"Boston," Hawk said.

We headed out of the boxing room Henry kept for us, the last sliver of the old gym he used to operate before going upscale. I walked over to an incline bench and added a couple plates to warm up. I cranked out a fast five and Hawk followed and then we began to slowly increase the weight on the next four sets. By the last set, we'd topped three-fifty.

"Not bad for a couple of old dudes," Hawk said.

"Speak for yourself," I said. "We're not in the AARP yet."

"I don't get older," Hawk said. "I youthen."

"You and Merlin," I said. I began to hum the first few chords of *Camelot*.

We continued over to the lat pulldown machine, and I watched as Hawk ran the key down to the lowest plate. He slid beneath the bar and cranked out twelve reps, slow and easy, holding the weight against his neck each time for a long count of three. He had complete control and mastery of the equipment. No wasted movement.

Henry Cimoli wandered out from his office, watched us train for a moment, and then shook his head in disappointment.

"That all you got to say, Henry?" Hawk said.

Henry tossed his hand up over his shoulder and walked back to his office.

"He loves us," I said.

"'Course he do."

I nodded and used my teeth to start unwrapping the tape from my knuckles. The front of my gray T-shirt was soaked.

"How's Pearl?" Hawk said.

"Susan will only call her Puppy."

"She'll come around."

"I'm still working on the house-training," I said. "She's pretty much only at my place. Susan claims the sounds of a yipping puppy might distract her patients."

"That and puppies leave little presents around your house."

"Lots of presents," I said. "We're working on crate training. And her sit and stay commands."

"I like that little dog."

"She fell asleep on your lap the whole drive back from New York."

"How you feel if this Pearl prefers me to you?"

"Never will happen."

"Don't be so sure," Hawk said.

We walked back to the locker room to shower and dress. I was headed to the office. Hawk was off to wherever Hawk goes.

Outside, he'd parked his silver Jaguar beside my Land Cruiser. Before he drove off, he looked at me from over the car. The rain beading down off his slick bald head.

"Man needs to be taught lesson," he said.

"Won't exactly be a paying gig."

"This is for Mattie?" he said. "Right?"

I nodded.

"Then whatever she decides, count me in."

6

AT FIVE MINUTES until ten, just as I finished *Arlo & Janis*,
Mattie opened my office door and held it wide. A man in a
black suit with a red tie entered the room. He was a smaller,
fit-looking guy with lots of black hair, a prominent nose, and
a toothy grin. He looked to me, stuck out his hand, and said,
"You must be Spense."

He had the face and manner of someone selling jewelry
on late-night television. I disliked him immediately.

I closed the pages of my morning paper, folded my arms,
and leaned back in my office chair. The rain fell pleasantly
outside, making tapping sounds against my bay window. The
man had a small black backpack slung across his shoulder.
When I didn't respond, he retracted his hand, set the backpack on the floor, and took a seat without being asked.

"My name is Greebel."

"You look like a Greebel," I said.

"What does that mean?"

"Do you have an appointment, Mr. Greebel?"

"I'm in the employ of a certain party who's asked me to
deliver a particular item."

"Sorry," I said. "Could you be any more circumspect?"

He motioned to the backpack. Mattie leaned against the doorframe.

"There you go," he said. "And there is an envelope inside to make up for a truly unfortunate misunderstanding."

"There was no misunderstanding," Mattie said. "A man whipped it out in front of a freakin' kid."

Greebel continue to smile. His teeth were so big and white that I wondered if they were capped. So I asked.

"No," Greebel said, the smile fading and his lips covering the chompers. "They're my own teeth."

"You must be the rock star at the dentist's office," I said.

Mattie pushed herself off the doorframe and walked toward my desk. She took a seat at the edge.

"A most generous gift," Greebel said. "Along with the return of the lost item."

"The backpack wasn't lost," Mattie said. "My client ran off. She was scared shitless."

"I don't know anything about that," he said. "But I hope this will all remain confidential. If you have any further questions, please contact my law firm."

"Were you sent by the Blackstone Club?" I said.

He shook his head.

"T. W. Shaw?"

He shook his head again.

"Jimmy Hoffa?" I said.

Mattie shook her head. "This guy wouldn't say shit if his mouth was full of it."

Greebel started to grin again, wearing a bemused expression while standing up. "Are we through here?"

"Perhaps your client, whoever that might be, might have started off by returning the bag to its rightful owner rather than playing a game of keep-away," I said.

"I apologize if there was any misunderstanding."

"The Blackstone Club, of which your client is a member, sent two men to follow my assistant here," I said. "One of whom was carrying a gun."

"I have no knowledge of that."

"No big deal," Mattie said. "They were fucking idiots."

"Amateurs," I said.

"I really have no idea what you're talking about," Greebel said.

"So your client isn't the Blackstone Club or T. W. Shaw?"

"Or the fucking Easter Bunny," Mattie said.

"My client will remain nameless," Greebel said, turning on a heel. "And I hope your client is pleased by the generous gift."

"And what if they're not?" Mattie said.

Greebel smiled even bigger. You could play "Sweet Rosie O'Grady" on those teeth. The lawyer held out his hands, showing his palms, and nodded at the backpack before leaving the room.

He left the door open, and we soon heard the hallway door open and close.

"What a freakin' douche," Mattie said.

"But a conscientious flosser."

Mattie scooted off the desk and reached for the bag. She unzipped it, removed the laptop and what looked like a small makeup bag. She continued to pull out notepads and packs of pens until she found the envelope. It was white and sealed and looked to be bulging at the seams. Mattie slit it with a fingernail and began to shuffle through a wad of cash.

"How much?" I said.

"Thousand bucks."

"Are you satisfied with the offer?" I said.

Mattie held my gaze. And then slowly shook her head.

"Nope," she said. "No fucking way."

7

LATER THAT AFTERNOON, Mattie and I met Chloe Turner at Joe Moakley Park on a green park bench overlooking Carson Beach. The rain had stopped and the sun returned, but most of the park and beach remained empty. Puppy Pearl romped and played across the wet grass while I sat down on a concrete retaining wall.

Pearl had taken to Chloe immediately, lapping her face with a thousand kisses, causing her to relax her shoulders and take in deep breaths.

"Thank you," Chloe said, sifting through her backpack. "But I don't want the money. I don't want to have anything to do with that man. I agreed to five hundred to show up. But this makes me feel dirty. I don't like it."

"Who told you about meeting this guy?" Mattie said. "About making money from massages?"

"This girl at school," Chloe said. "Can we not talk about it? I'll split the five hundred with you like I promised. But I don't want any more trouble. If my mom found out. Christ. She'd kick me out of the house."

I smiled at Chloe. She was a cute girl who looked much

younger than fifteen. She was as gangly as Pearl, with a chubby little girl's face. Lots of baby fat and wide-set innocent eyes under blond bangs and shoulder-length hair. She had on khaki shorts and a blue-and-white boatneck shirt like French sailors used to wear.

"What this man did was a crime," I said. "He should be arrested and go to jail."

"Taking the T to the Common to go to some fancy men's club," Chloe said, shaking her head. "What the hell was I thinking? I got what I deserved. He probably thought I was a whore."

"Don't talk like that," I said. "That's what he wants you to feel like. People like that feed on power and making others feel weak and useless."

"Can't we just let it go?" Chloe said. "Please."

Pearl had taken to running figure-eight patterns, bits of clipped grass across her brown flank. She seemed possessed of a demon or an adrenaline shot, looping and looping until she ran back to us and flopped on her back. Her small pink tongue lolled from her mouth. Pearl made Chloe smile as she wiped her eyes with the back of her hand.

"I don't want to quit," Mattie said. "I'm not good at it. Who's the girl?"

"Come on, Mattie."

"If you don't speak up," Mattie said, "he's gonna do it again to someone else. Some other kid. Only this time, that girl might not get away."

Chloe looked to me. I nodded.

"I can't pay you," Chloe said.

"What if we take this man's money as a down payment,"

Mattie said, sounding much more entrepreneurial than me. I wouldn't have asked for the money. But I wasn't Mattie. And this wasn't my case.

Chloe shrugged and reached down and pulled Pearl up into her arms. Pearl lapped at her face, kissing her nose and cheek. The tear stains disappeared instantly.

She looked to me. And then back to Mattie. She let out a long breath.

"Debbie Delgado."

Mattie nodded.

"You know her?" Chloe said.

"I know Sandy Delgado," Mattie said. "She was in my class."

"Debbie is Sandy's little sister," Chloe said. "She's a senior. I don't know her, really. She came up to me at a basketball game and said I was cute. Wondered if I thought about being a model."

"And how'd that get to a massage?" I said.

"She said this woman she knows is tied in with big people in New York," Chloe said. "Said this woman discovered some top models from Boston. And that she's always on the lookout for fresh faces."

"This was the woman you met?"

"Yeah," Chloe said. "Debbie said this woman wanted me to start networking. She didn't say, but I figured this was the guy who ran the agency or had something to do in that business."

"*Foot Fetish Weekly*?" I said.

Mattie shot me a very Mattie look. I remained quiet.

Pearl looked content, lying on her back like an infant, in Chloe's arms. She looked at me with sad brown eyes, letting me know her heart still belonged to me.

"What's her name?" Chloe said.

"Pearl."

"You just get her?"

"I've had her since I was a kid," I said.

Chloe looked to Mattie. Mattie shrugged.

"Don't ask," Mattie said.

Chloe set Pearl back onto the sidewalk, and the adrenaline shot kicked in again, Pearl running figure eights until she plopped down again with exhaustion. Her rib cage rising and falling with exertion.

"Does Debbie know what happened?" Mattie said.

"Yes," Chloe said, biting her lower lip. "She called me right after and said I'd embarrassed her. She said I screwed up."

"Wow," I said.

"Did she know about the backpack?" Mattie said.

"No."

"Did you tell her about what the man did?"

"No."

I crossed my legs at the ankles and leaned forward in a half-hearted stretch. Hawk and I had performed many walking lunges that morning, and it felt good to hang there for a moment.

"Can you ask her to meet you?" Mattie said.

"No."

"Can you ask her to meet us?" I said.

"I don't want to get in trouble," she said. "I just want all this to go away. When I think about that man and what he was doing, I want to throw up. I got a boyfriend. I didn't even tell him. He'd probably think I was a whore, too."

"Please don't say that," I said.

Chloe nodded.

"Can you tell Debbie you know another girl who's interested?" Mattie said.

I looked to Mattie and shook my head. Mattie, being Mattie, ignored me. I reached for Pearl and slipped the harness around her skinny brown body. She rewarded me with more kisses and a healthy dose of puppy breath.

"I know she's got a summer job at an ice-cream shop at the bottom of Pru Center. That's where we first talked about giving massages and how much it would pay. I tried to get on at the food court but they weren't hiring."

"Tell her you're sorry you got nervous, but you have a friend who's ready to make some fast money," Mattie said. "And tell her I'm seventeen."

"I don't know, Mattie," Chloe said. "What if she recognizes you?"

"It won't matter," Mattie said.

Chloe placed her hands on her hips and stared out onto the beach, where some kids had started a pickup game of volleyball. They laughed and played, someone setting up a large speaker beside some beach towels. Endless summer.

"Okay," Chloe said, nodding. "But watch yourself, Mattie Sullivan. Something about this man. I don't know. He was friendly at first. But something in him changed. He had a look, watching me as he took the towel off. I don't know. It was weird. Like an animal. It looked as if he wanted to hurt me. Hurt me real bad."

"No one's hurting you," I said. "Ever."

Chloe looked to me and then back to Mattie. "This guy really do all those things you said?"

"Leaping tall buildings in a single bound?" I said. "Out-racing locomotives?"

Mattie shrugged. "Yep," she said. "I don't want to say too much. It always goes to his head."

8

TWO DAYS LATER, I knocked off work and walked around the corner to join Wayne Cosgrove for a quick drink at Davio's. Wayne was late as usual, so I started early with a tall Allagash White. I'd yet to break the foamy head when Mattie sauntered in and took a seat beside me at the bar.

"Startin' a little early," she said.

I eyed the beer, then looked over to Mattie. "Thank God," I said. "You caught me just in time. I was about to chug this entire pint."

"You could at least wait until five. Or until you got home to let Pearl out."

"Pearl's with Susan," I said. "I'm on my own tonight."

"Good," she said. "We need to talk."

"I'm present in both mind and spirit."

"Busy?"

"As a beaver."

"You don't look busy."

I took a long sip of cold beer. "I spent half the day checking out our new pal, Greebel," I said.

"And?"

"He's a creep, too."

"And?"

"And I found no mention of a specialty in working with foot-massage enthusiasts."

"What about the other half of your day?"

I shrugged. "Background work on some cops for a defense case for Rita Fiore."

"Checking out the cops?"

"Some cops," I said, "are like Belson and Quirk."

"And others."

"Others," I said, "not so much."

"I think that Rita Fiore has the hots for you."

"Shocking," I said, doing a subtle Sean Connery. "Positively shocking."

I drained a little bit more of the beer, the foamy head soon gone. Little bubbles rose up and broke the surface as the bartender placed a bowl of mixed nuts on the bar. I decided I might never leave.

"I found Debbie Delgado," she said. "I waited all day until she came on at that ice-cream shop at Pru Center. I went up, ordered a strawberry cone, and basically shot the shit with her until some customers came up. I told her when she got a break, I wanted to talk with her about maybe hooking me up with her rich friends."

It was early evening at Davio's, and much of the dining room was empty. The large U-shaped bar had just started to fill up with the office crowd. Lots of men in loose ties speaking with women in sleeveless silk tops. I liked being among the office crowd after work. Their exasperated faces made me recall why I did what I did.

The bartender returned. Mattie ordered a Coke without ice. The bartender left, and I nodded at her excellent selection.

Mattie picked up a cocktail napkin and began to play with the edges. She had on jeans and her Sox windbreaker, hair pulled into a ponytail and her face scrubbed of any makeup. She looked as wholesome as Rebecca of Sunnybrook Farm.

The bartender set down the Coke and walked away.

"I waited around for like an hour, and finally Debbie comes out and sits with me in the food court," Mattie said. "I tell her that I've heard that she's got some kind of connection with a rich guy who likes to get his feet rubbed. Actually, I didn't say feet. I just said some rich guy that likes massages. And Debbie stopped me right there. She said I wasn't exactly the type. And I said, 'What do you mean?' And she says, 'You're way too old.'"

"You are ancient."

"I asked her how young are we talking," Mattie said. "And Debbie says, 'the younger the better.' Can you believe that crap? *The younger the better?* I didn't know what to say and just blurted out that that was pretty sick. And Debbie was like it was no big deal. She says the man just liked fifteen-, sixteen-year-olds."

"Yikes."

"Debbie said if I knew some girls who might be interested to let her know," Mattie said. "She says she got two hundred bucks with each new girl. And if I brought some good ones to her, we could split the money."

"Did she know what had happened to Chloe?" I said.

"If she did, she didn't mention it," Mattie said. "I asked

her if she didn't think the whole thing was pervy. She said the guy was super-rich, like crazy rich, and real stressed out. She said young girls made him feel like a kid again. It relaxed him. Like a sleepover or something. It was all real clean. Pillow fights and gossip and all that. Debbie says she did it once or twice and that it was no biggie."

"Did you find out his name?"

"I asked," Mattie said. "But she wouldn't tell me. I told her that he sounded like a fucking child molester. I said that if you're over eighteen, that's your own business. But kids, little girls, got no reason to be around some weird old man."

"And how did she reply?"

"She said I needed to grow the fuck up," Mattie said. "That the world wasn't all sunshine and rainbows. She said a man like this could change your life. He knew people. Powerful rich people that could make shit happen with the snap of their fingers."

"Ah," I said. "The rich are different."

I'd been studying the menu, contemplating a lobster roll with fries. If I didn't eat now, I'd have to stop by the Public Market on the way home. But if I did eat now, I'd be fully sustained for the evening. That way I could focus more on sipping Johnnie Walker on ice while I watched *The Magnificent Seven* on TCM. I'd seen the movie a hundred times and looked forward to a hundred more.

"That's okay," I said. "There are other ways to find this guy."

"Would you hold on one second?" Mattie said. "Christ. Let me finish."

I turned toward her on the barstool. "Do I sense dogged determination?"

"Duh," Mattie said. "I said screw it, took the T back to Southie, and found her sister, Sandy. I should've just gone to Sandy first. We go way back. To Gates of Heaven. To middle and high school. Both Sandy's younger sisters are fuckups. Sandy's been going to Bunker Hill when she's not working. Studying to be a nurse. Got a good head on her shoulders."

"Did she know about Debbie's new friend?"

"Nope," Mattie said. "But she knew something was wrong. She said Debbie had been acting weird and bragging about having all this extra money. Like a shit ton of money. She knew that money wasn't coming from slinging ice-cream cones. Sandy had seen Debbie out with some rich lady. Drives a fancy car, clothes outta Newbury Street window, lots of jewelry."

"A woman of means."

"Sandy says she had a British accent, too," Mattie said. "She doesn't know her name, but Sandy thinks Debbie has been working for the woman as a personal assistant. Running errands. Fetching coffee. Said it was her side hustle on her days off."

"Hmm."

"Bet your ass, hmm," Mattie said. "Chloe said the woman at the club had a funny accent. Right? She'd met the woman when she got the instruction on the massage and the cash."

"So all we have to do now is catch Debbie with this lady of means," I said. "And then hopefully connect this woman to Mr. Feet."

"Really, Spenser?" Mattie said. "I'm like five steps ahead of you."

"It's almost as if you'd been trained by a professional," I said.

"To add a little pressure," Mattie said, "I told her about what happened with Chloe. How the guy acted like he wanted a massage but then pulled off the sheet and started going to town. I thought Sandy might puke. She promises she'll call when Debbie's back with this woman."

"How often are they together?"

"Sandy says Debbie gets a ride home from her at least twice a week," Mattie said. "Hey. Tonight might be the night. I'll let you know. The Delgados live over on Fourth and G. I'll text you the address if I hear anything. What do you think? You think Susan will let you out of the house to come play?"

"I went to the woods because I wished to live differently."

"Does that mean yes?"

I tilted my head and nodded. "Yes."

Mattie left, nearly bumping into Wayne Cosgrove on the way out. Each one unaware of the other's significance in my life. I waved to Wayne and ordered the lobster roll with fries. And another Allagash.

Stakeouts gave me no pleasure on an empty stomach.

9

—

"YOU COME BACK much?" I said.

"Not much to come back to," Mattie said. "My sisters would rather take the T into town and stay with me. When they graduate, they'll be long gone from here. Southie ain't Southie anymore. It's Condoville for rich dipwads."

"Glad I'm not rich," I said.

"Or a dipwad," Mattie said.

"Thanks," I said. "I think."

It was dark, and we sat in the front seat of my Land Cruiser watching the twin doors of a triple-decker duplex in South Boston. The building needed paint and new windows and stood out on Fourth Street, where most of the old houses were either gutted and renovated or replaced with modern-looking condos. Mattie was right. The Old Southie of corner stores and dive bars was tougher to find than an authentic accent in *The Departed*. Many of those who'd grown up here could no longer afford it.

"What about your grandmother?"

"You know she's been sober four years now," Mattie said. "Can you believe it? But that life. That aged her a lot. She's got a lot of health problems. Diabetic. Can't walk across the street without losing her breath. You can't live on cigarettes and whiskey."

"Sorry to hear that."

Mattie nodded.

"Ever hear from Mickey Green?" I said.

"Nah," she said. "I heard he moved to Florida."

"He owes you," I said. "You were the only one who believed him. If it weren't for you, he'd still be in the can."

"I didn't care as much for him as I did getting the scumbag who killed my mom."

"You did great."

Sitting in the passenger seat, hidden in shadow, Mattie nodded again. I leaned back in the seat, the windows down. The street was dark except for the intermittent tall lamps and lights in windows. No one passed, and no one paid us any attention. We'd been there for forty-five minutes. I knew I'd made the correct decision about the lobster roll.

"Chloe may have been stupid about money, but she didn't deserve to see that shit."

"Nobody does."

"I remember when I was a kid getting a bad feeling from this priest who used to come around the projects," she said. "He ran some kind of youth program. Board games and watching movies and all that. After-school bullshit. You know. He used to always knock on my door and ask my mom if I wanted to join him and the other kids. And my mom always shut the door in his face. She said the man had the devil in his eyes and she'd seen it before."

"Your mom knew."

"Yeah," Mattie said. "But once, I heard this priest was taking a bunch of kids to the zoo. And my mom wouldn't let me go. I was mad and said screw it and decided to go anyway."

A city electric truck rumbled past, nearly taking off my side-view mirror, and then turned down G Street. It was very dark and quiet again. I heard a dog barking far in the distance, making me think of Pearl and wonder how she was doing with Susan.

"The priest had this big black car," she said. "But when I met him at the front of the projects, it was just him. I asked the priest if I'd gotten there early, and he acted like he'd already been to the zoo, dropped off the other kids, and come back for me. I'll never forget the look on his face when he opened up the door. Like my mom said, something was wrong with his eyes. His skin was also real white, like someone who never went outside. So white you could almost see through him."

"Translucent."

"Sure," Mattie said. "Anyway. He was sweating and smelled like bathrooms and old closets at Gates of Heaven. Like he'd crawled out of one and come for me. I got real nervous, told him I had to get back home, and ran all the way back to my apartment. Two weeks later, I found out he'd been watching some girls change into their swimsuits. He was reported, they canceled the after-school thing, and I never saw him again."

"Sometimes you just know."

"Is that something you're born with?"

"Maybe," I said. "I think the older I get, the better I am at reading people. Sometimes I'm wrong. But more often I'm right."

"Like if someone is lying."

"Lying is tough," I said. "Sometimes people are such good liars they believe it themselves."

"But you know when someone wants to do you harm."

"Yep," I said. "I usually know when they aim the gun at me."

"Smartass," Mattie said. "You know what I mean."

"Sure," I said. "You can see it in their eyes or the way they hold themselves. Men often stiffen up when they react to you. Like dogs. You need to develop a sense of awareness when you're in a bad place with bad people. Realize it may come at you from any side or all sides all at once."

"How come you didn't like being a cop?" she said. "I bet you were a good cop."

I shrugged. A pair of headlights appeared far off in my rearview mirror. We both watched the car come up fast and then disappear into the distance. A few seconds later, another turned behind us and moved slowly past my window.

"I liked being a cop," I said. "I didn't like taking orders."

"And you like working for yourself."

I nodded.

"Maybe being a cop wouldn't be so bad," Mattie said. "The guy who came to talk to me after my mother was killed was stand-up. The detectives that came later wouldn't listen. But the guy on patrol stayed with me and my sisters until my grandmother got there. In the same way I got the bad feeling about the priest, I had a good feeling about this cop. Even though my world had just been tossed upside down, he made me feel like everything was going to be okay. That I would live through this. You know? That's something else."

"Love all," I said. "Trust a few."

"You love all?"

"Maybe not all," I said. "But I appreciate the sentiment."

The second car stopped in front of the duplex. The side door opened and a young woman in a white hoodie got out. She headed up the steps, showing herself under a bright porch light, and pulled out some keys to unlock the door.

"That's Debbie."

"Nice car."

It was some type of Mercedes coupe with the top up. We were too far to see the license plate or who was inside.

"Can I say, 'Follow that car'?" Mattie said.

"Please do."

10

THE CAR WAS REGISTERED to a woman named Patricia Palmer. But it didn't take too many strokes of the keyboard the next morning to learn she went by Poppy. I'd clicked through so many party photos of Poppy Palmer on the Boston scene that I started to feel underdressed.

She was forty-three, born in Surrey, England, and operated some type of consulting company not far from the Quincy Market. It didn't appear she had ever been sued. Or arrested. I found a bland and vague company website that told me only that she worked with many Fortune 500 companies. Doing what, I had no idea. She was thin but muscular, with severe, somewhat masculine features and short black hair and black eyes. She kept constant company with men in tuxes and women in sequins.

In every photo, she seemed to be having a hell of a time lifting a champagne glass to fight illiteracy, poverty, cancer, blindness, hunger, domestic violence, and animal abuse. I didn't see Save the Whales, but maybe I hadn't been at it long enough.

Around lunchtime, I called Bill Brett, who took most of the event photos for *The Globe.*

He remembered the parties. But didn't know anything about Poppy. "Do you have any idea of how many of these things I've gone to? Jeez, Spenser."

"I have a birthday coming up," I said. "Catered by Karl's Sausage Kitchen. Front-page material."

He hung up. I kept scrolling through pictures.

I took a few notes, walked across the street to Starbucks, and returned with a tall coffee. I drank the coffee and put my feet up on my desk. After several minutes, I took them back down. I drank some more coffee and stood up. I looked across the street to an office building that used to be a completely different office building where a woman named Linda Thomas had once worked. I wondered what became of her.

I finished the coffee and began to click through the photos again. Most had appeared in *The Globe, Boston,* and *Boston Common.* Poppy Palmer seemed to have a dazzling array of cocktail dresses. Sequins. Silk. Backless and scoop-necked. And I noted, she was quite fit. Not fit in the way Susan Silverman was fit but more like a woman who might deadlift the back of a Buick.

I looked for people I knew in the shots. And names of the charities she supported. I'd been to enough of these things with Susan that I'd developed a mental Rolodex.

On the third viewing, I noticed that in three different shots at three different events, she stood side by side with the same man. He was medium-sized and silver-haired, with dark tan skin and a face that some women might consider handsome. His face looked properly craggy and distinguished, like a profile you'd see on a Roman coin. He seemed to be perpetually laughing, and in two shots had his hand on Poppy's waist.

The man's name was Peter Steiner.

I made a screengrab of the photo, zoomed in on his face, and emailed the picture to Mattie.

I went back looking at more photos of Poppy Palmer. And then started a separate search for Peter Steiner.

One cutline named him Peter Steiner of Steiner and Associates. Being a trained detective, I googled Steiner and Associates and found out it was an investment firm that worked with select clients to help them achieve their maximum potential. They listed no address or phone number, only a generic email for serious inquiries.

After a few minutes my phone buzzed. A text from Mattie said Showed to Chloe. That's the bastard.

I felt like giving myself a high five. Instead, I picked up the phone and called one of the people I'd spotted in the party photos, Bill Barke. Bill and I went way back to the old jazz clubs of Cambridge that had gone by the wayside.

"Spenser," Bill said. "You still owe me for those Sox tickets."

"It was a lousy game," I said. "They lost."

"Go cry to John Henry."

"Do you happen to know a guy named Peter Steiner?"

There was a long pause. "Do I know Peter Steiner?"

"Is that a rhetorical question or is your hearing going?"

"Sorry, I'm driving back to Plymouth in the convertible," he said. "Yeah, I've met Peter Steiner. What the hell do you want to know about Peter Steiner?"

"Who is he?" I said. "And what does he do beyond helping a select group of Bostonians reach their maximum potential?"

"He's a fucking hedge-fund guy," Bill said. "He lives in a
big brownstone on Comm Avenue. Flies to Florida on the
weekends in his private jet. Hangs out with ex-presidents,
CEOs, and has-been actors and athletes. He's one of those
guys. You know the type."

"Unfortunately."

"Ever seen his girlfriend?"

"Poppy Palmer."

"She's a real hot tamale," Bill said. "That accent kills me."

"She looks like she could break a man's pelvis with her
thighs."

"She does CrossFit, triathalons, and all that," Bill said. "I
think Steiner does, too. They're always back and forth to
some place in the Caribbean. Out of our league, pal."

"Ever heard anything untoward about him?"

"Untoward," Bill said. "You're always so damn formal.
What the hell do you mean 'untoward'?"

"Sex stuff."

"Nope."

"Criminal stuff?"

"I wouldn't invest my money with him," Bill said. "But
more because I think he's an arrogant hot dog. Not anything
I've heard."

"He appears to never meet a charitable event he wouldn't
attend."

"Some guys are like that," Bill said. "Probably thinks he
looks great in a tux."

I named some of the events where I'd spotted him and Poppy Palmer. I asked Bill if he knew anyone connected to those charities who might know more about him.

"Do you care if he knows you're asking?"

"Maybe a little."

"If it were me, I'd check in with Wayne Arnett," Bill said. "He's an auctioneer at these things and goes by the name Mr. Money Raiser. Susan probably knows him. He's very close with these people. Big guy on the social scene. Definitely knows Steiner. And he definitely loves to talk. I come out to raise money for the kids. But I'd rather be at home listening to old King Oliver 78s with my dog, Dixie."

"The reason we're friends."

There was another long pause. "Sorry to hear about Pearl."

"It's been a few tough months."

"Maybe you should think about getting a new one," he said. "Life's not worth living without a good dog."

"Already happened."

"And who's this?" Bill chuckled.

"A German shorthaired pointer," I said. "And her name happens to be Pearl, too."

"Of course it is."

11

AS SUSAN SILVERMAN happened to know everyone who was anyone, Susan just happened to know Wayne Arnett, AKA Mr. Money Raiser. And she arranged for us to meet him at the bar at the Eliot Hotel that evening.

"That's a terrible moniker," Susan said.

"What about the Maestro of Money," I said.

"Even worse."

We were walking together on Newbury Street. She'd met me at my office after her last appointment, and we'd left both of our cars to take an evening stroll. The light was golden, the evening cool, and a great many people were dining al fresco. The cafés and bars shoulder to shoulder and chair to chair. Susan wasn't into people-watching. She was more interested in the window-shopping, studying the mannequins and deciding which summer dresses she'd like to add to her closet.

"Auction Jackson."

"I kind of like that one," Susan said. "But it doesn't make any sense."

"I've attended many of those things with you," I said. "Few make sense."

"But some do," she said. "And as silly and trite as they may seem, they raise a great deal of money and do a lot of good."

"The Maestro of Money," I said. "I'm going to suggest it."

Susan had on a knee-length blue silk dress with tall leather heels that made her legs look about a mile long. Her skin was dark and tan, and she'd worn her black hair up off her neck. She smelled like good soap and summertime.

I began to whistle some Cole Porter as we strolled.

"Thanks for bringing my jacket," I said. I slipped into a linen navy sport coat to accentuate the jeans and T-shirt.

"Do you think the puppy will be okay?" she said. "I left her in the crate without water. Just like Janet told us."

"Janet knows dogs," I said. "She knew both Pearls and now knows the third."

"We shall see," Susan said, peering up a flight of stairs at a brownstone shop and taking in a cheetah-print Diane von Furstenberg. I was pleased to see a CLOSED sign in the window.

We continued along Newbury and turned onto Mass Ave and then into the Eliot. We found Wayne Arnett at the bar, sipping a martini inside a glass the size of a goldfish bowl. I liked the look of it and ordered two more. And then Susan corrected me. She wished to have a gimlet with fresh lime juice and Ketel One.

I had a gin martini. Straight up with extra olives.

"I like him," Arnett said. "I like this big guy."

"I do my best," I said.

Arnett looked very much like a professional charity emcee and auctioneer. He was in his mid-forties, short and slightly chunky, with black hair and artfully trimmed facial hair. Blue eyes and a dimple in his chin. He was impeccably dressed. A navy blazer with a starched white shirt, red bow tie, and creased khaki pants. His shoes were old-school wingtips kicked up on the barstool.

"So," Arnett said. "Peter Steiner."

"Peter Steiner," I said.

"What an asshole," Arnett said.

"Oh, yeah?" I said. "Do tell."

"I don't mean to speak out of school," he said, smiling and waving his hand around. "But something is amiss with Peter Steiner. Something is wrong with Peter Steiner. He purports to be an international man of mystery. A great financier. Someone who deep-sea dives and owns two private planes. But god knows, he gives me the creeps."

It appeared Wayne Arnett had begun without me. I looked up, signaled the bartender, and ordered him another cocktail. Spenser the Generous.

"You know, Wayne," Susan said. "Spenser thought you might change your name to Auction Jackson. What do you think?"

"You don't like Mr. Money Raiser?" he said.

"Miss Silverman is being cute," I said, placing a hand on Susan's knee. "She can't help herself."

Susan swatted my hand away. And Arnett shrugged and gleefully reached for his next cocktail. I liked very much where this was headed, as long as Mr. Money Raiser could remain on his barstool. Susan gave me the side eye and took a micro-sip of her gimlet.

"Do you mind saying why you're asking me about Peter?" he said. "I mean, there are plenty of other people who can tell you about Peter. And Peter and Poppy Palmer."

"Are they married?" I said.

"I don't think so."

"But they are a couple?" I said.

"Very much so," Arnett said. "They are what you call a dynamic Boston power couple."

I looked over at Susan and winked. She rolled her eyes.

"What does she do?" Susan said.

"Whatever Peter asks."

"She's devoted?" I said.

"Completely," he said. "She assists him in whatever he's into. She runs some type of modeling agency, I believe. Maybe a charity or two. But being this is Boston, and not New York, I don't know about the modeling thing. He, on the other hand, has quite the stable of investors. I really don't want to say. But there are some big names. Big, big names."

"I have at least a few hundred bucks in the bank," I said.

"Peter Steiner wouldn't even pick up the phone unless you were a billionaire."

"Damn," I said. "I'll make sure to buy a couple of scratch-off tickets on the way home."

Two comely women in lovely summer dresses came over and said hello to Arnett. He smiled and put on some high-octane charm. They were in their late twenties or early thirties and seemed to have walked out of an ad for La Perla.

Lots of flawless glowing skin and muscular calves. He introduced us as he rested his hands on their slim waists.

Susan watched me trying not to watch the women. She
seemed to find this hilarious. I turned a blind eye and drank
a little martini, completely unfettered.

When the women left, I said, "You're quite the charmer."

"Very beautiful," he said. "But nope. Still gay."

Susan laughed. "Are you with someone?" she asked.

"For five years," he said. "We share an apartment in the
South End and a cat named Perry Como."

"Love makes the world go round," I said.

"It sure does," he said. He sighed and finished off the
martini and then grabbed hold of the next. He drank some
more and turned to me with red-rimmed eyes. "I guess you
want to know about the incident."

"Absolutely," I said, having no idea which incident he
meant. "That's why I wanted to meet you."

"There was a woman who worked for him," he said. "I
can't recall her name. But she was young and very pretty.
Some type of artist, I believe. In some way or another, she
accused him of trying to force himself on her. This was
maybe ten years ago. I don't remember. I don't remember all
the details. But there was a lot of talk. It was all a big soci-
ety scandal. No one could believe that Peter had eyes for
anyone outside Poppy. They were such a dynamic and attractive couple."

"I know the feeling," I said.

"You think he was charged with something?" Susan said.

Arnett nodded. I looked to Susan and shook my head. I
could find no criminal charges against Steiner in Boston.

"I think it went away as fast as it had come up," Arnett said. "And obviously he and Poppy made amends. I know she told a lot of people that this woman was after Peter's money and had made up the entire story."

"You wouldn't happen to know anyone who might remember this woman's name?" I said.

"Perhaps," he said. "Whoever she is, I heard she left Boston. Most of her reputation as an artist had been built on her association with Peter and Poppy. God, what was her name? I remember them hosting a show for her at their house. You have seen Steiner's home, haven't you? Or at least heard about it?"

I shook my head.

"It used to be a school over on Comm Avenue," Arnett said, trying to point a finger in the direction of Commonwealth. "It's maybe an entire city block. Big old brownstone. I mean, there is Boston money and then there is Boston *money.*"

"Super-rich," Susan said.

"No," Arnett said, lifting his martini to us both. "Filthy rich."

12

"ONE OF THE PERKS of leaving Homicide and getting kicked upstairs in my ripe old age was not having to deal with a pain in the ass like you," Quirk said the next morning.

"You don't really mean that."

"You bet I do, buddy boy," Quirk said, refilling his mug from a pot in his office and taking a seat back behind his desk. "This is supposed to be the stress-free environment before they put me out to pasture."

"Never look a gift horse in the mouth."

"You mean the donuts?" he said. "When have you ever brought me a dozen from Kane's without strings attached?"

"Maybe it was just my way to let you know you are both valued and loved."

"Bullshit."

"Or maybe I might have questions about a certain individual and a certain case that looks like it may have been washed from the books."

"Aha," Quirk said. He raised his index finger, a substantial move, considering his hands were bigger than a Quincy bricklayer's.

Without a word, I reached onto his desk, plucked a lovely cinnamon-dusted, and took a bite. Knowing police head-quarters and Quirk's office all too well, I came armed with my own coffee from Starbucks.

"Ever heard of Peter Steiner?"

"Nope."

"Poppy Palmer."

"A poppy what?"

"Poppy Palmer," I said. Saying it slow, with careful enun-ciation on the alliteration.

"No, but I knew a fan dancer named Fanne Foxe."

I smiled. "Pilgrim Theater," I said. "In the old Combat Zone."

"Those were the days," Quirk said.

"Indeed."

Quirk eyed the box of donuts and then me, and then eyed the donuts again and the open door of his office. When the pressure became too intense, he lifted the lid and grabbed a Boston cream. "So," he said. "Steiner's peter and Poppy whosis."

"Exactly," I said. "So glad you're paying attention."

Quirk nodded. His office was as neat and immaculate as Quirk himself. The only thing new, besides an ever-expanding arrangement of framed grandkid pics, was a collection of bobbleheads near the window.

"Bobbleheads?" I said.

"You get one and you're fucked," he said. "Everyone brings me one now. Feel free to take one on your way out."

I finished my cinnamon donut and sipped some coffee. I pulled out a stack of papers from my office on Peter Steiner and Poppy Palmer and handed it to him. "I understand Steiner might have been charged with a sex crime some years ago."

"When?"

"Some years ago."

"Please," Quirk said. "Don't be too precise with me, Spenser. I like to really work at this stuff."

"If so," I said, leaning back into the office chair. "I'd like to connect with the investigator."

Quirk reached for his cleanly shaven square jaw. His full head of hair showed more salt-and-pepper these days, but didn't look all that different from when we met decades ago.

"This the guy you were telling me about?" Quirk said. "The one who whipped it out in front of a fifteen-year-old?"

"Bingo."

"Jesus Christ," Quirk said. "This guy must have money. Guys like that always get off."

"No pun expected or intended," I said. "But, yes, he's rolling in the dough."

"When did he assault the kid?"

"Two weeks ago."

"But the kid won't talk?"

"She'll talk to me," I said. "Not to the cops."

"Okay," Quirk said. "Besides being a decent guy, why should I bestow such a magnanimous favor as the assistant superintendent of Boston Police? Just for a fucking box of donuts?"

"Not just any donuts," I said. "All the way from Kane's."

"Christ," Quirk said. "You got me there. Let me make some calls."

I stood, pointed at him with my thumb and forefinger, and dropped the hammer.

On the way out, I took an extra donut with me.

13

I PICKED UP PEARL at the Navy Yard and drove back to my office before the lunchtime traffic. Right before noon, I parked somewhere in the neighborhood of Commonwealth and Dartmouth, slipped her into a training harness, and took her out for a little stroll.

She was a handsome dog. Perhaps the most beautiful of all the Pearls. Slick brown coat and intelligent eyes, a long, regal nose that immediately found the grass along the mall. Many people offered compliments as we walked. Lovely women stopped jogging to bend down and pet her.

I was enjoying this arrangement.

The address I had for Peter Steiner was on the north side of Comm Ave, an elegant four-story brownstone that dominated a space usually reserved for three homes. I read it had once been a hotel before becoming a private school in the fifties. It was a lot of real estate for an unmarried man with no family.

It was shady and cool under the large trees as we walked. Every so often, I would stop and command Pearl to sit and stay. I would walk back five paces, leash in hand, and then ask her to come. When she got to me, she got a small treat. When she came without being called, I set her back into a sit. We did this over and over.

I furtively glanced at Steiner's residence. I saw no one enter the door at the top of the stone steps or leave. The blinds in the home were half drawn, but as a professional investigator, I knew that peeping in windows was considered poor form.

Pearl and I crossed the street and walked around the corner of the building. I tried to look in the windows anyway, but the afternoon sun glared hard off the glass. Pearl sensed something, perhaps a clue, and dug her nails into the sidewalk.

I decided to let her take the lead. Ten yards later, we found half of a discarded bagel still in a wrapper.

I had to remove it from her mouth. No telling who'd eaten the other half and what they might pass on to Pearl. Pearl wasn't pleased.

We kept walking and soon found the public alley behind Steiner's place and decided to investigate.

On the backside, we found two cars parked outside. One was the Mercedes I'd seen drop off Debbie Delgado. The other was a light blue Rolls-Royce Phantom. Pearl and I noted the license tag on the Rolls. Or at least I hoped she did. She was still a detective-in-training.

I continued past the dumpsters and the other cars, still not being able to see inside the turreted windows facing the alley.

We continued along the alley all the way to Clarendon, heading back over Commonwealth to the mall. Pearl sat smartly at the corner until I let her know it was safe to cross.

She panted with the exertion as we crossed into the mall, and she promptly relieved herself. This was a lot of work for a puppy detective.

As I was jotting the tag number of the Rolls into my phone, it began to buzz.

"Where are you?" Mattie said.

"Teaching Pearl the finer points of investigating."

"Can you get back to the office?"

"We are headed in that very direction."

"Good," Mattie said. "I found another one."

"Another what?"

"Victim of that creep Steiner," Mattie said. "Amelia Lynch. She's eighteen now but says she was fourteen when it happened."

"He expose himself to her, too?"

"Worse than that," Mattie said. "Much worse."

"Sure it's Steiner?"

"This thing happened at his house," Mattie said. "Big place on Comm Avenue."

"I'm standing right in front of it."

"She thought she was going for a modeling audition," Mattie said. "It was that woman, Poppy Palmer. She talked her into taking some pictures in a bathing suit and all that kind of stuff."

"If you found her in less than twenty-four hours," I said, "how many you think are out there?"

"Didn't you say the more victims we find, the more that'll step forward?"

"That's generally the rule."

"Okay," Mattie said. "Let's keep looking. Let's get this asshole."

14

WE MET AMELIA LYNCH at a Dunkin' in Mattapan. As I considered all Dunkin' shops in the greater Boston area satellite offices, I made myself comfortable at a back table. We all drank coffee, but a corn muffin called to me from behind the counter.

As Mattie settled in with Amelia, I excused myself and bought the muffin. I split off a quarter, walked to the curb, and shared it with Pearl waiting patiently in the car.

It was a blazing hot summer in Boston at a cool seventy degrees. My windows were cracked to let in the morning breeze and smells of the city.

"She okay?" Mattie asked when I returned.

"She is now," I said.

"Amelia was telling me about first meeting Poppy," Mattie said.

"Pretty dumb," Amelia said. "She told me I had the looks and height to be a runway model in Paris."

Amelia had the height, a little taller than Mattie, with long, white-blond hair and wide-set blue eyes. Her skin was pale and her cheeks pink. She may have been eighteen, but she appeared and acted much younger. She spoke quietly, eyes down on the table or at her cup of coffee, dressed in ragged jean shorts, flip-flops, and a tie-dye T-shirt featuring Snoopy and a peace symbol.

It had been a while since I'd seen one of those.

"How did you meet Poppy?" I said.

"A girl in school told me about her," she said. "I told my parents, and they laughed. My dad said it sounded like a con job. My mom told me I was decent-looking but not quite model material. She thought my nose was too big."

"I think you have a terrific nose," I said. "Much better than mine."

Amelia smiled, nervously tucking her long hair behind one ear, showing off multiple piercings. I wasn't sure if telling a young woman that she was attractive was acceptable or creepy. I just didn't want to let her mother's comment slide. Kids, particularly teens, took everything to heart.

"So," Mattie said. "Amelia went anyway."

I decided to let Mattie handle the questions. And I began to eat the corn muffin to make myself appear useful. The woman behind the counter continued to stock the donuts. I remembered a time when people actually made the donuts. Now they just stocked them. They appeared each day, brought by the donut gods.

"It was at Mr. Steiner's house," Amelia said, still staring into her cup. "I was so nervous. I even went to the mall and got a manicure and a new summer dress. I did this makeup tutorial on YouTube and everything. I had my cousin take some pictures to make it look like I had a portfolio. This girl that set me up said Poppy had connections at Abercrombie and Lululemon."

"I'm old enough to remember when Abercrombie sold hunting boots and dog collars," I said.

Mattie rolled her eyes. I could power the lights at Fenway with the eye rolling from Mattie Sullivan.

"Tell him about the interview," Mattie said.

"Are you sure?"

"Yeah."

"I don't know."

"Spenser's been around," Mattie said. "He's heard it all. He's seen it all. He's like a doctor. He needs to know everything. Every detail about what happened at that house."

"It's true," I said. "Some are even convinced my soul is nearly ninety."

"How old are you?" Amelia said.

I told her.

"That's not that old," she said.

I turned to Mattie and stuck my tongue out. Amelia swallowed and reached for her coffee. She took a long sip as if it were filled with Old Forester instead of a double decaf latte.

"His house was like some kind of palace or museum," Amelia said. "I once took a field trip to the Winthrop, and it reminded me of being in there. Only without the paintings and sculptures. Big, tall ceilings and lots of marble. Like I told Mattie, Poppy was really nice to me. She took me upstairs to her private office, and we talked about all the people she knew and the places she'd gone."

"Buttering her up," Mattie said. "She's as sick as he is."

"Poppy told me she was Mr. Steiner's business partner," Amelia said. "And they owned a big-time modeling agency that had offices in Boston, New York, and Paris. I don't know if it's true, but I was impressed. I mean, no one had ever talked to me like that, telling me about traveling the world on private jets and meeting rich and famous people. She said they'd just hosted a big party with guys who played for the Pats and that one of her girls, she was always saying her 'girls,' had just landed a part on one of those CSI shows."

"Is that when you met Steiner?" Mattie said, leaning in to the table.

"Nope," she said. "That was the second time. The first was just Poppy. She said my pictures showed potential but all of 'em needed to be reshot by a pro. She said it was enough to show to Mr. Steiner and see what he thought. He had the real eye for talent. She told me Steiner had discovered Bridget Moynahan back in the day."

"I doubt Bridget Moynahan needed much discovering," I said.

Amelia took a long breath, and I noticed that her hands were shaking as she picked up her coffee. She took a sip and closed her eyes for a moment. When she spoke, her voice cracked a bit, and she placed her hand to her small chest.

"It took a lot going back and forth into the city," Amelia said. "Without my parents finding out. I had to do my makeup on the T. Which is a real mess. When Poppy called again, I was excited. She said she'd shown my pictures to Mr. Steiner and he wanted to meet with me. I really thought this was going to get me the hell out of here and on to New York or Paris. I'd read about things happening like this. Someone powerful spotting a nobody on the street, and the next thing you know they were making movies."

"Happened to Thelma Todd," I said.

"Who the fuck is Thelma Todd?" Mattie said.

"Pride of Lowell?" I said.

Nothing.

"The Ice Cream Blonde?" I said.

Still nothing.

I was attempting to leaven the situation. Mattie shook her head and kicked me under the table. The cups of coffee jostled.

"It was pretty much the same this next time," Amelia said, playing with the ends of her hair. The delicate features, sharp ears, and nearly white hair reminded me of something out of Tolkien. "We talked more about Paris and how it was really the center of the universe. Poppy told me about fashion week and all the girls going that year. She talked about these big fancy parties, and that's when she asked me if I'd like some wine."

"And how old were you?" I said.

"Fourteen," she said. "I didn't know what to say. The only wine I'd ever had was at communion. I said okay because I didn't want to seem like I didn't have any class. When she came back with a bottle, that's when I met Mr. Steiner."

I kept quiet. I finished the muffin, wadded up the paper, and looked over at Mattie. Mattie was listening to every word, her entire body turned to Amelia, watching her as intently as I imagined Susan Silverman would with a patient. Like me, she didn't take notes but recalled every word.

"He was so handsome," Amelia said. "And charming. He

looked like someone who should be playing polo or yachting out on the Cape. Polo shirt. Big silver watch. He gave me a hug and opened the wine. When we started talking, it was like being with someone I'd known my whole life. He asked me a ton of questions and told me how impressed he'd been with my photos. He apologized for being late. He said he was hanging out on the set of a Wahlberg movie that was shooting in Quincy."

"Hope it was better than his last," I said.

"I was so nervous I drank the wine fast," she said. "Without asking, he poured me another and then started to talk to Poppy like I wasn't even there. He kept on eyeing me and nodding, watching me like when I go with my dad to buy a new car. He told Poppy I looked European and worried I might be lost with all the girls from Sweden and Poland. He asked me to stand, stood back, and looked at me some more, and said I was still an inch too short for runway and that I wasn't developed enough for bathing suits and lingerie. He said most of his clients ended up doing catalog work and I might need to develop some and maybe come back later. I don't know why I did it. But I tried to change his mind. I told him that I was more grown-up than he thought. I said I had some pictures taken over the summer in a bikini that made me look lots older."

"Just what he wanted," I said. "It's called negging."

"It's called being a fucking asshole," Mattie said.

"Before I knew what was happening, Mr. Steiner said maybe Poppy could get some Polaroids of me. He said they had a small studio on the first floor."

I didn't speak. And neither did Mattie. A woman in a

housecoat and slippers wandered into the Dunkin' and asked for a dozen with powdered sugar and a coffee regular. Amelia turned to watch the woman and then back to the table and leaned in. "That's how it happened."

She didn't speak again until the old woman paid and left.

"They had swimsuits and bras and stuff already," she said. "They acted like the whole thing was normal. Just something you did. She gave me a black silk robe and told me to pick out what I liked. The room seemed legit. It had light stands and those silvery umbrellas and a big wall set up. So, I did like she said. I really wanted to make them happy. I wanted them to think I was good enough right then. I didn't want to wait."

"Was Steiner there?"

"Not at first," Amelia said. "He didn't come in until later. Poppy said he had an important business call and might not be able to make it. Poppy took a bunch of pictures of me in a bikini and then asked me to take off my top."

I took a long breath and let it out. I looked to Mattie. I needed to hear it. But I very much wanted to leave and wait with Pearl outside.

Amelia started to cry. After a while, she wiped her face with a napkin and coughed into her hand to compose herself. Mattie rested a hand on her knee and told her it was okay.

"I was so damn stupid," Amelia said. "So damn stupid."

"And that's when he touched you?" Mattie said.

Amelia looked to both of us and nodded. "Poppy excused herself, and I was putting my robe back on," she said. "Mr. Steiner told me I did great. He walked up behind me and wrapped his arms around my waist and kissed my neck. Before I could cover myself up, he had one hand on my boob and another down my bottoms. I don't know why but I just froze. He whispered into my ear that I was beautiful and so innocent. And I'd be famous one day."

"What happened next?" I said.

"What do you think?" Amelia said. "I got dressed and got the hell out of there."

"Did you ever tell anyone?" I said.

Amelia shook her head. Her blue eyes looked enormous and very clear. "Not until I heard Mattie was asking around about him and Debbie Delgado. The girl who introduced me to Poppy was the one who got Debbie into all this. I figured maybe I could help now. Maybe do something and make it right. I don't freeze up so easy anymore."

"Will you talk to the cops?" I said.

Amelia nodded. Mattie nodded back.

Now there were two.

15

TWO DAYS LATER, Boston Police Homicide Captain Lorraine Glass walked into my office and stood in front of my desk with a decidedly unpleasant expression.

"Quirk says you have some questions for me," she said.

"Yes," I said. "Why has it taken you so long to be won over by my obvious charm and winning personality?"

"About Peter Steiner."

"Oh," I said. "Him."

"Please skip the regular bullshit," she said. "Quirk said to talk to you. And I said I'd stop by. So here I am."

Glass stood over me, dressed in a black pant suit with a cream top under the jacket. I knew she had a gun, but the jacket covered it nicely. She was average height and trim, with short brown hair and angular features. She didn't wear any makeup or jewelry besides a digital sport watch on her wrist.

"May I offer you a coffee or a bottle of water?"

"Nope."

"Hot towel," I said. "Wine spritzer?"

"Like I said," Glass said. "Skip the bullshit. I don't like

you, Spenser. I've never liked you. I know you're big pals with Belson and Quirk. However the hell that happened was way before my time. I've worked very hard to get to where I am. I am not, nor will I ever be, part of the boys' club. And if I find out you're working for some scumbag attorney who works for Steiner, I promise you I'll come back here and kick your balls from here to Haverhill."

"Haverhill is quite a long ways from the Back Bay."

"And I got a leg to do it."

I waved a hand in front of my client's chairs. She took a seat, and I closed my laptop and leaned forward onto my desk. "My balls are safe," I said. "I don't work for Steiner."

"Who do you work for?"

"I don't need to tell you," I said. "But in the spirit of cooperation and our blossoming friendship, I'll tell you I'm working with another victim."

"So you know about the others?"

"I know two. I also know there are others."

Glass shook her head and leveled her eyes at me. She ran a hand over her face and took a long breath. "Not including those first charges?"

"I found no charges against Peter Steiner or his significant other, Poppy Palmer."

"That's because the charge was expunged," she said. "You know how that works, don't you?"

"Money."

"Money," she said. "And a good attorney. And having an entire rock-solid case deep-sixed by the goddamn DA's office."

"Who was the victim?"

Glass shook her head, offering the thinnest of smiles. "You know better than that," she said. "Victims of sexual battery are confidential."

"So Steiner raped someone?"

"Yep."

"And this was your case when you were on sex crimes?"

She nodded. "I hadn't been a detective long," Glass said. "If I had the same case now, I could've done more with it. But even then, as green as I was as an investigator, I still did good. The case was good. It was more than enough to prosecute."

I stood up and stretched, walked to the wall, and straightened one of my two Vermeer prints. It was of a young woman seated at a piano, a much older man standing beside her. I believed the man was her instructor, his mouth hanging open in song.

"One of the vics worked for Steiner," she said.

"One?"

"There were two."

"One was his personal assistant."

"That's right," Glass said. "What else do you know?"

"I know she was an artist," I said. "And that Steiner had promised to be her patron."

"Yeah," she said. "He's a real philanthropist. He's known to pull out his johnson faster than Quick Draw McGraw."

"Please don't ruin Quick Draw for me."

"Too late," Glass said, smiling. "Already have. This thing that happened—"

"Allegedly?"

"Not even close," she said. "This thing that happened

wasn't just Steiner. It was Poppy Palmer, too. They'd offered the victim a place to live and work close to Steiner's home. Some kind of fake residency. Even had an official name for it. One night, Steiner and Palmer come over and either get her drunk or drug her. We're not sure. But the things the victim recalls about that night are so sick and twisted, I wouldn't even wish them on you."

"Steiner and Palmer," I said.

"She's the recruiter."

"She's procured other young women for him."

"Do your clients want to make a case?" Glass said. "I would be thrilled to put them in touch with detectives at Sex Crimes. That idiot DA is long gone now. He was a drunk and a gambling addict and left the office in shame."

"I remember," I said.

"Steiner's people got to him easy," Glass said. "Makes me want to puke. But I sure found out fast how this goddamn town worked. I'd like to have a second shot at this guy."

I nodded. Glass shuffled in her seat. Her black suit jacket was slightly open, and I could see the butt of a very large revolver. She noticed me noticing and grinned.

"Don't fuck with me, Spenser," she said. "This thing with Steiner is important. I've never forgotten what he did."

"We're on to something."

Glass stood and smoothed down her jacket over the gun. She was a good head shorter than me and had to look up when I stood, too. But something about her made her feel substantial in the room. Her feet shoulder-width apart and hands on her hips. "You better be."

"You mentioned a second victim?" I said.

"Second vic was the woman's younger sister," she said. "Girl was fifteen. Son of a bitch used the older girl to rope in the younger one. The kid sister thought she could trust Steiner because her sister worked for him. Neither one of them knew what the hell was going on. Steiner and Palmer working them at the same time. I wish I could tell you more, but that'd give you too much."

"You want me to work for it."

"Work for it a little more," she said. "Find some more people to talk. And then I can maybe reach out to the sisters and see if they want to join up."

"I'd like that."

"I'm sure they would, too."

I offered my hand. Glass looked down at it and then back at me. Her hands remained on her hips. "Frank Belson swears you're okay."

"Frank is a very smart man."

"Says you helped find Lisa when she went missing a while back."

"True."

"Well," she said. "You haven't done shit for me. I figure it's about time you start."

16

I HAD DINNER WITH SUSAN and Hawk that night at Harvest in Harvard Square. Since I'd just run six miles up and down the Charles with Hawk, I felt confident to order the fried haddock with french fries and coleslaw. Susan had the roasted beet and red endive salad with lobster bisque, and Hawk had a dozen Island Creek oysters from Duxbury and a bottle of Iron Horse.

"Prepping for a big evening?" I said.

"Don't need no oysters for that," Hawk said.

"But it doesn't hurt," I said.

Hawk selected another oyster off the ice and slurped it from the shell.

"Like a Boy Scout," Hawk said, turning to study a woman standing at the bar. She had long brown hair and wore a very short blue romper. The silky material rode up high enough to know her area code. "Always prepared."

The woman glanced at Hawk and smiled. Hawk said something about needing to earn another merit badge.

"You know I'm right here," Susan said.

"Did you hear something?" I said.

Susan gave me the side eye. "Don't bother with the oysters tonight, haddock boy."

Hawk laughed. He refilled his champagne glass from a silver bucket. I was still working on a pint, and Susan had barely touched her glass of Riesling. She had on a purple silk camisole that showed off her lovely tan shoulders. Her dark black hair pinned up high on top of her head.

"Haddock should be on the state flag," I said, forking off another bite.

"Save some for the puppy," Susan said.

"Heard you still not calling that dog Pearl," Hawk said.

Susan finished a small spoonful of bisque. She patted her lips with her napkin. "I advocated calling her something else," she said. "Not to conflate Pearl's memory."

"Pearl's memory is conflated with our two Pearls and the Pearl I had as a kid."

"As a trained therapist," Susan said. "I'd say you're trying to evade grief."

"Maybe."

"Maybe his ass just crazy," Hawk said. "Only so many blows a man can take to the head."

I cut off a small portion to save for Pearl. I ate a few french fries, considering the discussion. "Makes as much sense as anything," I said.

"Reincarnation?" Susan said.

"I think I used to be a big-breasted white lady back in the day," Hawk said. "I think about them all the time."

"What about a big-breasted black woman?"

"I think about them, too," Hawk said. "And Asian. And Latina. I don't discriminate."

"It's okay to be sexist," Susan said. "As long as you're not bigoted?"

I drank some beer. "If Hawk and I didn't discuss women, we wouldn't have anything to talk about."

"You talk about sports and music," Susan said.

"I turned this white boy on to Fathead Newman."

"I already knew about Fathead Newman."

"Bullshit," Hawk said. "You only knew about 'Fathead' Newman as a sideman to Ray Charles. Not as a solo artist."

Susan looked to me. I turned to her and grudgingly nodded. She drank some Riesling. I worked on the haddock. And Hawk worked on his Iron Horse.

"This conversation on sexism and ogling women isn't over," Susan said.

"What if I ogle you all the way home?" I said.

"That," she said, "is not only permitted, it is encouraged."

Hawk shook his head and stood up. "Excuse me," he said, heading toward the woman at the end of the bar, champagne glass in hand. Something he said made the woman throw back her head in laughter.

"You never told me what you found out about the woman Wayne Arnett mentioned."

"Had a visit from my biggest fan today," I said. "Captain Lorraine Glass. Can you believe that woman still doesn't like me?"

"You're an acquired taste."

"I have explained that to her," I said. "She's still hesitant."

"What did she have to say?"

I told her about my conversation with Glass.

"Sisters," Susan said, shaking her head. "That's horrible."

"Yep."

"But pretty common," Susan said. "A sexual predator will often use a family member like a sister or even the child's mother to get close to them. The child will blame themselves and not tell what happened. The proximity to family and the predatory grooming makes it all the more shameful and scary. They feel alone and isolated. What happened to the case?"

"The DA dismissed it."

"Who was the DA?"

I told her. Susan knew many stories about him from Rita and how he'd been the reason for her leaving the DA's office and going into private practice.

"It was either a bribe or blackmail," Susan said.

"Probably," I said. "Steiner appears to have unlimited resources."

Susan sipped some more Riesling. I looked over to the bar to see how Hawk was doing with the woman in the mini-romper. She was feeling his biceps as he flexed.

"But Peter Steiner is probably used to dealing with the morally compromised or greedy."

"True."

"And you are neither."

"That is true, too."

"You'll help Mattie and her friend until he's punished," she said. "While finding out if there are others."

"That's the idea."

Susan tapped at her chin with her forefinger. She closed one eye as if giving me a long, careful consideration. I smiled back.

"It's almost as if you like me," I said.

"You are a taste I have acquired."

"Hawk left half his oysters."

Susan reached out and pushed the platter toward me.

17

TWO DAYS LATER, Mattie and I were back in South Boston looking for Chloe Turner. Calls, texts, and emails had gone unanswered.

"Maybe she's on vacation," I said.

"Sure," Mattie said. "That's it. She left Southie and jetted off for the South of France."

"Did you try her sister?"

"Of course I tried her sister," Mattie said. "You think I'm a freakin' idiot? That's how we got into this shit in the first place. She says Chloe's been home all week. And now Chloe has decided to ghost me. After all we did for her."

"I had to put on a coat and tie for the sycophants at the Blackstone Club."

"If she's scared, she should just say so."

"She was scared."

"But she said if we found more victims, she'd talk," Mattie said. "This is complete bullshit. You can't let a guy like Steiner do whatever the hell he wants."

I parked along L Street where it met Sixth. Mattie and I got out of the car and crossed the street to the triple-decker duplex where Chloe Turner lived. We barely made it to the sidewalk before a middle-aged woman in a sleeveless pink top and blue jeans walked out onto the porch and down two steps. Her blond hair had been touched by a curling iron, and she'd put a lot of time and effort into her makeup. Her fingernails were long and red. I had a chance to study them as we got close and her index finger pointed straight at my chest. "You that Spenser guy?"

"I'm incognito," I said. "Usually I wear a cape."

"She said you were big," the woman said, shaking her finger. "Said you looked like a pro wrestler with a big neck and a busted nose."

I turned to Mattie. "Chloe's mom?"

Mattie nodded.

"So shines a good deed in this weary world," I said.

"Mattie," the woman said. "Is this the guy?"

She looked at me. "This is the guy, Mrs. Turner."

"You should know better," Mrs. Turner said to Mattie. "Your mother brought you up to have more sense. God rest her soul. Don't bring these people down here to make trouble. I had to miss work yesterday because of all this crap. Knocking on doors, asking people personal questions. You're not a cop. You're just a freakin' kid."

"I'm twenty-two," Mattie said.

I introduced myself and handed her a business card. I explained that Mattie worked for me. As Mrs. Turner studied the card, I noticed she had on very tall, very pointy suede heels. The kind that could twist into the back of a grown man's hand and make him beg for mercy.

"A private investigator?" the woman said. "Bullshit. You can get those cards printed anywhere."

I opened my wallet and showed her my license. It had both my photograph and an impressive and complex watermark.

"Look, I heard about the backpack," Mrs. Turner said, hand resting on one hip. "And Chloe admitted to me about the shit she'd pulled. Taking the T into town and going to some fancy club. I told her she got exactly what she deserved. What did she think she was doing for five hundred dollars? Playing Parcheesi?"

"Did she tell you what the man did?" I said. "It wasn't Parcheesi."

"More like pop goes the weasel," Mattie said.

"Yeah?" Mrs. Turner eyed me and nodded. "She told me enough of it. And I heard his side of things from the attorney who showed up two days ago."

"The esteemed Counselor Greebel?" I said.

Mrs. Turner nodded. She pulled out a pack of Marlboro Lights from her purse and fired one up with a plastic lighter. She turned her head and blew smoke off the porch.

"That Greebel guy is a creep," Mattie said.

"He said the guy thought Chloe was eighteen," Mrs. Turner said. "Whose fault is that, Mattie? My own daughter acting like a goddamn whore."

"That's not what happened," I said.

"Oh, yeah," she said. "What the fuck do you know, Ace Ventura? This is my little girl we're talking about. She's a good kid when she's using her head. Going to give a man a rubdown for five hundred dollars. Do you really think I like my neighbors knowing about this crap?"

"This man is a predator," I said. "Your daughter was lucky to have gotten away."

"That's why she never should have gone in the first fucking place," Mrs. Turner said, pointing two fingers at me now, the cigarette stuck between them.

I looked to Mattie. She placed her hands into her Sox pitcher's jacket. Her red hair pulled into a ponytail. Her jaw working on some bubble gum.

"What did this Greebel guy tell you?" I said.

"Nothing," Mrs. Turner said, shrugging.

"Did he offer you more money?"

"More money?" she said. "No."

"Did he threaten you?"

Mrs. Turner didn't answer. She touched her tongue to her upper lip and turned to Mattie. She just shook her head. Mattie leaned against the railing and looked over to me. Mrs. Turner stood in heels as tall and thin as matchsticks.

"How'd he threaten you?" I said.

"I don't want trouble."

"Too late," I said. "This guy sexually assaulted your daughter. This guy Greebel is trying to intimidate you."

Mrs. Turner took in a long drag of the cigarette, turned her head, and blew out the smoke. "He knew I had a job with the city."

I nodded.

"He said if you guys kept on making trouble, maybe I wouldn't have that job anymore."

Mattie blew a pink bubble, and it quickly popped. Mrs. Turner just stood at the porch and stared at me. "I don't want trouble," she said again.

"He hurt some other girls, Mrs. Turner," Mattie said. "We know he raped at least one."

"Jesus," Mrs. Turner said, cigarette burning down in her fingers. "Jesus Christ."

"All of 'em kids," Mattie said.

"This wasn't Chloe's fault," I said.

"This guy Greebel said he was connected with some powerful people," Mrs. Turner said. "He said you were a bottom-feeder looking for money. And that if you tried to blackmail them, you'd get taught a lesson."

"Eek."

"You a toughie?" Mrs. Turner said. She smiled for the first time, eyeing me. She was more attractive when she smiled, again touching her upper lip with her tongue.

I shrugged in a weak attempt to appear modest.

"Can I please talk to Chloe?" Mattie said.

"She's not here," she said. "She got scared. She's with her loser father. Like he's gonna do something. Someone comes after Chloe, and he'd probably throw his back out getting out of the way."

"Can you tell her to call me?" Mattie said.

Mrs. Turner looked to Mattie, smoke scattering off the porch and down the street, and then back to me. I stood straighter to make sure she knew I was indeed a toughie.

She nodded slowly. "But please let this go," Mrs. Turner said. "No cops. Not here with my little girl."

18

MATTHEW GREEBEL, attorney at law, kept an office in a high-rise on Atlantic. I parked at the parking deck next to the Harbor Health Club and walked across the street. I rode to the twelfth floor of a tall glass building, where I found a heavyset woman with henna-colored hair who was blowing her nose.

"I'm here to see Matt," I said. "He's expecting me."

"And who are you?"

"I'm that one in ten dentists who doesn't approve of Matt's toothpaste," I said.

"Excuse me," she said.

"It's pretty urgent," I said. "He has a lot invested in those pearly whites."

The woman wiped her nose and eyed me, picking up the phone and telling Greebel that his dentist was here to see him. I winked at her, and she told me to take a seat. I didn't feel like sitting and walked to one of the large windows and looked out onto the Financial District, the Quincy Market, and far into the North End. Looking out at the North End made me think of Mike's Pastry and a peanut-butter cannoli.

I looked at my watch. Perhaps on my way home to check on Pearl.

"Who?" Greebel said, walking out from his office. He had on a white dress shirt, a blue power tie, and pleated black pants. He placed his hands on his hips and stared at me. "What do you want?"

"To continue our conversation."

"There's nothing to continue," he said. "We're done."

"You and your client might be done," I said. "But I'm not."

"No offense," Greebel said, scratching at his neck and looking to be in bad need of a shave. "But I really don't give a fuck."

I turned to his older, portly secretary. She was still snuffling into a Kleenex.

"He always talk like this?"

She shrugged and looked back to Greebel. Greebel eyed me, nodding, and appearing to be contemplating his next move.

"Gretchen, call security."

She nodded and picked up the phone again. I walked away from the window and over to Greebel. I could smell his cologne within ten feet. As he stared at me, I noticed he had some lettuce stuck in his teeth.

"Sure you don't want to talk first?"

"I'm sure," he said. "I don't usually run such small errands. You continue to harass me, and I'll call the police."

"You ran an errand down to Southie yesterday," I said. "To harass the mother of Chloe Turner. Made me wonder why an attorney in a big high-rise is driving all around Boston to protect his client. Must be some client."

"You have any more issues, take it up with the club."

I smiled and walked up even closer to Greebel. His breath was most unpleasant. I detected both onions and tuna fish.

"The club isn't your client," I said. "You're a fixer for Peter Steiner."

He snorted. "Who?"

"Peter Steiner," I said. "He had Chloe's bag. He sent you and the cash. Did you help him on the rape case as well?"

"I don't know what the fuck you're talking about."

"You will not harass Chloe Turner or her family ever again," I said. "Nor will you harass any more of Peter Steiner's victims."

"Please." Greebel gave a smug little chuckle.

"Or I'll come back here," I said. "And I will knock those caps right off your rotten teeth."

"Go ahead," he said. "Threaten me. You heard it, Gretchen. You heard it."

Gretchen heard it. She nodded, phone still cradled to her chin.

"No intimidation, no payoffs, no more threats," I said. "I'm coming for Peter."

"You're making a very big mistake."

"Please threaten me with something more original."

Greebel must have felt the lettuce in his teeth, as he used his pinkie to dislodge it. He inched closer to me, craning his neck to look up at me. The teeth, the unshaven jaw, the breath, and the cologne were hard to take. Yet I stood my ground.

"This is the big leagues, pal," he said. "I checked up on you. You're a minor-league slugger at best."

"I would recheck my sources."

"Ha," he said. "Just don't say I didn't warn you."

"Tell Steiner to keep it in his pants," I said. "Or else I'll tie it in a knot and hang it from the tallest branch of the Liberty Tree."

"What?"

I smiled and began to whistle "The Sons of Liberty" on the way out. Johnny Tremain would be proud.

19

HAWK CALLED ME bright and early the next morning. I'd just walked into my office, turned on the lights, and set a cup of coffee on my desk. Puppy Pearl trailed behind me, sniffing under the couch for a squeaky toy she'd left on her last visit.

"You got donuts?" Hawk said.

"Contrary to wild and slanderous accusations, I don't eat donuts every day."

"Seems like a waste of time to climb those steps then."

"Where are you?"

"Parked in the alley watching two ugly motherfuckers been watching your office since sunup."

"Where are they?"

"Out front the Restoration Hardware in a big-ass black truck," Hawk said. "Don't think they shopping for drapes."

I walked to my window and stared to where Berkeley Street had passed Boylston and on toward what was once, a long time ago, the Museum of Natural History.

"Who are they?"

"Don't know," Hawk said. "I got word from Tony that some serious money down on your white ass."

"Nice to be wanted."

"Not like this it ain't," he said. "Couple of sluggers in from Providence."

"You want me to come down?" I said. "Or you want to come up?"

"You already said you ain't got no donuts," Hawk said. "Shit, man. Get with the program."

I walked back to my desk, slid open my right-hand drawer, and extracted my new Smith & Wesson .357 Magnum. I slid it into my jacket pocket. Pearl found her squeaky toy, and in the tradition of her predecessor, plopped up on the couch and went to work.

"I can wait," I said. "Make them sit for a while."

"Or maybe, in twenty minutes, you decide to take a little drive."

"To somewhere where we might communicate better?"

"Now we talking."

I told him I'd head over the river to the boathouse at Magazine Beach. Hawk grunted. He seemed to like the idea.

"Across from the Shell sign," Hawk said.

He clicked off before I could answer. I found a leather holster for my .38 and strapped it to my ankle. If I'd planned better, I would've removed my bazooka from storage and hoisted it onto my shoulder. Sluggers in from Providence deserved a warm welcome.

I drank my coffee and responded to a few messages. After

ten minutes, I heard the outside door open and pulled the .357 at the ready.

It was Mattie. She held up her hands.

"Jesus Fucking Christ," she said. "What are you? Nuts?"

I nodded toward the couch, where Pearl was working on the rubber toy and trying to get the remnants of peanut butter I'd slathered inside.

"Can you watch her?"

She nodded. I took the stairs down to my Land Cruiser, and the engine turned over with a mighty roar on the second try. Classics had style but were often temperamental.

I took Storrow over to the BU Bridge and Cambridge.

I had spotted the truck two blocks down Berkeley Street. It was a big black Chevy with a grill guard and camper over the bed. The driver was good, not overly aggressive, and I wasn't completely sure it was them until I crossed the river. The traffic was light, and despite their best intentions, they had to stop behind me with a single car length between us. The windows were tinted.

It appeared he'd been too lazy to remove his snow tires from the winter.

I turned onto Memorial and soon pulled into the parking lot by the Riverside Boat Club. The large truck got caught at a light across the street while I crawled out of my car, stretched, and headed toward the boathouse.

It was a lovely early morning on the river. Most of the first-light joggers and dog walkers were gone, and all that remained was one old man in a scally cap sitting on a park bench under some tall trees. He was tossing peanuts to a squirrel. I didn't see Hawk. But one didn't often see Hawk. I knew he was there.

"Good day," the old man said.

"We'll soon find out."

I took a leisurely stroll through the racing shells up on racks and on toward the river. A crew of female rowers headed down the Charles with a motorboat following close behind, words of encouragement shouted through a bull-horn. They pulled strong and hard onto the slick silver surface. A small wake headed to the rocky shoreline.

I stopped and stared across the river to the Mass Pike and on toward the stadium lights of Fenway. The air was warm and sluggish. Geese hunted for bugs around the reeds. I took in another breath of air, hand in my pocket feeling the .357 as another crew rowed out from under the River Street Bridge. Two men walked past the boathouse and between the shells and on toward the river.

One white. One black. Both had beards and wore sun-glasses. The white man had on an army-green tank top. The black man wore a maroon-colored tropical shirt. Festive.

"Hey, asshole," the white man said.

I didn't move, as I wasn't overly fond of his greeting.

"You," the black man said. "Old man."

I was really starting not to like these guys. I turned as they entered my personal space.

"Lovely morning," I said. "Are you here to feed the squirrels or geese?"

"You're that guy they call Spenser?" the white man said. "You don't look so tough."

"Same could go for you," I said. "You should go up in size

on that tank top. Makes your belly look like the Pillsbury Doughboy."

"Oh, yeah?" the white man said.

"Fuck him up, Buddy," the black man said.

Buddy's tank top didn't do much to hide his belly or the clear outline of a pistol tucked under the tank and into a pair of camo cargo shorts. From over their shoulders, I watched a silver Jaguar slide into the parking lot, the engine purring low and effortless.

"Yeah, Buddy," I said. "Fuck me up."

"From now on, mind your own goddamn business," the black man said.

Buddy took a big step toward me and moved into a fighting stance. He lifted his chin at me. "Come on, old man."

"You guys the best Greebel could find?"

"Who the fuck is Greebel?" Buddy said.

"Peter Steiner?"

They didn't answer. The black man looked to me and shook his head. He turned and spit as Buddy took a step toward me. It was too close for my liking, and I bopped him twice, very hard and very fast, on the schnoz. Blood ran down to his chin, but he moved forward undeterred. He wiped the blood and flicked it away with his fingers.

"Fuck him up, Buddy. Kill his ass."

Buddy feinted a right to my midsection, and I countered with a fist to his throat. He landed a solid punch to my right ear, hard enough that I could hear the Bells of St. Mary's. The man was close enough to smell, which was most unpleasant, and I head-butted him twice, knocking him from his center of gravity and back on his heels.

There was a hard snick of a gun. And Buddy stopped to catch his breath.

"Now you gonna stand there and take the beating, old man," the black man said. "You understand? Take that shit."

I saw Hawk only slightly before they did. He had slipped into a crisp Burberry trench coat, long enough to hide the sawed-off 12-gauge in his hands.

"Hey, young brother," Hawk said. "Drop that gun. Down on your knees. Hands on your head."

The younger man started to argue. But when he turned to Hawk, he nodded and did as he was told.

Hawk kicked the gun away, found a park bench along the path, and took a seat. He had the shotgun trained on the man's back. He looked up to me and Buddy and said, "Continue."

"What?" Buddy said.

"Y'all got paid to kick this man's ass," Hawk said. "Just giving you the space and opportunity."

"His name is Buddy," I said.

"Course it is," Hawk said. "Bud-dy."

Buddy let out a long breath, shook his hands, and then lifted them as fists. He motioned to me again with his head, a gesture I found most annoying. He stood maybe two inches taller and probably weighed eighty pounds more than me. His beard was big and burly like a logger from Oregon or a hipster from Brooklyn. He smiled as he circled me, and I noticed the glint of a gold incisor.

He grunted and came toward me, arms flailing. He landed one against the meat of my left shoulder and I tapped another on his bloody nose and two in his stomach. His stomach was large but not altogether soft, and the blows didn't seem to have much of an impact.

"Come on, Buddy," Hawk said. "Teach this man a lesson."

I saw Hawk in my peripheral vision and shook my head.

"Man's old," Hawk said. "Probably needs one of them Rascal motor scooters."

Buddy came at me again, loose and fast, hands flailing. I reached out and grabbed his thick hair and collared him into a headlock. He was strong, but not strong enough, and I twisted him down hard and fast into the pathway like a prized steer. I held Buddy's head in the crook of my arm and squeezed in an attempt to unscrew his head from his body. I had on jeans and Red Wings that morning and walked the man counterclockwise into a subservient hold that would've brought admiration from Gorgeous George.

Down the pathway, I saw the old man feeding the squirrels had moved closer onto another green bench. His entire body turned to us as he cracked a peanut and ate it.

When Buddy's face began to turn a bright shade of purple, his partner took exception.

"Let him go," his partner said. "Shit, man. Let him go."

Hawk stood and walked close to the man with his hands on his head. He pressed the end of the 12-gauge against the back of his head. "Shhh," Hawk said.

Hawk pulled the gun from Buddy's waist as he struggled to breathe. Hawk tossed the pistol far into the river. So far, I didn't even hear a plop.

"Got to admire the progressive nature of these fools," Hawk said.

"White and black," I said, loosening my hold by a milli-meter.

"Ebony and ivory," Hawk said. "Y'all had enough? Ready to head back to Little Rhody? Had enough big-city fun?"

I let go of Buddy's head and stood up. He moved into a seated position and gasped for breath.

The black man, still on his knees, stared at Hawk. He looked away and shook his head, spitting again.

"Nobody told me you'd be here," the young black man said.

"You know who I am?" Hawk said.

The black man nodded. Buddy tried to stand, but I kicked his feet out from under him and told him to stay still. He sat back down hard. He looked up at me and tried to muster a hard look without success.

"Me and this white boy an old-school tag team," Hawk said. "Your ass ready?"

The black man looked down at his partner and shook his head. "Naw, man," he said. "Not you."

Hawk turned and tossed the black man's gun into the river. This time I heard a heavy plop.

"Long ride back to Providence," Hawk said.

"Might I recommend a book on tape?" I said.

Hawk nodded. *How to Lose Friends and Not Influence People.*

Hawk pointed the shotgun at both men, explained the damage it could do at close range, and told them to run, not walk, back to their truck. They did as they were told. Hawk slid the shotgun up into its hiding place in his trench coat.

"An overcoat in June?" I said.

"You think I'm too eccentric for Cambridge?"

"Not by a long shot."

As we passed the old man on the park bench, he looked up and cracked a peanut. He stared at me and Hawk and tipped his scally cap.

"How'd we do?" I said.

"Nice show," the old man said, lifting his sack of peanuts to me.

I took a handful and offered a few to Hawk while we walked away.

"Maybe we should join the circus," Hawk said.

"Plenty of time," I said.

20

LATER THAT AFTERNOON, I took Pearl home and changed out the bloody shirt for a fresh one before meeting Rita Fiore at Legal at Long Wharf. She was waiting at the bar, keeping the full attention of the bartender who appeared to be rightfully taken with his customer.

"What are we drinking?" I said.

"A mojito," Rita said.

I ordered a Sam Adams on draft and an ice water.

"Ice water?" she said.

"Had an early-morning workout."

Rita looked as stunning as always. She had on a black pencil skirt that hit right above her knees and a cream-colored silk top that showed off her arms and highlighted her other assets. Her red hair was pinned up on top of her head, and she wore a pair of emerald earrings bigger than a cat's eye. She smelled like Paris in April.

"What's the occasion?" she said.

"I hadn't seen you in a while."

"How's the background work coming?"

"It's coming."

"But you're not done?"

"Close," I said. "But no cigar."

Rita sipped on her mojito. There was a lot of fresh mint nestled among the crushed ice. I knew it probably looked much better than it tasted. I never cared for mojitos. The bartender brought me the beer and winked at Rita. Rita winked back at him.

"Flirting in my presence," I said. "I'm hurt."

"You'll always be my number-two backup."

"Number two?"

"Sixkill has moved to the top of the charts."

I grasped my heart to let her know how much she'd wounded me. "I grow old, I grow old," I said. "I shall wear the bottom of my trousers rolled."

She peered down at my neatly cuffed blue jeans over my Red Wing boots. She looked up at me and grinned. "Too late," she said.

I drank some beer and set the cold glass against my swelling knuckles. Along the docks, sailboats stirred in the early-afternoon breeze. A nearly cloudless day on the harbor.

"The reason you've been slow on my case—" Rita said, crossing her lovely pale legs.

"Is because of Susan."

"My legal case," Rita said, running a finger up and down her wet glass. "Is because you have found another."

"Never."

"Peter Steiner?" she said. Her green eyes were very large and very beautiful and very judgmental.

"Oh, no," I said.

"Oh, yes," she said. "Do I need to remind you that Boston is but a small town?"

"I was reminded of that only this morning," I said. "Assistance had to be brought in from Rhode Island."

"Is that why there is a slight bruise against your neck and your right hand is swollen?"

"Old lady tried to take my parking spot."

The bartender returned, and we both ordered lunch. Crab cake salad for Rita, and I had a tuna burger with fries and coleslaw. The bartender acted as if I didn't exist, keeping eye contact with Rita.

"Peter Steiner should be rotting in prison," she said.

"Please," I said. "Don't hold back on my account."

"He's this city's version of the Marquis de Sade."

"Yikes."

"Yep," she said. "And everything you heard from Lorraine Glass about my former boss royally fucking up the case is spot-on."

"Did he fuck it up," I said. "Or did he drop it?"

"Was he paid?"

I nodded.

"Maybe," she said. "But we're talking about a man who had more skeletons in his closet than the Haunted Mansion at Disney."

"Glass said they had everything they needed."

"She's right."

"I didn't know you and Glass were friends."

"There is much about me you don't know, buster," Rita said. "You could fill an encyclopedia with it."

A crowd of schoolkids had gathered in front of the aquarium. An exasperated young woman counted heads as the
kids milled about the docks, playing at the edge of the water,
seagulls swirling overhead. Above them a marquee to the
IMAX theater boasted a film about great white sharks.

"Can I get him now?" I said.

"Hard to get traction on an old case that already went to
the grand jury."

"That's something I didn't know."

"DA made a deal with Steiner," she said. "He admitted to
solicitation. Two years later, he had the charge expunged."

"These girls weren't prostitutes."

"They were sisters," Rita said. "One was fifteen."

I told her about Chloe Turner, Debbie Delgado, and Amelia Lynch, although I didn't mention any of their names.

"You're thinking of a class-action civil suit?" she said.

"Precisely."

Rita nodded. She drank some mojito at a much faster
rate than Susan enjoying a glass of white wine. She sipped
even more and raised a finger at the young bartender. His
service was polite and prompt. He could not keep his eyes
off Rita, and I didn't blame him.

Rita nodded and pursed her lips. Her makeup was flawless.

"Have any of these girls been taken out of state?" she
said.

"Not that I know of."

"But you think there are others?"

"I'm sure of it."

"I recall Steiner having some kind of compound in

Miami," Rita said. "Only rumors about what he did down there. Maybe a private island? Horny old wealthy men are the worst. Lots of young women. A hedonistic fuckfest."

"Please," I said. "Slow with the legal terminology."

"Do you know anyone in Miami?"

"By chance, I happen to know the special agent in charge of the FBI's Miami office."

"Does he like you?" Rita said.

"Surprisingly enough," I said. "He adores me."

"Adores?"

"He likes," I said. "And most importantly tolerates."

"That's where I'd go," she said. "You'll have much better luck with the Feds. I don't know who Steiner knows now. But I still don't trust the Suffolk DA's office to follow through. Do you have any idea of the wealth this guy has?"

"Like a dirty Scrooge McDuck."

"Only it's not golden coins he wants to swim in."

"Sick," I said.

"And well insulated."

The bartender served us our lunch. He asked Rita if there was anything else he could do. *Anything else at all.* She cut her eyes at me and smiled.

"Hold that thought, kid," she said. "I'll let you know."

21

SUSAN WAS AT MY APARTMENT when I returned to the Navy Yard. She had Pearl out in the common area, sniffing the grass and getting used to going outside to take care of her business. After the puppy made a deposit, Susan bestowed praise befitting a Nobel Prize winner.

"You know," I said, "she's accomplished that task many times before."

"Not with me," she said.

"She hasn't been locked up long," I said. "I've only been gone a few hours."

Susan scooped up Pearl in her arms and kissed her on the nose. "Too long for the baby."

"Now she's the baby?"

"She's precious," she said. "I just don't know if she's Pearl."

I nodded and followed them up to my apartment on the second story of what had been a shipping warehouse. I re-filled Pearl's water dish and made a vodka gimlet for Susan and scotch for me, with lots of ice and lots of soda. Pearl had brought home the lost squeaky toy from my office and ran around in circles, tossing the toy up and down and growling at it.

"So," Susan said, resting a hip against my kitchen counter. "Florida?"

"Boca Raton," I said. "Steiner has a tropical retreat near there."

"When?"

"We leave tomorrow morning."

"*We* meaning—?"

"Me and Mattie."

"I had assumed you and Hawk," Susan said. "Or you and me."

"Sorry," I said. "This is all business."

"I don't mean to slight Mattie," Susan said, "but Hawk is often a better companion in your line of work."

"I investigate," I said. "I don't break glass unless there's an emergency."

"And you're taking Mattie because this is her case?" Susan said.

"I'm coming along in an advisory role only," I said.

"And in case she needs to break the glass."

I nodded. I drank some scotch and walked to the freezer to fill a plastic baggie with ice. My hand had swollen into a fist that looked like I'd inflated it at the thumb.

"It's awfully nice of you to foot the bill," Susan said.

"There's money left over from L.A.," I said. "Gabby Leggett's mother has been most grateful."

"As she should be," Susan said. "I heard Gabby's doing much better. Back home with her family and taking therapy."

Susan squatted to the ground and snatched away Pearl's

toy while managing not to slosh her drink. She tossed it far over the couch and Pearl chased it with much pep and vigor.

"Has Mattie ever been on a trip like this?" Susan said.

"Mattie has never left Massachusetts," I said. "The farthest south she's been has been Braintree on the Red Line."

Susan nodded. "So there's that, too."

"We're going to stay at the old hotel at the Boca Raton Resort," I said. "Not a bad place to broaden her horizons. It will be good for her to travel. See the world outside the Commonwealth."

"Sure you don't need a sexy Jewish shrink on the trip as an adviser?"

"Quick trip," I said. "I hope. I'll drop the pup with Janet before our flight."

Susan twisted her mouth and closed one eye, contemplating the situation for the next few days. "Or," she said.

I drank some scotch. I leaned against the kitchen counter alongside Susan and waited.

"Maybe she could stay with me."

"The Puppy with No Name."

"Just for a few days," she said. "Right?"

"The puppy howls when she's in her crate," I said. "There is much weeping and gnashing of teeth. What will your patients think?"

Susan set down her drink and reached for Pearl. She cradled the pup on her back up close to her breast. Puppy Pearl rewarded Susan with lots of kisses on the nose and eyes. Susan laughed and did not try to stop her.

"Fuck 'em," she said.

22

BY NOON THE NEXT DAY, we'd landed in Fort Lauderdale. Two hours later, I waited for Mattie in the lobby of the Boca Raton Resort and Club. I had already unpacked and changed into khakis and a blue polo shirt. As I stood by the concierge desk, I began to wonder if I should have packed an ascot. Or at least borrowed one from Hawk. The lobby had a certain Old World elegance, with high white ceilings, marble columns, and potted palms.

"Jesus, Spenser," Mattie said, coming up behind me. "Are you sure we can afford this?"

"I can afford this," I said.

"But you'll expense it," she said. "It's part of the case."

"Of course."

"The guy at the front said they got five pools," she said. "And a private beach."

"Pity we won't have time to enjoy them all."

Mattie had on the same thing she'd worn on the plane: a V-neck T-shirt with red and white stripes, skinny jeans, and black Chuck Taylor low-tops. Some classics never change. She had her hair in a ponytail and a notebook in hand.

"What are we waiting for?" she said. "Let's go find Steiner's house. You already know the address."

I nodded. "Patience," I said. "Time to learn the hard facts about sleuthing."

"What's that?"

"Not much glitz and glamour," I said. "First stop is the county courthouse, and then we need to stop by the local newspaper. I've learned it's best to get the lay of the land before storming the castle."

"Is that what we're going to do?" Mattie said. "Storm the castle?"

"Probably not," I said. "But I do hope to get a pretty good view of the drawbridge. And maybe of Steiner, too."

Mattie leaned in and whispered in my ear. "I've got a phone next to my toilet."

"All the comforts of home."

"Two sinks, a freakin' huge bathtub, and a view of the ocean," Mattie said.

"Business trips don't have to suck."

"This doesn't suck," Mattie said. "Not by a long shot."

We walked out to the porte cochere, and I handed the valet my ticket. I whistled "Moon Over Miami" while we waited, although I knew it to be geographically incorrect. I knew the Connee Boswell version but didn't recall Betty Grable singing in the film. Perhaps I was too transfixed by her legs.

"Maybe when this is all over, we can expense the trip to Peter Steiner," I said.

"How often do the bad guys get what they deserve?"

"In my experience?" I said.

Mattie nodded.

"Fifty-fifty," I said.

"But you try anyway," she said. "I kept on thinking what Chloe and Amelia told us. It makes me want to puke."

"Don't clutter your mind up with it," I said. "People like Steiner are a virus."

"Your mind is clear?"

"And my heart is pure," I said. "That's why my strength is the strength of ten."

"Cool your jets," she said. "Don't get too ahead of yourself."

I shrugged. The valet brought around my car, which was silver, appropriately dull, and generic enough for the work that needed to be done.

We wheeled away from the hotel, and I headed toward I-95, which would get you anywhere you wanted to go on the East Coast. South Florida was not Boston, and I immediately turned the air conditioner to full blast.

"But later?" Mattie said. "When we're done with work."

"The pools?"

Mattie nodded.

"All work and no play makes for a dull sleuth."

"You think?"

I slipped on my sunglasses. "I know."

23

NO MATTER HOW MUCH and how well I flirted with the clerk, we found no misdemeanor or felony charges against Peter Steiner in Palm Beach County. Not so much as a parking ticket. We did, however, learn that eighteen months ago, a man named Jorge "Pepe" De Santos sued Steiner for breach of contract. According to the suit, Steiner withheld payment to De Santos for landscaping services at his compound in Seagrass, Florida, and still owed him five grand.

"Well, that was one big waste of time," Mattie said, walking back to the car. The sun very high and hot over the parking lot.

"The devil thrives in the details."

"Not this bastard."

"Can you believe that woman wasn't taken with my charm?"

"I think you annoyed her," she said. "Maybe you're better in Boston."

"My charm defies borders."

Pepe De Santos owned a company called Fighting Fitz-patrick Landscapers Inc., which sat at the end of a dead-end street in Lake Worth. The sky seemed bigger and bluer here, expansive, with momentary white clouds passing overhead. One-story ranch houses with small palms and palmettos lined the mostly residential street.

Fighting Fitzpatrick Landscapers consisted of two white single-wide trailers and a large metal barn. Small plants and trees sat in plastic buckets among giant mounts of soil and mulch. A sprinkler *click-click-click*ed, watering a grouping of flowers in long flats. Several white pickup trucks were parked along the chain-link fence, with trailers loaded with riding lawn mowers and weed trimmers. Men in dirty white shirts and work pants came and went from the big metal barn.

I asked one where to find De Santos, and he pointed inside.

As we walked into the open barn, I thought I heard the music of Pérez Prado playing. But since I only knew "Cherry Pink and Apple Blossom White," I couldn't be positive. Hawk would've known. He had spent a considerable amount of time in Cuba.

A wiry little man in shorts and no shirt stood at a workbench, sharpening a long mower blade. The blade was held in a large vise, the man's hands large and streaked with grease as he worked a file back and forth.

"Mr. De Santos?" I said.

He nodded, picked up a cigarette, and turned down the radio. His skin was very dark and leathery. He had a full head of black hair flecked with gray. His muscles knotted and corded like an old fisherman's. He looked like the kind of guy who might've had his prize marlin eaten by sharks.

"Pérez Prado?" I said.

He shook his head. "Beny Moré."

"Ah."

"My father's favorite," De Santos said, with the slightest accent, taking a drag off a cigarette and setting it on the corner of the workbench. "So romantic."

The barn smelled of dirt and old oil, a little freshly cut grass, too. Weed trimmers and blowers hung from the ceilings, along with an armada of riding lawn mowers parked along the concrete floor. Everything was neat and orderly. Every tool had its place in a long stretch of pegboard. Three men covered in sweat and grass stains walked in behind us.

De Santos waved them away with a hand. "How may I help you?"

"We came to talk to you about Peter Steiner," Mattie said.

The corded muscles in De Santos's neck and shoulders stiffened. He lifted the cigarette but didn't take a drag. Beny Moré sang on. I couldn't tell Beny Moré from Pérez Prado from Xavier Cugat. All I knew is that Xavier Cugat always had a Chihuahua when he took photos.

"I have nothing to say about that man," De Santos said. He picked up the file and continued to sharpen the blade. Somewhere outside a truck started, and you could hear the jostling of the trailer following behind.

"We don't work for Steiner," I said.

"Yeah," Mattie said. "Steiner is a complete creep."

De Santos stopped sharpening again and lifted his eyes to both of us. He took a drag from the cigarette. "How can I be sure?" he said.

I showed him my license.

"You are a long way from home," he said. "And who is she?"

"My boss," I said.

De Santos shrugged and took a seat on a stool by the workbench. The air was heavy with smoke and the tang of sharpened metal. "That man wouldn't pay me for two months' work," he said. "He is a thief. I've kept this business going because people know I do good work. And I do what I promise. Just like the man who had this business before me."

"You mean you're not the original Fighting Fitzpatrick?"

De Santos laughed and let out a little smoke from the side of his mouth. "The business is very well known," De Santos said. "Mr. Steiner turned longtime customers against me. He tells them lies about my work. He says that I walked off the job and left his estate a mess. All lies."

Mattie asked what happened as a heavyset Latina in khaki pants and a T-shirt adorned with a shamrock walked into the barn. She held a white paper sack, looked to us and smiled, and dropped the sack onto the bench.

De Santos fired off something to her in Spanish, nodding to me and Mattie.

Without missing a beat, Mattie, also in Spanish, seemed to clarify something for him. He looked to the woman and nodded.

The woman looked to us and then back to De Santos as if deciding what to believe.

"I didn't know you knew Spanish," I said.

"You never asked," Mattie said. "Mr. De Santos doesn't trust us."

I touched my chest with my right hand. "Don't I look trustworthy?"

Mattie turned back to De Santos and the woman and spoke to them for a long while in both Spanish and English. True to her Boston upbringing, she used her hands a lot. She said we were investigators working for young girls Peter Steiner had abused.

The woman nodded at De Santos and left the metal barn.

De Santos didn't touch whatever lunch he'd been brought. His resolve was impressive. The food smelled wonderful, and I hadn't eaten since the flight.

"I couldn't go there another day," De Santos said. "This man is the devil."

"How?" Mattie said.

"Please."

Mattie reached into her pocket for her cell phone. She thrust the phone forward and scrolled through several images.

"They're just kids," she said.

"The girls I saw were young, too," he said. "One day I saw two girls swimming in the pool. They were both completely naked. Children. Just children. Not developed. Not of age. I saw Steiner come outside in a robe. He took the robe off and jumped in to join them. I ignored them and kept working in the flower garden. What I saw later turned my stomach. Steiner's gray head between the legs of a young girl. I gathered my men and my equipment and left. I sent him a bill for the weeks of work I'd done. He refused to pay."

"Was that the first time you saw him with kids?" I said.

"No," De Santos said. "But it was the worst. Something I couldn't ignore. Steiner has many friends. Many who join him in this. I have worked in this county long enough to know how to keep to myself. Mr. Fitzpatrick worked on the Miami estates of many drug lords and never said a word. But this is different. This man is different. It is a secret world behind his gates. And if you speak out against him or say a word, men will come for you. They have harassed me many times."

"What kind of men?" I said.

"Men with expensive haircuts and dark suits," he said. "They come from Miami and threatened my business and my family if I ever discussed what I saw. They spoke to me like I was some orange picker who didn't know the law. I have lived in this country for forty years, Mr. Spenser. They were not the police. They had no right to come into my home and tell me what to do."

"Why not go to the police?" I said.

"In Palm Beach County?" De Santo said, snorting. "Only more of the same. Men like Steiner own the police and the judges. Perhaps I saw judges and politicians in his pool."

"Did you?" Mattie said.

De Santos gave a small, noncommittal shrug. "Here, you are either moneyed or not. I'm just the hired help. Same as you. I will never get paid for my work. And lawyers are very expensive. More than I make."

"I am well aware," I said.

"Steiner knows he never has to pay me," De Santos said. "He tells lies to put me in my place."

"What do you know about these men who came to scare you?" Mattie said.

"Dark cars like men in government," he said. "Dade County license plates."

"Do you think they were cops?" I said.

"They didn't say they were," he said, finishing the cigarette. He crushed it in a Café Bustelo can filled with sand. "Or if they were not. They reminded me of those men who investigate aliens."

"That's bullshit," Mattie said. "You're a citizen with rights."

"Aliens," De Santos said, smiling and pointing upward to the sky. "Men in black."

"Maybe Peter Steiner is from another planet," I said.

"I know he is not a man," De Santos said, squinting into the smoke. "This man has no heart. No soul. And no honor."

"I'd like to see where he lives."

De Santos held up a hand and walked over to a tool kit on the bench. He handed me a plastic card with SEAGRASS EXPRESS written on it. "No one gets on the island without one of these."

24

I BOUGHT CUBAN SANDWICHES and Cokes at a gas station, and we drove onto Seagrass. I used the pass De Santos had given me to enter the gates, and soon we found our way onto the isthmus that ran parallel to Florida's east coast. It was a sliver of real estate between Palm Beach and Boca with a two-lane road running north and south. I estimated most of the houses cost more than the GDP of Bora-Bora.

The estates were immense, barrel-roofed, with unfettered views of the Atlantic. The lawns full of palm trees, seagrape, bougainvillea, and birds-of-paradise. We weren't on Comm Ave anymore.

"I didn't know people lived like this," Mattie said.

"Ever been to Marblehead?"

"No."

"This is like Marblehead with palm trees."

We found Steiner's compound within five minutes. The avenue was long and narrow, with no shoulder or turnarounds. It appeared as if it was almost designed for people who put a premium on privacy. There were little to no places where a respectable snoop could park, eat a sandwich, and sit on a house.

"How am I expected to do my job?" I said.

"You drive," Mattie said. "I'll eat."

"That defeats the purpose of a stakeout," I said. "The best part is eating. Or drinking coffee."

"Too hot for coffee," Mattie said.

I made a U-turn in front of another waterfront mansion and doubled back to Steiner's address. This time I drove slower and more carefully, not being able to see much behind the large iron gate and twisting brick driveway. Tall palms dotted the property, and a long stucco fence faced the main road.

"Can you drive up to the gate?" she said.

"Cameras would catch us."

"Is that a bad thing?"

"It's a bad thing if we wish to remain discreet."

"Isn't one of your rules of detecting 'bother the crap out of someone until they do something stupid'?"

"Rule number eleven."

"Do you really remember the numbers?"

"One day, I'll write them all down," I said. "For posterity."

"But that's what you do?" she said. "When you don't have jack shit?"

I shrugged and kept on heading north. That was pretty much the action along the Seagrass strip. Cruise north and then south and then do it all again. Maybe head on down to the malt shop and hang out with Potsie and the Fonz. There was little to see outside the tall gates, fences, and high shrubs. A common man had to rely on his imagination.

"Do you think he's here?" Mattie said.

"That's what I was told."

"I'd like him to know we are here, too."

"You're the boss."

"But what would you do?"

I thought about it, driving north and then doubling back again. "I'd find a way to say hello," I said. "And get under his skin."

"Like a big Fuck You."

"Sure," I said. "Something like that."

I slowed in front of Steiner's compound and pulled into the expanse of patterned brick before the iron gate. I stopped in the shade of two palms, let down the windows, and turned off the ignition. It was very quiet, the smell of the sea strong.

"What now?" Mattie said.

"We wait for someone to tell us to buzz off."

"And what will you say?"

"I'll ask to speak to their boss," I said. "Tell them I'm a master of the art of shiatsu."

"What's that?"

"A Japanese massage technique."

"I don't think you're his type," she said. "Big and hairy."

I reached behind my seat for the sandwiches and handed one to Mattie. I unwrapped the other while watching the big gate not ten feet away from where I'd parked. I finished my sandwich in record time while Mattie worked on the first half.

"He already knows we're onto him," Mattie said.

I nodded.

"I can't believe he threatened Chloe's mom like that," she said.

"I can."

"Creep."

"A well-moneyed creep," I said. "The worst."

"I don't know how you do it."

"Eat an entire Cuban sandwich in under three minutes?"

"Not go bullshit on these people," she said. "I want to climb that fence and take a baseball bat to Steiner."

"Can't do that."

"Why not?"

"That's called assault," I said. "You can go to jail for that. Trust me. It happens."

"Don't men like this bother you?"

"They do."

"But you don't show it."

I nodded. "I don't like what they are and what they do," I said. "But if I allow their behavior to influence me, then I might get sloppy."

"Do something stupid," she said. "Like knocking a bastard's teeth in with a baseball bat."

"Precisely."

"I don't know if I can do it."

"Takes time," I said. "And a few years of experience."

Mattie finished the first half of her sandwich. She wrapped up the second half in wax paper and placed it back in the bag. "I don't like all this sneaking around," she said. "I'd rather go straight to it. Cut out the bullshit."

"The bullshit is what some might call investigating."

"You can't arrest anyone," she said. "You can't make a case against these creeps."

"But I know people who can."

Mattie nodded, her Sox cap down far in her eyes. Beyond the gate and the well-manicured lawn, the light began to turn a soft gold. The sea shimmered blue and endless off the sea wall, a gentle roiling among the sailboats and pleasure crafts.

"How can Steiner live with himself?"

"Susan would say because he's a sociopath," I said. "And I would agree."

"No feelings?"

"None whatsoever."

"But kids," Mattie said. "Christ."

I was about to ask Mattie for the second half of her sandwich when our presence drew the attention of a white Ford Explorer with a light bar on the cab. The patrol car stopped. Two white men in uniform got out and walked toward our rental.

"Mission accomplished," I said.

"Now what?" she said.

"Don't you recall Spenser's lesson number twelve?"

"Bullshit your way through anything."

"Ah." I smiled. "You were listening."

25

THE BOYS FROM SEAGRASS PD were polite enough to let us follow them to their office in our own car. I didn't challenge the invitation, as that was the point of the exercise. I'd been there all of ten minutes when Chief Jimmy Goodyear strolled in and took a seat in a rolling leather chair. Being a trained detective, I had noted his name on the door.

Mattie sat outside the glass office, annoyed that the chief wanted to talk only to me. I explained it was probably not an issue of gender but age.

Goodyear appeared about as old as me and looked like most cops I knew. Potbellied, big-mustached, with sandy, thinning hair and the ruddy face of a guy who liked one too many whiskeys after a short day of work. He laced his hands atop his desk and looked up.

"So," I said. "I think this is where you tell me that you don't take too kindly to strangers around here."

"Why were you and that young lady parked outside Mr. Steiner's compound?"

"I'm an eccentric billionaire," I said. "I heard Steiner had the Midas touch. Lately, I've been thinking of investing in orange groves and pork bellies."

"Funny," he said. "You don't look like a millionaire. Not with that mug."

"I earned my money the old-fashioned way," I said. "I inherited it."

"Nope," he said. "Not buying it. Who's the girl? And why were you driving her to see Mr. Steiner?"

I leaned back in my chair. It was chrome and black and designed with all the comfort of the Spanish Inquisition.

"Am I being charged with something?"

"I don't know," he said. "This is a private community, Mr. Spenser. It appears you entered our gates under false pretenses."

I smiled. "Not buying the eccentric-billionaire story?"

He shook his head. "Not one damn bit," he said. "I've been around enough of those assholes to know one when I see one."

I nodded. The wall behind Goodyear and the wall behind me were made of glass. The two walls that sandwiched us were filled with many framed photos of ball players and fishing trips, cheap golden plaques handed out at annual rubber-chicken dinners with the Jaycees.

"How old is that girl?" he said.

"Old enough to work for me."

"And what do you do, sir?"

I told him and told him that we'd just arrived from Boston that morning.

"Bullshit," he said.

I pulled out my wallet again to show off my shiny official license. He took it over the desk, studied it, and returned it.

"And she is your—"

"Assistant," I said. "Although technically this is her investigation."

He smiled and leaned back into his chair. "She looks like she's fifteen."

"She's twenty-two," I said. "And in college."

"Studying to be a gumshoe?"

"Haven't heard that term in a while," I said. "But yes. With a minor in the art of the low country masters. Why did you think we were here?"

Goodyear let out a long breath and scratched at the stubble on his cheek with his right hand. His big sandy mustache drooped over his upper lip like a walrus. "I'm sorry," he said. "Lots of people come and go from that place. Sometimes we try and persuade them to rethink their life choices."

"Ah," I said. "You thought I was a pimp."

"I didn't say that," he said. His ruddy face colored even more. "No, sir. I didn't say that."

"If I were a pimp, I'd wear a white suit and straw hat," I said. "And I'd drive a big car with a horn that played 'Flying Down to Rio.'"

"Put yourself in my shoes," Goodyear said. "Older man showing up with a young girl at Steiner's place. Obviously, you know his reputation."

I told him I did and offered a few select details of what Steiner had been up to in Boston.

"You won't be able to catch him," he said. "Sorry. Not now. Not ever."

"That's a bit pessimistic," I said. "I'm more of can-do kind of guy."

"Yeah?" Goodyear said. "Stick around here awhile, and you'll be cleared of that."

I crossed my left ankle over my right knee. I'd removed my ball cap and rested it on top of my shoe. "What can you tell me?"

"Sounds like you know the story."

"Don't be so sure."

"Steiner has more money than Jay-Z and Beyoncé and keeps quite a stable of pals who've become accustomed to his lifestyle."

"And what is that lifestyle?"

"On the record?" Goodyear said. "Or off?"

"I'm not a reporter," I said. "We flew down here to learn more about Steiner."

"I hear that man has parties that would make Caligula's goat puke."

"Caligula had a goat?"

"Oh, come on." Goodyear nodded. "You know he did."

"Any formal charges?"

"A few."

"Any stick?"

"Nope," he said. "Funny thing. The victims come to recant their stories pretty fast."

"How many of the victims were kids?"

"Two," he said. "One was sixteen. Her parents wouldn't allow her to testify. The DA backed away faster than a four-alarm dumpster fire. Besides, what had *allegedly* happened didn't technically happen in Seagrass."

"I sense some sarcasm in that 'allegedly,'" I said. "Where was the girl assaulted?"

"I've seen bigger men than you get waylaid by this fella," he said. "You sure you want to take these people on?"

I nodded.

"You do look like you'd be fair to middlin' in a fight."

"A little better than that."

Goodyear let out a long breath. His eyelids drooped heavily as he weighed his next thought. He pulled at the walrus mustache and leaned back in his chair. "Ever heard of Cerberus Security?"

I shook my head.

"Big-time outfit out of Miami," Goodyear said. "No offense, but they're not like you. I'm talking hundreds of employees in lots of different countries. They work for Saudi princes and professional ballplayers who shoot their career to hell in one night. Cerberus has computer hackers, financial specialists, bodyguards, and people that make people like you disappear."

"Eek."

"Steiner has Cerberus on speed dial," he said. "This is the place where cops go when they decide to make some real money. Ex-military, maybe some ex-spooks, too."

"I've dealt with men like that before."

"Okay, tough guy," Goodyear said. "But my advice to you is have a nice stay in Boca. Have a piña colada or two by the pool and then fly on back to Boston. Tell your client that you didn't get what you need."

"I can't do that."

"Why not?"

"For all we have and are," I said. "For all our children's fate."

"Is that from a book or something?"

"Or something."

"Good luck," he said and tossed me back my license. "Snoop all you want. His people might get in your way. But I won't. I can't stand the cocky bastard. I've had so many threats by his people, the city keeps a lawyer on retainer. You'll never catch him. Not here. Seagrass is just a waystation for him. He stays here just one night or maybe two and then he's gone."

Goodyear knew how to string out a tale. I turned around and saw Mattie pacing back and forth in the small police department lobby. When she spotted me, she relayed a look of great annoyance. I held up a hand to wave, and she turned her back.

"Steiner flies down here and then jumps on a private jet to his island."

"What island?"

"His fucking island," Goodyear said. "Remember when I said this son of a bitch had more money and clout than you can imagine? Peter Steiner bought an entire island in the Bahamas. No law. No rules. That's where he takes these girls. God help them."

26

I WAS BACK IN MY HOTEL ROOM, speaking with Susan. A thunderstorm had moved into Boca, and the back gardens were awash in long sheets of rain. The rain tapped hard at the banana trees, palms, and hibiscus outside my window.

"An entire island?" Susan said.

"Apparently besides being a whiz with investments, he also plays Mr. Rourke to horny old billionaires."

"Pedophiles."

"The chief wasn't sure what happens on the island, but that's the working theory."

"How's Mattie?"

"She turned a cold shoulder at the chief's office," I said. "She didn't like that the chief wanted to speak to me first."

"You said it was her case," Susan said. "Perhaps you should have insisted."

"The chief thought Mattie was much younger."

"So?"

"He thought I was her pimp," I said. "Bringing her to Steiner's compound."

"Were you wearing a white linen suit?" she said.

"No," I said. "But I am thinking of buying one. Think of how dashing I'd look, taking you out for a stroll on the Harvard Square, and popping into Charlie's for a burger and a cold one."

"I won't go walking with you in a white suit," she said. "And I'd prefer a cocktail at the Russell House Tavern when you get home."

"One more day," I said. "And tomorrow won't be any easier. I'm meeting with Special Agent Epstein alone outside the FBI office. It's impossible to bring Mattie to get what I need from him."

"Have you tried to explain that to her?"

"Working up the courage."

I'd bought two beers at the hotel bar, and the first one was already empty. I planned to meet Mattie in thirty minutes at SeaGrille at the Beach Club. I had enlightened her about how a long day of sleuthing demanded an evening of fine dining. I looked at my perfectly made king bed. The hotel was lovely but absolutely worthless without Susan.

"How's Pearl?" I said.

"The puppy is a terror."

"That little bundle of energy?" I said. "Never."

"She ate the heel off those Manolo Blahnik shoes we bought in Beverly Hills."

"The ones you wore when we—"

"Exactly."

"I'm pretty sure we broke that chair," I said.

"And your little pup also has been leaving little presents upstairs and downstairs," she said. "I had to have Janet take her today just to get in my last few patients."

"This stage is the toughest," I said. "She's no different than the first two Pearls. It'll take another few months for house-training, and this is the worst time for teething. She doesn't know your Manolo Blahniks from a rawhide bone."

"She needs to learn."

"Give her time."

"I didn't ask for another dog," she said. "Pearl was Pearl. This dog isn't her."

I waited for a moment and could hear her breathing across the many miles up the Eastern Seaboard. I tried to craft my words carefully for Susan and Pearl.

"You feel disloyal," I said. "To Pearl."

"Are you trying to shrink the shrink?"

"No," I said. "I'm just trying to understand why you won't accept her."

"I'm doing my best," Susan said.

"I know."

"Love," she said.

"Love."

27

THE NEXT MORNING, I met Nathan Epstein at the Puerto Sagua diner in South Beach.

Epstein had changed little since I'd seen him last. He was still thin and balding, with round, dark-rimmed glasses. Although he had developed a nice tan since moving from Boston to become the special agent in charge of the FBI's Miami office.

"May I recommend the perico breakfast platter with a side of Cuban toast?"

I studied the description on the menu. "You may," I said.

The diner was out of sync with the rest of the neighborhood. It was more a time capsule from the sixties: Spinning barstools fronted a Formica-topped counter. Glass cases displayed guava pastries and empanadas. A small refrigerator held only Hatuey beer.

"Surprised to hear from you."

"One foot on sea, and one on shore," I said. "To one thing constant never."

"Well," Epstein said, lifting his coffee. "That sure explains it."

"Peter Steiner," I said.

"No small talk?" Epstein said. He had on a light blue guayabera and well-worn khakis. He didn't look like a federal agent. He looked like a tourist in from Topeka.

"Long drive back to Boca," I said.

"I never heard of Peter Steiner," he said. "But I looked him up."

"And?" I said. The waiter wandered over and refilled our cups of café con leche.

"I can neither confirm nor deny we have a file on him as thick as the Dade County phone book."

"Might you confirm or deny if the substance of the file is financial or with possible violations of the Mann Act?"

Epstein took a long sip of coffee. He set down the mug and thought about the question.

"Theoretically?"

"Of course."

"Theoretically, a file that big would contain many indiscretions."

I nodded. The waiter reappeared, and I ordered the perico with an extra side of Cuban toast. Epstein had the same.

"Is there an active case on Mr. Steiner?" I said.

"Since I'm just hearing about him, I will let you draw your own conclusions."

As we waited for breakfast, I told him every detail, from Chloe Turner's missing backpack to the Blackstone Club, all the way through to Captain Glass's experience with the Suffolk County DA's office.

"Mr. Steiner appears to be well insulated."

"Like an Igloo cooler."

"I only had time to read the file once," Epstein said, "but it appeared my predecessor decided to drop the investigation with little or no explanation."

"Meaning?"

"This guy has to have some powerful friends," he said. "A lot more powerful than the Suffolk DA."

"The cop up in Seagrass said he takes VIPs to his own Fantasy Island in the Bahamas."

"Yep," Epstein said. "Apparently that's been going on for a while. Again, theoretically speaking, that island might be a hell of a way to gain access to rich sickos with specific tastes."

"He uses the jet and the island and the girls to rope in new clients."

"On the way over, I called up an agent who worked the case," Epstein said. "He said they called his plane the Lolita Express."

"Wow."

"Yeah," Epstein said. "Plenty of American elected officials, foreign heads of state, and international CEOs lined up for the journey."

"Sounds like a timeshare pitch," I said. "Come for the sun and fun but leave your money with Steiner and Associates."

"Something like that."

Epstein tapped his fingers against the laminated menu. As impassive as a sphinx.

"There's more?"

Epstein shrugged. He looked like a riddle wrapped in an enigma inside an empanada.

"In your experience," he said. "Isn't there always more with guys like Peter Steiner?"

"Always."

"And if you had a big island under your control, where you catered to every whim of these VIPs, wouldn't you perhaps tape a few of these encounters? You know, for posterity and safekeeping."

"Jumping Jehoshaphat."

"Yep."

"How many?"

"At least three blackmail cases. But in every one of them, the so-called victim walked away," Epstein said. "Nobody wants us to look into what happens on Fantasy Island."

"As a veteran federal agent, what would you surmise?"

"About the same as what your pal Steiner is into in Boston," Epstein said. "Booze, blow, and underage girls."

"How young?"

"One of the reports says he brings some in from Vietnam," Epstein said. "Some from Russia. Maybe as young as twelve. You sure know how to find some real heroes, Spenser."

"What else can you tell me?"

Epstein leaned back and placed his hand on his chest. "Might I remind you I am the special agent in charge of the Miami Field Office."

"So?"

"So," he said. "It would be highly unethical and perhaps illegal to divulge information from a confidential and active case."

"Active?" I said.

"It is now."

The waiter returned with our breakfast and set the hot plates in front of us. He refilled our water glasses and coffee, and as he walked away, Epstein grinned like the Cheshire cat.

"So who are these guys Steiner blackmailed?"

"Very rich. Very famous. You'll know the names," Epstein said. "But none of them will ever talk. Steiner has everyone by the short hairs."

28

FOR A YOUNG WOMAN who possessed a high disdain for the good life, Mattie Sullivan appeared to have settled in nicely at one of the pools at the Boca Raton Resort. I found her at a table shaded by a large striped umbrella and working on the first quarter of a tall club sandwich.

"The mark of a good hotel," I said. "A solid club sandwich."

"I had to eat," she said. "What took you so long?"

I told her about the meeting with Epstein and what I learned. I even told her about the ingredients of eggs perico.

"When do we head back?"

"Tonight," I said.

"Seems like a waste," she said. "Lounging by the pool while we have work to do."

"You're a hard boss."

"Bet your ass," she said. "Want half of the sandwich?"

"I just ate," I said.

"Want half the sandwich?"

I took a quarter and stretched my legs out from under the umbrella. I had on a pocketed navy T-shirt, khaki shorts, and running shoes. Having decided not to go full native, I wore a Sox home cap. Something I seldom wore back in Boston.

"You think Epstein will reopen the case?" Mattie said. "Or is he just bullshitting you?"

"I know Epstein," I said. "He doesn't care what I think. And is low on bullshit."

"Bullshit is how this asshole keeps his party going," she said. "I never in my life heard of someone owning their own island. That's nuts."

"Apparently so is the guest list."

"If we can show some of the Boston girls going to that island?"

"Or if we can just prove some of the girls from Boston were taken down here."

"Gotta be lots more."

I nodded. I finished the quarter sandwich. Mattie closed one eye and smiled. I picked up the final quarter.

"I knew you had it in you, champ."

I tried to smile with great modesty. Lounge chairs ringed the oval pool without a single open slot. Kids frolicked. Parents drank tall tropical drinks. Six young women in bikinis seemed to be celebrating with bottles of champagne being delivered poolside. If you tuned your ear hard enough, you could hear the surf on the beach. Or perhaps that was wishful thinking.

"Can you even call these men victims?" she said. "They're not being forced to do anything by Steiner. If he gets them on tape, that's their own damn fault."

"Agreed."

"I don't give a damn about these guys Steiner is black-mailing."

"The enemy of my enemy is my friend."

"You know where I grew up," she said. "I seen a lot of sick stuff. I heard a lot of sick stuff. My mother was hooked on drugs. Fucking Jumpin' Jack Flynn. I know what's out there. I know evil is real."

"But still."

"How do they do this without anyone stepping up?"

"Why do people in power continue to shield the bad guys?"

"Yeah," Mattie said. "That's another kind of sickness."

"You want to do this kind of work," I said, "get used to it."

Mattie sat back in her chair. She had on a one-piece bathing suit, cutoff blue jean shorts, and rubber flip-flops. White sunglasses and a Sox cap pulled down into her eyes.

"I don't know," she said. "This thing with Chloe has me thinking."

"About not following in my footsteps?"

"You have to fight with one hand tied behind your back," she said. "I don't know if I'd like that."

I nodded.

"I got one more year at Northeastern," she said. "Maybe after. I dunno. Maybe after, maybe trying to get on with the cops."

I widened my eyes.

"I know, I know," she said. "But like you said, there are some good ones. Maybe you could introduce me to your friend, Captain Glass."

"You bet," I said. "And Martin Quirk, too. Although in full disclosure, I wouldn't call Glass a friend. As hard as it is to believe, she can't stand me."

"I believe it," Mattie said. She smiled and reached for a few french fries.

Beyond her shoulder and up at the pool's bar, I noticed a woman staring at us. I had on sunglasses and a ball cap and stared back without her knowing. She had on a large straw hat and a tiny black bikini. She seemed to be in excellent shape, with adnominal muscles that could grate a block of Parmigiano-Reggiano.

The way her entire body turned to us, watching us straight on, made me feel uncomfortable. No furtive glances or subtle looks. This woman was staring right at me. Although I knew it was difficult for women to contain themselves around me in my best T-shirt, I felt an odd sensation at the back of my neck. My muscles bunched up, looking from the woman to the other side of the pool, where a man in a khaki suit leaned against a stucco wall. I scanned the perimeter of the pool, seeing two more men wearing suits. Odd dress for ninety-two degrees in the shade.

"What is it?"

"I'll be back."

"What is it?" Mattie said. "Christ, Spenser. What the hell is it?"

"Don't turn around," I said. "But Poppy Palmer is sitting directly behind you."

"Bullshit."

"And she's got three friends with her."

"What do we do?"

I stood up and winked at Mattie. "What else?" I said. "I'm going to introduce myself to her."

"I'm coming, too."

"I'd rather you not."

"Just try and stop me."

I didn't.

29

THE OUTDOOR BAR was square-shaped and sat about twenty people under a vaulted roof of polished wood beams. Every seat had a fine view of the pool and the beach. And Poppy Palmer appeared every bit content under the wide straw hat with a tall, blue drink in hand.

"What's an evil woman like you doing in a place like this?" I said.

Poppy viewed us like we were a curiosity. Mattie stood firm-footed beside me, arms crossed over her chest. She looked as if she wanted to make Poppy eat her big hat.

"Or didn't you want to be noticed?" I said.

"Were you hoping I wouldn't notice you outside my home?" Poppy said. Her accent thicker and decidedly less posh than I expected. I was no Henry Higgins, but she sounded like she'd grown up working class somewhere outside London.

"Go fuck yourself," Mattie said.

I held up my hand, hoping to offer a wittier and more nuanced retort.

The man in the khaki suit pushed himself off the poolside wall and approached the bar. He sidled up beside Poppy with his back turned, asking the bartender for a Perrier with a twist of lemon. His hair was salt-and-pepper and buzzed close to his head. He had on silver sunglasses, his face pock-marked with acne scars. As he turned to look at me, I noted a slight bulge on his right hip.

Mattie noticed it, too. She nodded at me.

"Professional," I said. "Doesn't drink on the job."

"You have no idea," Poppy said.

"I have some idea," I said. "Did you come here to intimidate me with your bikini? Because you should know, my heart belongs to another."

"She looks like a hooker," Mattie said.

I placed a light hand upon Mattie Sullivan's shoulder. Poppy's nostrils flared, but she grinned.

"I am a member of the club," she said. "I have every right to be here. And every right to have you and this little trollop tossed out on your asses."

"What's a trollop?" Mattie said.

"Kind of like a hooker," I said.

"Takes one to know one," Mattie said.

"Do you want to tell me what's on your mind, Poppy?" I said. "Subtlety is often lost on me."

Poppy nodded behind my shoulder. Two more men walked up to the bar. One was a young muscular black man in a navy suit and the other was a thin Latino in a suit as pink as the inside of a conch shell. Not many men could pull off the pink. I pointed to him across the bar and nodded my appreciation.

"Don't ever come to my home again," Poppy said. "You

have business with Peter, you take it up with Peter in Boston. But this is where I live, and you're only causing trouble and embarrassment for me."

"Trouble and embarrassment," I said, "is in my Google profile."

"You are insufferable," Poppy said.

"True," I said. "And you are an accomplice to a sexual predator."

"That's slanderous," she said. "What on earth are you talking about?"

At close range, it appeared that Poppy's breasts had been surgically augmented. They stood at attention like a pair of Tomahawk missiles. She had some kind of scrawl inked onto her rib cage and wore a diamond stud in her navel. She did not appear to be a woman of means. Or style. She was what Susan might call tacky.

"You help Steiner procure young women," I said. "But soon, both of you will be whistling 'Stone Walls and Steel Bars.'"

"My attorney will have a restraining order on you and this gawky young woman by this afternoon."

Mattie's face flushed. Her jaw clenched as she took two steps forward.

"That gawky young woman has the temperament and drive of a pit bull on Dexedrine."

"I know who she is," Poppy Palmer said.

Mattie hugged her arms tight around her body as if she didn't trust her fists being free. "You don't know a damn thing about me."

"You're a trashy little girl from Southie," she said. "You grew up in the housing projects with a deadbeat mother who got herself killed. I would think that would make you more cautious."

Mattie knocked the blue drink from Poppy Palmer's hands. The glass shattered across the polished concrete. Poppy didn't flinch, only smiled slightly. "Whoops," she said.

My smile dropped. I looked into her flat, black eyes. "Then you know who I am, too," I said. "And my reputation."

"Of course."

"Then you know I don't quit."

"Weren't you shot in the back a few years ago?" she said. "Left to die in an icy river?"

That wasn't a story that many people knew. Or one that I liked being known. It wasn't best for business. Poppy Palmer could see I was taken aback and grinned. A waitress had walked up on us and started to rake the broken glass and blue ice into a dustpan.

"Things like that happen every day," Poppy said. "People come and go. People disappear. This little girl with you is a reckless child lost on a battlefield."

"This little girl isn't lost," I said. "She's with me."

Mattie rested her hand on my right arm. I nodded at Poppy. I nodded at the three men. Neither of them acknowledged they even saw me from behind the sunglasses.

"Then leave," Poppy Palmer said. "You can walk away from here now, fly home to Boston, and go back to your small lives. I'm warning you. This will all come to a fast and violent end. All I have to do is snap my fingers."

I nodded. "And I'd hate to get blood all over that man's pink suit. Not many people can carry off the pink."

"You against three of my best?" she said. "I'd like to see you try."

Poppy Palmer's nostrils flared even more as she breathed in and out. Small black straps covered her freckled, slightly peeling shoulders.

"Is that it?" I said. "Because I'd rather lie in the sun and catch up on my reading, if you don't mind."

"Do as you like."

Poppy touched the top part of her upper lip with her tongue and laughed. A trail of sweat ran down from her temple and across her cheek.

Mattie and I walked back to the table under the striped umbrella. The waitress had cleared away the fries and the last bit of the club sandwich.

"What was that woman saying to you about being shot?" Mattie said.

"Something that happened not long before I met you."

"Was it bad?"

"Yeah."

"Real bad?" Mattie said.

"Took me a while to get back on my feet and in shape," I said. "Susan helped. And so did Hawk."

"How'd she know about that?"

"Boston is a small town."

"You don't believe that," she said. "Something's worrying you. I can see it all over your face."

We watched as Poppy Palmer stood up from the bar and exited, three men trailing behind her. The black man in the blue suit walking up and placing a silk robe across her sun-burned shoulders.

"Do you think if I tossed those guys into the pool, we'd be invited back to the Boca Raton Resort?" I said.

"Probably not."

"Then I shall restrain myself," I said.

30

BACK IN BOSTON, I dropped Mattie at her apartment and headed straight across the river to Cambridge and Susan's. Pearl welcomed me home with much yapping and yipping, and Susan welcomed me home with something even more substantial. I awoke before daybreak to Pearl rattling her training crate and took her for a brief walk on Linnaean Street.

I'd slipped into Susan's silk kimono adorned with tsunamis and koi to hasten the process. Since this was Cambridge, the few who passed by paid me little or no mind.

I let Susan sleep and fed Pearl and filled her water bowl. Checking Susan's fridge, I was delighted to find she'd visited the farmer's market and stocked up on vegetables, eggs, and freshly made sourdough bread. I diced up an onion, a green pepper, and tomato to sauté in a good amount of butter. Once they softened, I added four farm-fresh eggs. The coffee perked and the toast browned in the oven.

Once I finished, Pearl trailed me to the small breakfast nook, where I tore off a small bit of toast and tossed it to her. I read *The Globe*, an actual physical newspaper, until Susan walked into the room.

"You stole my robe," Susan said.

"I think it makes me look like Toshiro Mifune."

"A little tight in the chest and arms."

"I take it you want it back?"

Susan nodded. I shrugged, stood, and dropped the robe. Susan giggled. I was completely naked.

"I'm being harassed in my own home," she said.

"Would you like me to put on a T-shirt?"

"Pants would be nice," Susan said, shielding her eyes and going straight for the coffee. "Pants would be greatly appreciated."

I walked upstairs and dressed in jeans and a black T-shirt. When I returned, I handed her a snow globe I'd brought her from the airport. It featured both a flamingo and an alligator.

"I don't know what to say."

"It screamed of you," I said.

"I'll find a wonderful spot on the back of the guest toilet."

"Perfect," I said.

Susan looked at my empty plate and to the kitchen and then back to my plate. I stood up, sautéed the rest of the onion, pepper, and tomato, and mixed in more scrambled eggs for her.

"And what's this?"

"Huevos pericos," I said. "Another gift from South Florida."

Susan took a seat, snatching the front page from me. I took the funny papers and had gotten nearly through *Arlo & Janis* when she tapped at the paper with her fork. I let down the edge of the paper shielding my face. I'd seen William Powell do it once in a movie.

"How was it?"

"Didn't I tell you last night?"

"We didn't talk much last night."

Susan ate more huevos pericos and offered a small bite to Pearl. I raised my eyebrows but said nothing. "And?" she said.

I told her about Boca and what we'd learned among the salty air and palm trees.

"That woman confronted you at the hotel?"

"She did."

"That's insane."

"It is," I said.

"What do you think she hoped to accomplish?" she said.

"I think she wanted me to say 'eek' and jet on back to Boston."

"Which you did."

"But I did not say 'eek.'"

"So you found out Peter Steiner abuses young girls wherever he goes, and even has a private island to entertain special guests and those he and Poppy Palmer would like to blackmail."

"Correct."

"And you got word from your Fed pal that he'll reopen the investigation his predecessor bungled."

"That's about the tall, short, and sideways of the situation," I said.

Susan appeared to be finished with breakfast. I stole the other half of her toast before she could stab my hand with her fork. "And just what do you think Poppy Palmer gets out of all this?" she said. "Besides the money."

"I don't know," I said. "I get the money. But the rest is more a question to you."

"She either has serious daddy issues," Susan said, "or she is a predator as well."

"Working as a team."

"She's taken a serious interest in stopping you," Susan said. "Very personal."

"Maybe she was just interested in seeing me in the flesh," I said, deciding not to worry her with Poppy's threats. "Given my national reputation."

"I saw your reputation earlier," Susan said.

"And?" I said.

Susan waffled her hand in a so-so gesture.

I folded the paper and set down the funny papers. I raised my eyebrows at Susan, and it made her smile.

"Changing the subject," Susan said. "It sounds like Peter and Poppy have been cultivating their lifestyle for years."

"Typical sociopath, Dr. Silverman?"

"Evil is a relay sport when the one you burn turns to pass the torch."

"Freud?"

"Fiona Apple."

"Is it fair to say Peter Steiner experienced some serious trauma as a kid?"

"That's one theory," she said. "Wherever and however a person felt most vulnerable or afraid as a child, they often want to master these feelings. So sexually abused children may grow up into hypersexual adults or conversely sexually avoidant adults. Not with every case, but with many."

"If what we've heard is even halfway true, finding new victims is a compulsion."

"We all have sexual feelings, but life experiences and personality disorders affect what we do with them."

I nodded and drank the rest of my coffee. "Are you going to bill me your hourly rate?"

I stood to refill both our cups of coffee. I added some milk and sugar to Susan's cup. It was the absolute least I could do.

"I would," Susan said. "But this is Mattie's case. Pro bono."

"And me?"

"Meet me upstairs and we'll work something out."

I left the coffee on the table and did as I was told.

31

I WAS SEATED AT MY DESK listening to Sarah Vaughan and tapping along to the music with an unsharpened pencil when Captain Glass called.

"Spenser," she said. "Where are you?"

"Strolling with the one girl," I said. "Sighing sigh after sigh."

"Are you drinking on the job?"

"Sumatran roast," I said, lifting a mug. "With a little sugar."

"Listen up, bud," she said. "The victim I told you about. I spoke to her. And she says she'll talk to you."

I dropped my unsharpened pencil and picked up a pen.

"Just you," she said. "Don't bring along that Southie Nancy Drew. Okay? This thing that happened was ten years ago. It's taken her some time to make sense of it all. Steiner and Poppy Palmer made her life a living hell. She can't take any more trouble from that freak show."

"Would any of her troubles be facilitated by a certain security company in Miami?" I said.

"Who'd you talk to?"

"I often work in strange and mysterious ways."

"Strange is right," Glass said. "Woman's name is Grace Bennett. She has a studio in the Seaport. I warned her you could be a real pain in the ass."

"Ah," I said. "You like me. You really like me."

I was about to ask her for contact information. But Glass had already hung up.

Just then, Mattie walked into my office. She'd been doing a little online research for me in the anteroom to my office. "Anything?" Mattie said.

I told her. And the condition of me going alone.

"That's bullshit," she said.

"Maybe," I said. "Consider me a surrogate sleuth."

"But if she won't talk to me or the Feds, what good is she?" Mattie said. "We need every victim we can find."

"I'll try and make the case."

Mattie walked over and took a seat on the edge of my desk. She reached over to the computer and shut off Sarah Vaughan. She mashed a couple buttons, and soon there was some electric drumbeat and the sound of a woman whose voice seemed well autotuned. Sarah didn't need autotune.

"You're going to try and work the ole Spenser charm?"

"My charm is timeless."

"It better be."

With that, I took the stairs down to the back alley and drove to the Seaport.

Grace Bennett lived on the fifth floor of a rehabbed brick building off Sleeper Street in what developers call a live/work space.

It was hard for me to think of the area as anything but

the old Fort Point Channel, a bunch of warehouses by the docks and piers. But with new branding came new hotels, restaurants, shops, and art galleries. She buzzed me in immediately and pulled back a large metal industrial door to let me in.

Bennett was a young black woman, tall and thin, with lots of curly hair and nice dimples. She wore cut-off jean shorts and a red T-shirt that advertised Raising a Reader. Her feet were bare, and her hands covered in blue paint. Her skin was light, and her eyes were green. There was something about her that reminded me of a young Dorothy Dandridge.

"You look different than I expected," she said.

"What did you expect?"

"Humphrey Bogart in a trench coat."

"The stuff dreams are made of," I said in my best Bogart.

She gave me a confused glance and led me to a chair by a long bank of industrial windows, not unlike those in my new place in the Navy Yard. But her view, with windows that looked out to a nearly identical brick warehouse across the street, wasn't as stunning.

"I guess you know everything," she said.

"Actually," I said. "I know next to nothing."

"Lorraine didn't tell you anything?"

I shook my head and took a seat in a wide, comfortable blue chair. "I'm not even allowed to call her Lorraine. Only Captain. Your Highness, if I'm being informal."

"She's not as mean as she acts," Grace said. She sat in an identical chair across from me and tucked her bare feet up under her. "She was actually very kind to me and my sister during this whole thing."

"Actually, for some reason, that doesn't surprise me."

"Damn," Grace said. "This was a long time ago. Did you know I had to leave Boston?"

I shook my head.

"Moved to Cleveland for a while."

"I would make a Cleveland joke," I said. "But I happen to like it."

"It's not bad," she said. "Right?"

I nodded. A calico cat wandered in from the workspace along a far wall where there were a few easels and several large paintings. I wasn't close enough to see what they were or what style, but they looked very modern to me, with bright and bold colors. Most of what I knew about paintings had come from those who'd spent their lives trying to steal them.

The cat hopped up in my lap and expected me to reward it with a good scratch. I obliged. I didn't think Pearl would mind.

"I worked for that son of a bitch for almost two years," Grace said. "I was young, naïve, and ambitious as hell. That's what got me. I was told I was one art show away from fame. I trusted them. I let them flatter me. I introduced them to my little sister. God. It's so awful. I was so stupid and selfish to let that happen."

Grace began to cry. I continued to scratch the cat and waited to hear more.

32

"DOES ALL THAT MAKE SENSE to you?" Grace said.

"My girlfriend is the shrink," I said. "But I understand a little bit about sociopaths and manipulations. Especially when the victims are teenagers."

"I wasn't a teenager when I went to work for Peter," Grace said. "I had an art degree from BU and had been working on my own for almost a year. Peter and Poppy came to one of my shows in Cambridge and bought one of my paintings. When I heard who they were, I was impressed, flattered, and grateful. Can you believe it? It was a large piece no one expected to sell, and they took it home that night. A week later, Poppy called me to have a drink and help her hang it. Have you seen their home?"

"Yep," I said. "Big enough to dry-dock the *Queen Mary*."

Grace finished cleaning her hands with mineral spirits and clapped her hands for her cat. The cat sprung from my lap and into hers. I'd never had a cat but appreciated their athleticism.

"When did you start working for Steiner?" I said.

"Almost immediately after my show," Grace said. Her arms were long and muscular, paint splatters on her biceps. Her eyes seemed even a deeper shade of green in the sunlight. "Although I could never grasp what I was supposed to do. Basically, I just ran errands. I picked up dry cleaning. Ran to the package store. Answered the phone. I didn't ask a lot of questions. I got paid good money, Mr. Spenser. And God knows I needed the money."

"Was there anything unusual about the arrangement?"

"Nothing," she said. "The only thing odd was that I couldn't really tell what the hell Peter and Poppy did. Peter always talking about his big mysterious clients. Poppy was always on the phone, interviewing new models, trips to New York. I went to Paris with them twice. But if you're asking if I sensed anything odd, no. I thought they were just typical rich white folks in the Back Bay."

"No shortage of those types."

"I grew up down in the 'Bury." Grace said. "Both my parents came from Jamaica. My mom taught art at Roxbury Prep. My dad drove a truck. That kind of thing. I never thought I'd be living in a world like what Peter and Poppy showed me. A private jet to Paris? I mean, *come on*. I thought that shit was only in the movies."

"Did Poppy ever ask you to model?"

"Once," Grace said. "I told her I was flattered but too old. She seemed to be always working with the teenagers for shoots. Besides, I'm a painter. An artist. I didn't have any interest. Would you like any coffee?"

"If I have any more coffee, I'll blast off for the moon."

Grace shifted in her chair and caused the cat to jump to the floor. The cat offered a judgmental look as it licked a paw.

"Do you mind talking about the incident?" I said.

"Whew," she said, biting her lip in thought. "Yeah. I guess that's why you're here. Right? You really think you can do something about those people? I had to shut it out of my mind. I had to move on. Saw a shrink for years. Still seeing one. It's not a part of my mind I care to open back up."

"Steiner had never made advances?"

"Nope," she said. "Honestly, I didn't see him that much. I had my own little office at their place on Comm Ave. I took phone messages for him. He was charming and sort of funny. A real flirt. But nothing out of the ordinary. He never said anything sexual or offensive. In fact, I never thought he thought of me one way or another until they set up that residency for me."

"Ah."

"Yeah," she said. "Should've known. Three months at a cute little brownstone in the South End. All to myself where they said I could open my mind and create. Only they didn't say they'd require me to party with them and join in their fun and games."

"Fun for them but awkward for you."

"Awkward was the best of it," she said. She pursed her mouth and closed her eyes. "I had been there nearly a week when they showed up late one night. Unexpected, of course—I was already in pajamas. Poppy had brought a case of wine and kept refilling my glass. I must've had two gallons of rosé."

"God help you."

"Not a fan of rosé?"

"Between rosé and nothing, I'll take nothing."

"She may have added something into it," she said. "I don't know. I don't remember much of it. I was very sick and confused."

It was very quiet in the large space. The sunlight cast gridlike patterns on the old floors, worn and scraped from years of abuse. The cat found the sun and stretched itself to maximum length.

"What I do remember is Poppy taking me back to my bedroom and undressing me," she said. "I told her I was going to throw up, and she laid me on the bed. I blacked out for a while. I don't know for how long. I don't know what she did or what happened. When I came to, Peter was there, sitting on the edge of the bed rubbing my thigh. I was naked."

"Was he dressed?"

"He had his shirt off," she said. "That's all I know. I screamed and forced them out of my room. I locked the door and placed a big chair in front of it. I tried to stay up, but I finally fell asleep. When I woke up later that night, the house was quiet. And when I got up the courage to walk downstairs, I found they were gone."

"When did you go to the police?"

Her eyes were very wet as she inhaled a long breath and stared down at the cat. She smiled for a moment, watching it in the sun, and then looked back to me. "Not until I found out what they'd done to my sister."

"This was after?"

"No," she said. "I didn't know what they did to Bri until I

told her what had happened to me. She was ashamed and embarrassed. She blamed herself. She still blames herself even though I was the one who caused everything. I was too damn ambitious and stupid to look after my own sister."

"Captain Glass said she was fourteen?"

"Fourteen when she first met them," Grace said. "Fifteen when she was raped. I didn't know how long Poppy had been grooming her. She promised Bri and my mother that Peter Steiner wanted to look out for her education. They said that Peter was a big-time donor at Harvard and could assure that she got in. Do you know what something like that would mean to our family? My mother had to put herself through a community college. Harvard?"

"Will Bri speak to me?"

"No."

"The more victims we can find, the stronger the case."

Grace shook her head, stood, and wiped her eyes with the back of her hand. "My family has been through all this before," she said. "We were promised we would get some kind of justice. Both of us had to sit in offices for hours and hours remembering every sick detail of what those people did. Or tried to do. I knew something was wrong. Bri would come to see me, and Poppy would take her out shopping to Newbury Street or Copley Place. They'd come in with bags and bags from Neiman Marcus, Chanel, and Gucci. We laughed about it. It seemed like it was absolutely nothing to Poppy. She said she and Peter didn't have their own kids and she loved to lavish their friends. *Lavish*. She used that word a lot."

"Do you want to tell me what they did to Bri?"

I was still seated. Grace stood over me, the cat twisting and turning back through her legs.

"Not really," she said. "Poppy was there for it. She's the one who wanted Bri to feel comfortable with her body. That everything they did was normal and natural."

"Was this at Steiner's house?"

"Yes," she said. "Several of his houses. And with his friends."

I tasted metal at the back of my throat. I felt I'd been holding my breath and let out a long, steady exhale. I told her I was very sorry. I wish I'd said more, but that was all I had at the moment.

"Captain Glass said you were harassed."

She nodded and told me about two men visiting after she filed charges. They knew where her parents worked and threatened to have both of them fired.

"I'd like you both to meet a lawyer friend of mine," I said. "She's putting together a class-action suit. Perhaps some federal charges to follow."

"I don't know you," she said. "And I don't know this lawyer. Is he even any good?"

"She," I said. "Her name is Rita. In a courtroom, she's as relentless as a nuclear winter."

The calico cat wandered back between us and rubbed its flank against Grace's leg. She reached down and stroked its back and tail. The cat purring in the sunlight.

"How many girls are there?" she said.

"Two," I said. "You and your sister would make four."

"Let me talk to Bri," she said. "I sure would love to see these creeps exposed."

33

I PICKED UP A TAIL as soon as I headed north on Atlantic.

I'd spotted the car earlier outside Grace Bennett's building, and now it was three car lengths behind me as I passed the Boston Harbor Hotel and the Aquarium. It was a white Dodge Charger or Challenger. I couldn't really tell at this angle.

Perhaps it was my friends from Providence we'd met that fine morning in Cambridge. Or perhaps it was someone sent north from Cerberus Security in Miami. Or maybe I was just paranoid, and some poor bastard just happened to be headed in the same direction through the city, up to the North End, and over the Zakim Bridge.

When I crossed the bridge and turned toward the Navy Yard, the car followed. When I slowed down and took a turn into the Navy Yard, the car followed. But when I turned down into the warehouses by the old docks, the car accelerated around and passed me. Still, I couldn't get a good look inside or get a look at the plate. But now I could tell it was a Dodge Charger. Progress.

I parked my Land Cruiser and headed toward my building, a four-story brick warehouse right down the marina from

Old Ironsides. I liked my new digs, but sometimes I missed the closeness to the Public Garden. I'd worn my Braves ball cap that morning and my .38 on my hip. It was a warm mid-afternoon with a nice salty breeze off the ocean.

I was already onto thinking about making a nice snack of some feta, kalamata olives, and flatbread when I heard a yip. Pearl was across the street in a common area, wandering about alone.

I looked both ways and called to her as I headed to the street.

At the same time, the white Charger turned around the south end of the old warehouse and doubled back toward me. Pearl sat down in the middle of the street in a perfect, practiced sit. She was proud of herself as she waited for me.

The car sped up.

I ran toward her.

I picked her up like an authentic Pete Rozelle football and dove over the sidewalk and into the grass.

The car raced past me, and this time I made an effort to see the plate. There wasn't one.

I brushed myself off and picked up Pearl again. She licked my face and nuzzled my neck as the car squealed into the distance. I could rush back to my car and follow, but I knew they'd be long gone on the interstate or well into Charlestown within seconds.

I carried Pearl into my building and up the side steps to my condo. She was hot and panting. There was no telling how long she'd been outside wandering about. I checked her for injuries, but she seemed no worse for wear.

On the second floor, my door was open.

I set Pearl onto the floor and pulled out my gun. She looked up at me and tilted her head.

I pressed my index finger to my lips.

I didn't leave doors open. I did not let Pearl roam free.

Susan was with patients all day. Our dog walker wasn't working with Pearl until later in the week. There was no way she'd gotten out on her own unless puppy Pearl was decidedly more intelligent than her predecessors.

I listened before I entered. I took a deep breath and ran into the condo, toward the kitchen island and some cover. Still nothing. I waited several moments. Pearl had followed. She barked at my back until I picked her up.

So much for the element of surprise.

I got up and checked the large open space. I checked the bathrooms. I checked under my bed and in my closet. I returned to the kitchen and checked in the refrigerator for good measure and found a cold beer.

No one was there. But they'd left my condo a complete mess.

My bed had been stripped of sheets with mattresses tossed to the floor. Cushions from my couch had been pulled away and cut open. Closets and drawers ransacked. A small desk by the bank of windows overturned. First-edition books and treasured record albums littered the floor. Even my collection of wooden animals I'd carved had been knocked across the room.

The air was still and warm. Pearl had followed me in and sniffed at the toppled books. I picked up a rare copy of *The Faerie Queen* that Rachel Wallace had given me and set it back upon the shelf.

"Sniff us out a clue, Asta," I said.

Pearl looked up at me, tongue hanging from her mouth and panting hard. I walked to the kitchen, poured some cool water into a stainless-steel bowl, and called Quirk. I drank half the beer while I waited for him to come onto the line.

"Did they take anything?"

"Nothing that I can see," I said. "But the inside of my condo looks like it was hit by an F-4."

"You still working on that billionaire sicko?"

"Yep."

"Think it's his people?"

"We'd be fools not to."

I told him about Florida. I told him about Cerberus Security and Poppy Palmer reminding me that I wasn't invincible or immortal.

"The deuce you say."

"I know," I said.

"How in the hell would she know what happened to you?" Quirk said. "Took a hell of a lot to keep that business quiet."

"Unless a certain someone is on their payroll."

"Don't get paranoid, Spenser," he said. "That guy's long gone."

"I'm not sure if he's ever been gone," I said. "Just waiting."

34

"DOES THIS LOOK like a fucking doggie day care?" Henry Cimoli said.

"I've been a member here since Cotton Mather invented the reverse squat," I said. "You've had some questionable clients over the years."

Hawk and I sat in Henry's private office at the Harbor Health Club. Hawk and Pearl were playing tug-of-war with a new rope toy.

"Well, just make sure the hound doesn't take a crap under my desk," Henry said. "Even keeping you two bozos around, I have standards."

Henry shook his head, left the office, and closed the door behind him. Hawk tossed the rope toy into the corner, and Pearl romped over to fetch it. She shook it with all her tiny might. Had the toy been vermin, it would be quite dead.

"Security cameras?" Hawk said.

I shook my head. "Two men," I said. "Dark clothes and wearing masks."

"Car plates?"

"Car didn't have plates," I said. "White Dodge Charger."

"Your boys from Miami?" Hawk said.

"Probably."

"Explain the white car."

I nodded.

"Who are these dudes?"

I told him the little I'd learned online. A multinational security company that provided bodyguards and investigative services for heavy hitters and major corporations.

"You must be getting real close to the center of that Tootsie Pop."

I nodded. I picked up Pearl and rubbed her ears. She seemed not to pay any attention, chawing at her toy, slobbering onto my T-shirt. I didn't mind. Nor did she. Hawk and I were both covered in sweat.

"You need to talk to Mattie," Hawk said.

"I know."

"Don't care what she says or wants," Hawk said. "This is some dangerous shit. This ain't about trial and error."

I nodded. I tried not to think about how those men might've treated Pearl while tearing up my apartment. I'd twice checked her over for injuries but could find none.

"What's y'all's end game?"

"Snoop until I have enough for Rita," I said. "And enough for the Feds."

"Simple enough."

"Yeah," I said. "I wish."

Hawk leaned back in Henry's old wooden office chair. It was the same chair Henry had used since he'd trained me back in the dark ages. A lot of the gym had changed over the years. Better and more modern equipment, the removal and then reinstatement of the boxing ring. But Henry's office was Henry's office, right down to the framed pictures of famous fighters from Massachusetts. From Willie Pep to Marvelous Marvin Hagler.

"Who's backing this motherfucker?"

"Don't have names," I said. "But it appears Peter Steiner has great support from some cops and dirty politicians. He definitely had the former DA deep-six the charges against him from Grace Bennett and her sister."

"Kid was fifteen."

I nodded.

"Wouldn't mind being in a locked room with this Petey," Hawk said. "Might be able to knock some sense into him."

"I'd be careful with his friend Poppy," I said. "I think she has the ability to crack coconuts with her thighs."

"Not these coconuts," Hawk said. "Mine are made out of titanium."

"Of course they are."

Something in the corner of the room had caught Hawk's attention. Pearl was squatting and leaving a growing stain on Henry's new carpet.

"I won't tell him if you won't."

I found some paper towels and cleaned it up. I sat back down across from Hawk. Maybe it was my imagination, but Henry's office still had the faint trace of cigars. In the myriad framed photos, I'd nearly missed a new picture of Henry and Zebulon Sixkill. Henry and Sixkill out fishing somewhere off the coast of Revere.

"I'll meet you back at your office."

"Can't pay you," I said.

"When you ever pay me?"

"Mattie promises to be a handful."

"Reason I like that kid."

I nodded, got up, and walked over to Pearl. I slipped a harness over her neck and around her skinny body.

"These people aren't like that crew that came over from Providence."

"Think they badder than those Ukrainians in Marshport?"

"Maybe."

"Badder than those military fucknuts we met up with deep down in Georgia?"

"Don't know," I said. "Guess we'll find out."

Hawk nodded and reached down and picked up Pearl. He rubbed her head, and she licked his face.

"Ain't nobody mess with my little girl."

35

HAWK DROVE TO SUSAN'S while I drove Mattie home later that day.

"If there's any trouble."

Mattie didn't answer.

"If you see anything."

Still more silence. Mattie sat in the passenger seat of my aging yet classic Land Cruiser. Her arms were crossed over her chest while she took in the wonderful scenery along the Mass Pike.

"We just have to take precautions," I said.

"Did you take precautions when you worked with Sixkill?"

"No," I said. "But I wish I had."

"I am not Sixkill."

"I would never confuse you for a large, muscular Native American."

Mattie didn't laugh. But Mattie seldom laughed. I took the exit toward Fenway and the neighborhood where Mattie kept a small apartment.

"These people aren't like the toughs from Southie," I said. "They're not a bunch of leg breakers of even Jumpin' Jack Flynn's caliber."

"Please don't say that name."

I nodded. I slowed at a traffic light. My air conditioner was on the fritz, and we had the windows down. In my rearview mirror, I could see Pearl panting in the backseat.

"Until we know what we've got," I said.

"We know what we have," Mattie said. "You would've never heard about Peter Steiner or Poppy Palmer if it weren't for me."

"True."

"And if you really live by the code, then you should respect mine, too," she said. "I'm the one who gave my word to Chloe Turner and Amelia Lynch. I'm the one who made a promise that we'd get that bastard. Now what am I supposed to do? Sit around and hide while you and Hawk go out and bust some skulls? That's not what I signed on for. That's bullshit."

"Maybe," I said. "But as good of a detective as you may be, you're not equipped to deal with this crew. These are men who've made a special trip to Boston to scare and intimidate us. That's their only job."

"You taught Sixkill to shoot."

"I did."

"And fight."

"Sixkill could already fight," I said. "But Henry and I taught him to fight better."

"Why don't you teach me?"

I knew where this was headed and was fine with the direction. I'd had a similar conversation with Susan when we'd discussed how to help Mattie. Many of my ideas Susan called old-fashioned and sexist. I had simply asked if Susan might take Mattie shopping since she seemed to rotate a few different T-shirts, jeans, and her Sox pitching jacket.

"I will."

"But not now."

"Hawk and I have been doing this since the Pleistocene era."

"Got to start somewhere."

The traffic started to move, and I flowed with it. With the flow came a little fresh, while not cool, air into the car. I could hear Pearl panting and smell her puppy breath. I hit a small pothole and the rear suspension groaned with age.

"You haven't even asked what I've been up to," Mattie said.

"What have you been up to?"

"I haven't just been paying your overdue bills and writing invoices," she said. "If you'd taken two seconds to wonder, I might have told you I found two more victims of Peter Steiner."

I glanced at her for a moment but then turned my eyes back on the road. We headed past Kenmore Square and the big Barnes & Noble under the CITGO sign. It was hot and very bright, driving toward the setting sun.

"And both of them said they'd talk to Rita."

"When did this happen?"

"They both did the massage thing last year," Mattie said.

"Amelia Lynch put me in touch. I met with them this morning at Quincy Market. Some pretty sick stuff, Spenser. One of them has actually been on that freaky-deaky island."

"And?"

"Like I said, some sick stuff," Mattie said. "Steiner keeps a staff out on his place. They bring these old creepazoids cocktails, rub their saggy old shoulders with oil. But they get paid. It's a lot of money. More money than their parents make in a month."

"Can you get them to Rita's?"

"Hmm," Mattie said. "Thought you said to take it easy for a while. Let you and Hawk handle the man business and all that."

"I never said 'man business.'"

"But you implied it."

"I implied that Hawk and I were more skilled dealing in these matters," I said.

"Doesn't mean I can't contribute."

I nodded and weaved in and out of traffic. I turned down along Mattie's street, right off the Northeastern campus, and slowed in front of her building. We sat for a moment, the car running, the windows down. Pearl rambled up into Mattie's lap and then wandered over to mine.

"I like that dog," Mattie said.

"Me, too," I said.

"I'll watch my back," she said. "I've been doing that my whole freakin' life. And I'll see about getting the girls to Rita's."

"If you notice anything at all."

"I'm not the one with the reputation for making trouble," Mattie said.

"Not yet."

"Yeah," Mattie said, grinning. She pulled her ball cap down in her eyes and then reached for the door handle. "But I'm working on it."

36

SOMEONE AT CONE, OAKES had set a platter of mini-sandwiches in the center of a very large conference table. I guarded the sandwiches as Mattie ushered in a middle-aged woman and two teenage girls. They didn't seem to notice me as they turned their backs and took in the mesmerizing view high above Boston.

The woman was heavyset, with thick brown hair accented by a single white streak framing her face. She wore an ankle-length blue summer dress adorned with floral swirls and a lot of jewelry. The jewelry was large and chunky, beads and blocks around her neck and on her left forearm. Her name was Rosie Lagrasso from Revere. She was loud and boisterous, oohing and ahhing over the view.

Rita Fiore entered the room and sat across from me.

She looked to the sandwiches and then back at me.

"Well," she said.

"Well," I said.

"From Monica's in the North End."

I raised my eyebrows and gave a nod of appreciation.

Mattie joined us at the table with Rosie Lagrasso and

her daughter, Haley, and Haley's friend, Maria Tran. Maria Tran was Vietnamese and looked much younger than sixteen. She was a thin, slight girl with long black hair and glasses. She had on a T-shirt that read AERO SOCAL '87. She couldn't have weighed more than sixty pounds soaking wet.

Haley Lagrasso looked a lot like her mother. She had on jeans and a man's white tank top. Her thick brown hair had been lopped off right below her ears, wild and frizzy in the summer heat. She wasn't at all pleased to be there that morning, staring down at the table and tapping her nail-bitten fingers.

Introductions went around. Rosie Lagrasso complimented me on having such a nice office.

Rita snorted but didn't correct her.

One of Rita's paralegals came into the conference room and set a microphone jacked into a laptop beside the sandwich platter. She clicked away on her keyboard and nodded over to Rita. Rita, with her red hair piled high on top of her head, looked like Mary, Queen of Scots, in a white summer suit and a baby-blue silk top.

I made a move for the sandwiches. Without looking in my direction, Rita moved the platter away.

"Shall we begin?" Rita said.

She stated her name and her title of senior litigator at Cone, Oakes and that she was joined by Haley Lagrasso and Maria Tran. Lagrasso had been accompanied by her mother, Rosie, and Tran's parents had signed a waiver to approve her involvement. Rita first asked Haley how and when she met Peter Steiner.

"Maria introduced me to him," she said.

"Bullshit," Maria said. The word sounded strange coming out of such a small girl.

"You told me about him," Haley said. "You're the one who gave me the business card and told me about the pool parties."

"Whatever." Maria rolled her eyes and threw herself back into the conference chair. "You asked me because Amelia told you."

"Where were these pool parties?" Rita said.

"Some hotel in the West End," Haley said. "I don't remember the name. This was a long time ago. Very fancy, with the pool on the roof."

Maria named the hotel. I knew it. It wasn't far from the old jail.

"When?" Rita said.

"Like, last year," Haley said. "Right after school was out. You got five hundred bucks just for showing up. It was like some kind of private party. This woman gave me a uniform and told me what I needed to do."

"Can you describe the uniform?" Rita said.

"A red bikini," Haley said. "All the girls were wearing them. Maria had one on, too."

"I wore my own," Maria said. "Okay?"

I looked over at Mattie and noticed she was taking notes. I seldom took notes but wondered if perhaps now was the time to start.

"And what were your duties at these parties?" Rita said.

"Make sure these old creepy men had stuff to drink," she said. "I had to go back and forth to the bartender. Champagne. Beer. I'd walk around and ask these old guys if they needed anything. We called it Daddy Disco because of all the old music they played. Those old men loved to dance."

"Did they know you were a minor?" Rita said.

"No one asked," Haley said.

Rita looked over to Maria.

"They knew I wasn't sixteen," Maria said. "Poppy Palmer gave me a ride to the hotel once because I couldn't drive. That's when she paid me for each of the girls I'd gotten to work the event."

"Did she say what the event was for?" Rita said.

"She said the men were important clients of Mr. Steiner's and that we were to see they had a good time," Maria said. "We were told to smile and be polite, spend time with the men if they wanted to talk to us. Maybe rub some suntan oil on them if they asked."

"Ick," Mattie said, looking up from her notepad and leaning forward. "Tell Miss Fiore what you told me about the cabanas."

Rita looked over to Mattie and held up the flat of her hand. Rita wasn't fond of anyone butting into her depositions.

"Sure," Maria said, adjusting her glasses on her delicate face. "Some of the men had these cabanas on the rooftop. The girls were told they could make tips if they gave massages. It was a lot of money. Maybe five hundred extra dollars. That's a lot of money where I come from. More money than my mother makes in a week for giving manicures."

"Did either of you participate in the cabanas?" Rita said.

Maria didn't answer. Haley looked down at her hands.

"Go ahead," Rosie said. "Go ahead. That's why we're here, dammit. Tell them what that awful woman told you to do."

"I got drunk," Haley said.

"And," Rosie said. "Tell them."

"And I kissed this old man," she said. "While he touched me."

"Where?" Rita said.

Haley explained the fondling in great detail. I looked over to Rita. Rita took in a long breath. She was no stranger to lurid tales, but I could tell it sickened her. It sickened me, too. I was no longer interested in the sandwiches.

"Maria?" Rita said.

"Yeah," she said. "I rubbed the fat man's back. He offered me a thousand dollars to touch him. You know. Down there. But I didn't."

"Did anyone try to force you?"

"No," she said. "But Miss Palmer told me there was more money if I made any of the men happy. Some of the girls were told to get in the pool and play around. Some of the men handed out money if we took off our tops."

"Good God," Rita said. "These are children."

Mattie met Rita's gaze across the table and nodded. Rita nodded back at Mattie.

"How many of these parties did you go to?" Rita said.

Haley was crying now but trying to compose herself. Her mother was staring up at the ceiling and mumbling to herself, perhaps seeking a higher authority. Rosie reached into her purse and pulled out some Kleenex for her daughter. She handed it to her, and the girl blew her nose.

"Three," Haley said. She said it so softly, we could barely hear her.

Rita asked her to repeat her answer.

"Three," she said.

"And did men touch you at each event?"

Haley nodded.

"Please speak up," Rita said.

"Yes," Haley said.

"What about the island?" Mattie said. She'd been good about holding her questions, but there was little that could stop Mattie Sullivan from getting to the point.

"What about it?" Maria Tran said.

"What can you tell us?" Rita said, raising her eyebrows at Mattie.

"I only went once," Maria said. "One weekend. I told my mother I was going to the beach with friends. Mr. Steiner had a fancy black car take me to a private airport. From the private airport we flew to Miami and then on to Nassau."

"And what happened there?" Rita said.

Maria shook her head. She looked over to the Lagrassos and then back to me and Mattie.

"Not with him here," she said. "Okay? This stuff is too personal."

"But you will tell me?" Rita said.

Maria nodded. Mattie continued to write down some notes. I felt like a voyeur and very much wanted to leave the room and let them continue.

"Were there other girls on the trip?"

"Six," Maria said.

"Can you recall their names?" Rita said.

"No," Maria said, quickly. "I can't tell you. I made a promise. And I don't want any trouble. The only reason I came here with Haley is because of Carly Ly."

Mattie had told me that morning that the girls wanted her help in exchange for talking to Rita. Maria reached into her back pocket and unfolded a piece of paper, spreading it out with her hands. It was a missing-person bill looking for a young woman named Carly Ly, also fifteen and also from Revere.

"Oh, God," Rosie said, putting her hand to her mouth. "So awful. Just so awful."

I read the bill and passed it over to Rita. The photo was of a smiling, pretty Asian girl with short bangs and braces. She'd been missing since the second of May.

"What do her parents think?"

"I don't know," Haley said. "Her father doesn't speak English."

"My mother says they went to the police," Maria said. "But they've heard nothing back."

Mattie nodded, looked across to Rita and then leaned in to the table. "Tell them what you told me."

"I heard Carly was taking more trips with Mr. Steiner," Maria said. "She dropped out of school this winter and had gone to work for him full-time. I think she was on that island a whole lot of times. I don't know. I just couldn't do it anymore. I should've never done any of it."

Rosie shook her head. "So young," she said. "So stupid. What were you girls even thinking?"

Haley had her head down, picking at her short nails. Maria just stared at Rosie.

"I needed the money," Maria said.

Haley kept on crying. "They were so nice to me, Mom," she said. "They made me feel like they cared."

"I care," Rosie said. "I care."

Rita reached over and pushed a button on the laptop and snapped it shut. I stood up and so did Mattie. She came up to my shoulder, crossing her arms and looking across at Rita.

"Where are you two going?" she said.

"To find Carly Ly," Mattie said.

I grabbed as many sandwiches as I could carry in a napkin and followed her out. As I left the room, Rita started recording again. "Okay," she said. "Let's take it from the top. Maria, tell me about meeting Poppy Palmer."

Chloe Turner, Amelia Lynch, Grace and Bri Bennett, Haley Lagrasso, and Maria Tran. Now there were six.

37

I SAT WITH MATTIE and Carly Ly's father in the back of a Vietnamese restaurant on Revere Beach. He was a smallish man with jet-black hair and enormous gold glasses. He had a lot to say, although I needed one of his waitresses to translate.

"He says the police are of no help," the woman said.

It was raining outside on the beach, along with a lot of thunder and lightning.

"Did she ever mention working for a man named Peter Steiner?" Mattie said.

Mr. Ly held up his hand. He understood what was being asked. He nodded and then spoke for a long while. We waited and listened.

"Yes," the woman said. "He never met Mr. Steiner, but he has been of no help, either. Steiner told the police that Carly didn't show up for work and he hasn't heard anything from her."

Mattie looked over at me. Rain dappled her Red Sox jacket.

"Does he know his daughter dropped out of school?"

Mr. Ly grew even more agitated and spoke for a long while. He threw up his hands and went on and on. He was visibly upset.

The translator looked to us and said, "Yes."

"All that for a yes?" I said.

She nodded. The woman was in her late twenties, with shoulder-length black hair, and wore an apron over a T-shirt and jeans. Between translations, she would disappear into the kitchen and bring out another order to the mostly empty restaurant. A white couple, looking very Cambridge, sat at a booth by the window sipping pho.

Thunder rattled the windows and the front door. The rain hammered the pavement and street along the beachfront. *How it clatters along the roofs, like the tramp of hoofs.*

"What did the police tell you?" Mattie said.

More talking from Mr. Ly. He was subdued this time, talking low and quiet, shaking his head and giving an elegant shrug. I understood the shrug.

"They say she ran away," the translator said. "Because she had packed her things and taken a travel bag."

"Ah," I said.

Mattie cut her eyes over at me and nodded. She didn't take notes this time. Maybe it was the office setting that inspired the note-taking. Or maybe it was in response to Rita's professionalism.

"Did she say anything about the Bahamas?" Mattie said.

Mr. Ly shrugged again. He gave a very short answer.

"He says Carly didn't like to talk to him," the young woman said. "She kept many things to herself."

Mattie asked whom Mr. Ly had spoken to at the police

department. He nodded, stood up, and disappeared into the kitchen. The restaurant smelled very good, of Asian spices and fresh herbs. If I hadn't eaten a pile of sandwiches on the way over, I would've ordered a nice banh mi.

"He has a card," the translator said. "He and Carly never got along. She hated working at the restaurant. But she didn't have the choice."

"Did you know her very well?" I said.

"Of course," the woman said. "I'm her older sister, Lilly. And before you ask, she didn't tell me much, either. All Carly wanted to do was get far away from here and start her own life. The more she protested, the more my father asked of her. I think working for this Steiner man was her way out."

Mattie was chewing gum. She was thinking hard about something, waiting to ask her next question. She was impatient—however, properly aggressive.

"Is this like Carly?" Mattie said. "To just leave?"

"Very much," Lilly Ly said. "Very much."

"Without calling?" I said.

She nodded. Mr. Ly returned from the kitchen with a business card from a Revere Police Department patrol officer. It appeared no one had thought to send out an actual detective to investigate.

"Did she ever tell you about Peter Steiner?" Mattie said.

"Why?" Lilly said.

"Well," Mattie said. "Let's say he is a person of interest."

Lilly swallowed and nodded. Her father said something to her in Vietnamese, and she got up and went to the window to check on the customers. While she was gone, we were all silent. Mr. Ly sat quiet and still, looking out the window at the rain until his daughter returned.

"I believe she was in love with him," Lilly said.

No one said anything. Mattie was getting better about listening, especially when she was on to something important.

"She talked about this Steiner man a lot," Lilly said. "She told me he was very rich and very handsome. She said he was witty and clever and smelled very nice."

"The same has been said of me," I said.

Mattie kicked me under the table.

"Could she be with him?" Lilly Ly said. "Is that what you think?"

I nodded. Mattie nodded.

"She's only fifteen," Lilly said. "She has no experience with men. She has little experience outside Revere. Our mother is dead, and our entire life has been this restaurant. If she's safe and you find her, would you have her please call home?"

We promised.

Mr. Ly started talking again, very rapid and with a lot of intensity. We listened although Mattie and I had no idea what was being said. When he finished, he smacked his hand against the table in exclamation, stood, and walked back to the kitchen.

"I'm sorry," Lilly said.

"For what?" I said.

"For what he said."

"What exactly did he say?" Mattie said.

"He believes Mr. Spenser is a policeman," she said. "And

he does not like policemen. Or trust them. He had many bad experiences back in Vietnam."

Mattie worked over her gum. A woman walked into the restaurant carrying a plastic bag over her head but still soaked from the rain. Mr. Ly brought her neatly packed bags of take-out and rang her up.

"I would like some pictures of Carly," Mattie said.

Lilly nodded.

"And would you show me where she lived?" Mattie said. "Her bedroom?"

Lilly pointed back to the kitchen. "We have a living space behind the restaurant. Give me a moment and I will take you."

I thanked Lilly as she walked up to her father. They looked to be having a serious debate about the request.

"She's on the island," Mattie said.

"The worst being a best-case scenario."

My cell began to pulse in my pocket. I checked the screen, the call coming from a Boston number I didn't im-mediately recognize. I took it anyway.

"Goddamn it, Spenser."

"My father used to call me that," I said.

"They showed up," a woman said. "They fucking showed up at my studio and knew we'd talked. They knew every-thing. I can't have this. Bri can't have this. Don't you ever fucking call me again."

"Grace?" I said.

"Damn right it's Grace," she said. "They said they know where Bri lives, too. I will never speak to you again. And forget about Bri. She's scared shitless."

"Did they threaten you?" I said.

The line went dead. I looked up at Mattie.

"Check the girl's room," I said. "I'll be in the car. I have to make some calls."

I walked up to the register, where Mr. Ly eyed me from a barstool. I asked him for a cup of coffee to go. As I waited, a golden Lucky Cat smiled as it raised its paw up and down in a show of peace and friendship.

I thanked Mr. Ly. He said nothing.

I ran out into the rain and back to the Land Cruiser. I left word with Henry to have Hawk meet me at Grace Bennett's in the Seaport.

38

GRACE BENNETT WAS SO THRILLED to see me, she tried to slam her big industrial door in my face.

Always prepared, I stuck a Red Wing steel-toed boot in the frame to stop it.

"Hero's welcome," Hawk said.

I tried to talk sense and logic through the door, with little success. Grace threatened to call the cops if I didn't leave. I looked to Hawk and shrugged.

"Man," Hawk said. "She do love you."

"Who's that with you?" Grace said.

"Woody Strode," I said.

Hawk grinned. I winked at him. He'd always admired Woody Strode.

"What do you want?" she said.

"I want to know who threatened you."

"What does it matter?"

"Because my friend Woody and I are prepared to stop them."

Hawk began to whistle "You've Got a Friend in Me."

I looked to him. "Really?"

Hawk shrugged again. The door slowly rolled back. Grace Bennett was wearing short navy shorts and a V-neck white T-shirt. Her curly hair pulled back into a loose ponytail. Her chest sweating with a light sheen.

Hawk stepped up. "Well, well, well."

"Who are you?" she said, looking up at him.

"Let us in, babe," Hawk said. "I'd be happy to tell you all about myself."

Grace walked away but left the door wide open. We stepped into her warehouse apartment and studio. A radio played some classical music from somewhere in the open space. If I'd been a much more cultured man, I might have named that tune.

"Rachmaninoff," Hawk said.

"I was just about to say that."

"Mm-hm," Hawk said. He moved on into her studio as if he'd been invited. He found one of her larger paintings and studied it for a while. He had yet to remove his sunglasses and stood as still as a mountain, taking it all in.

"He doesn't look like an art lover," Grace said.

"Maybe," Hawk said. "But I know you dig you some Préfète Duffaut."

Grace moved up closer to talk, standing a good head shorter than Hawk. She looked him up and down. Hawk was wearing a tight black T-shirt, form-fitting black pants, and cowboy boots. He was looking decidedly Hawkish today.

"Who the hell are you?" she said.

"The man of your damn dreams."

Grace began to smile. She had a very nice smile.

I stood by her open kitchen area and leaned against the

counter, feeling like a stranger in a strange land. I took off my ball cap and shook the rain off the brim. "What did they tell you, Grace?"

Grace looked over to me and then back at Hawk. Hawk hadn't moved, still staring at her big painting of a colorful city of little shacks, palm trees, and a wide starry sky. I could spot the Caribbean influence and some religious themes, but that was all I had.

"Only one man," she said. "And he threatened to kill me."

"He say anything else?" I said.

"He gave me the address where my mother and Bri live in Roxbury," he said. "Told me to let sleeping dogs lie."

"Poetic," I said.

Hawk stepped away from admiring the art and glided over to where we stood. Like everything Hawk did, the move was effortless and smooth. The muscles in his big arms shiny with rainwater, looking contained and ready at any moment.

"You promised to keep this between us," Grace said.

"I did."

"You promised everything I said was confidential."

"It was."

"Then how the hell did they know?"

I shook my head. I leaned against the granite counter. The rain intensifying outside, falling hard on her windows and down onto the street between the two warehouses. I played with the hat in my hand for lack of an answer.

"I pulled open the door," she said. "The man grabbed me by the throat and put a gun to my head. He walked me back here and made me kneel on the ground as he told me what would happen to my entire family. How does that sound to you?"

"Did he say who sent him?" I said.

"We both know goddamn well who sent him," she said.

"Did he say anything about me?" I said.

Grace swallowed. She looked to me and Hawk and then slowly shook her head. "I told you everything he said. He threatened me and then left."

I nodded.

"Miami Blues," Hawk said.

Something about the efficient and direct threat reminded me of someone I knew all too well. Hawk stood close by, hands resting on his hips. I could hear him breathing, smooth and cool, waiting for the answer.

"He was a white man," she said.

"Always fucking things up," Hawk said.

"About y'all's age," she said. "He was dressed in gray."

I glanced to Hawk. Behind the sunglasses, he was still and impassive. It didn't even appear he was breathing.

"All gray," she said. "Suit was gray, shirt was gray, tie was gray."

"Notice anything else?" I said.

"Face had a weird look to it," she said. "Reminded me of a dead man. Like he wasn't getting the right circulation. And he had a ruby stud in his left ear."

Hawk didn't say a word. I looked at him again. We both knew but neither of us were about to say it.

"You look like that's someone you know," Grace said.

I nodded.

"Will he do as he says?" she said.

I nodded again.

"Who is he?"

"A man who almost killed me," I said. "But I had other plans."

Hawk took off his sunglasses and tucked them into the neck of his shirt. He gave me a long, hard look. "I thought you and Ruger had an understanding."

"Me, too."

"That man not like you and me," Hawk said. "Man like Ruger doesn't have a code to live by."

"Certainly seems that way," I said.

Hawk looked over at Grace and smiled. Susan said Hawk's smile could turn most women's knees to jelly. Grace looked a bit unstable as she smiled back. Hawk turned to me. "If it is him," Hawk said. "This time, you're gonna have to finish it."

I nodded again.

"Ain't no other way, babe."

39

"WE CAN OFFER Grace Bennett protection," Quirk said. "And I will personally reach out to the police in Revere about this missing kid. Jesus, Spenser. Anything else we can do for you?"

"I put on a pork roast this morning," I said. "Could you send over a prowl car to check on it?"

Quirk didn't respond. I stood at the open door of his office, with Captain Glass and Detective Lee Farrell seated close to his desk. Farrell had been recently reassigned to Sex Crimes. He was a slender man of medium height with blondish receding hair and a neatly trimmed mustache. I'd known him a long time.

"I'd like to interview Bennett and her sister," Farrell said. "And all these kids Mattie has rounded up. She's good."

"Tenacious," I said. "She's tenacious."

"And she wants to be a cop," Glass said.

Quirk raised his eyebrows and offered a look of approval from behind his desk. "No kidding," he said. "Tell her to come talk to me sometime. Her IQ can only improve the sooner she shakes working for Spenser."

Glass grinned. Farrell, being a true friend, did not.

"What else do you have?" Quirk said.

I told him about the Gray Man.

"You sure?" Quirk said.

"Uh-huh."

"Have you told Susan?" Farrell said.

"Nope."

"Christ," Quirk said.

"Who's the fucking Gray Man?" Glass said.

Quirk gave her the CliffsNotes version. "Some weirdo as-sassin that has a hard-on for Spenser," he said. "Shot Spenser in the back on the Weeks Bridge. Spenser fell into the river and nearly died."

"Terrific," Glass said. "You think he's on the payroll of the security company?"

"I've never known his real name," I said. "Or his national-ity. But what I've gathered, he's exactly the type they like to employ. Peter Steiner and Poppy Palmer know I've been mak-ing inquiries, and they're not comfortable with anyone they can't threaten or bribe."

"I tried to find the old case file at the DA's office," Glass said. "You'll be shocked to know it disappeared."

"What about our records?" Quirk said.

"Not a trace," Glass said.

"Christ," Quirk said. He got up from his desk and walked to his window, fingering open the blinds and looking out into the parking lot. "No reason we can't nail this pervert and let Rita Fiore sue his balls off at the same time."

"Exactly what I was thinking," I said.

"And Poppy Palmer?" Farrell said. "What about her?"

"Rita's suing her, too."

"She's the roper?" he said. "She procures the girls."

"She's assaults them, too," I said. "They work as a team."

"That's a new one," Farrell said. "A man and a woman pe-dophile team. Might be something Susan could figure out."

"It might take all the shrinks in Harvard to make sense of those two."

"Thank God that's not our job," Quirk said. "I don't give a damn about Steiner's money or his motivation. Or who the fuck he spends time with on the links. I want these sickos locked up."

Quirk was a man of great clarity. Farrell and Glass stood, and she walked past me out the door.

"Sorry about Pearl," Farrell said.

I nodded.

"How's the new pup?" he said.

"Even more," I said. "Stop by and meet her sometime."

Farrell shook my hand and left. Quirk and I were alone. He looked up at me from his desk, his bricklayer hands folded before him. "Close the door."

I did.

"Sit."

I sat.

"This isn't a fucking joke," he said. "Or a goddamn game. You need to warn Susan."

"I will."

"She needs to know this fruit case is back," Quirk said. "We can send some guys to watch her, too."

I nodded.

"And don't you dare quote me on this, Spenser," Quirk said, lifting his eyes to me. "But if that nut job comes for you, you got to put him down fast. All that chivalry and knighthood bullshit doesn't mean jack squat."

I nodded. "Hawk agrees with you."

"Me and Hawk in agreement?" Quirk said. "What's the world coming to?"

40

I BROUGHT A PIZZA and flowers to Susan. And a basted bone to Pearl. Her chewing had grown worse, two antique chairs recently falling prey to her sharp little teeth.

"You certainly know the way to a girl's heart."

"I had a hard time deciding on the beef knuckle or the ham bone."

Susan swatted me on the nose with the summer bouquet. I marched the pizza upstairs to her kitchen, Pearl sniffing and following behind me. I placed the pizza box in the oven and unwrapped the ham bone for Pearl.

Pearl snatched it up and marched away with it in her mouth as if just receiving an Oscar.

I turned on the oven, found a bottle of Ipswich in the refrigerator and a bottle of Chianti in the pantry. I opened the wine, poured a glass, and cracked open my beer off the edge of the counter.

Susan was still dressed for work in her shrinking outfit. A black silk jumpsuit with tall black heels. She pulled out her earrings and kicked off her heels, snatching up the wineglass.

"Long day."

"The last client was especially trying," she said.

"It's funny," I said. "I can talk to you about my work. But you can't talk to me about yours."

"You find that funny?" she said. "That's why therapists often need therapists."

"But you don't."

She took a seat at the kitchen table and drank a little wine. "I often only need a little time to clear my head."

I drank a little beer. Pearl padded up to me and rested her head against my leg. She looked up at me, and I rubbed her long ears.

"Seems familiar."

I nodded.

"Do you really believe it's her?" Susan said. "Or is that just something that makes you feel better?"

"Does it matter?"

Susan watched as Pearl climbed into my lap and began to lick the bottle of beer. I thought about tilting it a bit to give her a sip.

"Don't even think about it," she said.

Susan headed back to the oven and checked on the pizza. When she returned, she leaned against the counter and took a sip of the Chianti. Pearl had stopped angling to drink my beer and settled into my lap. I stroked her smooth, almost hairless skin, and she let out a long, content breath. I also took in a deep breath, far from content, and let it out slowly.

"I have good news and bad news," I said. "Which one do you prefer first?"

"Who in their right mind likes bad news first?"

"Masochists," I said. "Fatalists. It makes them happy."

"Since I'm neither," she said.

"You'll be happy to know that tonight's pizza came from Armando's."

"I saw the box."

"And I did not add anchovies."

Susan thought about it and then raised her glass. "And now for the bad."

"Perhaps we should wait until after we eat."

"That bad?"

I waffled my hand over the table. Pearl watched the motion with great curiosity and then glanced up to Susan. I drank the second half of my beer and set down the bottle. "He's back."

"He?"

"Ruger," I said. "The Gray Man."

"And what does that have to do with us?" she said. "That business was finished a long time ago."

"One might think."

"You let him go," she said. "Twice. You could've killed him. Or had him prosecuted."

"A wedding gift for his daughter."

"An inappropriate gift," she said. "Considering what all he'd done."

I started to get up, and Pearl sprang off my lap. I was headed to the refrigerator when Susan turned and grabbed me a new beer and cracked off the top on the countertop.

"Explain," she said.

I told her more about the run-in with Poppy Palmer in

Boca. I told Susan that Poppy had known a lot about my shooting. And then I explained about the visit to Grace Bennett's earlier that day. She listened intently to every detail.

"You treated a dishonorable man with honor."

"It certainly appears that way."

Susan walked to the table and sat down. She closed her eyes and shook her head. "There are times when I can deal with this insanity clinically," she said. "I can compartmentalize who you are and what you do and realize that's just part of the package. But right now, at this point in our lives, I've had enough."

"Meaning."

"I am asking you to do something I seldom ask of you."

I waited.

"Let the police handle this," she said. "You and Mattie have done a fine and admirable job finding these victims. You have put these girls and their parents in touch with perhaps the best attorney in Boston, someone they could never know or afford. And now you've delivered pertinent and important details to Lee Farrell. Do you really believe Lee won't do everything he can to make sure Peter Steiner and all his associates go to jail?"

"Nope."

"Then step back," Susan said. "Please. This man is paid to kill people. If he took Steiner's money, he'll finish this. You are a living reminder of everything he's not. He'd be delighted if you are dead. You probably shouldn't have let him go the last time."

"Hawk and Quirk agree."

"What else is there to do?" she said.

"Find more victims," I said. "Make sure nothing happens to any of them. Make sure that Carly Ly is found and brought home."

"None of that is your job."

"And how would that look to Mattie?" I said. "If I quit."

Susan gulped down the wine and reached for the bottle. She refilled the glass almost to the rim.

"Do you remember how long it took you to recover?"

"Not something easy to forget."

"I can't do that again," she said, starting to cry. "I refuse to lose you and be left caring for this crazy little nibbling hound well into my golden years."

Pearl wandered over and placed her front paws on Susan's knees.

"No way," she said. She knocked Pearl away, wiped her eyes, and tried to stop crying. "If something happens to you, this dog can't live here. She's your dog. Your responsibility. If you want to make her Pearl, you'll just have to stick around."

Pearl scrambled up into Susan's lap and began lapping up the tear streaks. Susan laughed and cried and finally kissed the little puppy on its head. She gulped down some more wine.

"Goddamn you both."

"I can't do it, Suze."

"I know."

"But if it's really him, I know what needs to be done."

"Is that any comfort?"

"To me, it is," I said. "Now how about some pizza?"

41

THE NEXT MORNING, Hawk and I were parked along Commonwealth Ave drinking coffee and eating corn muffins from Dunkin'. Dunkie's to the locals.

"Why muffins over donuts today?" Hawk said.

"I usually call an audible once I get to the counter."

"Good call," Hawk said.

I nodded. I drank some coffee. Hawk was behind the wheel of his Jag since Steiner's people were already well aware of my preference for vintage SUVs.

"Mattie won't be pleased I chose you over her for the job."

"This ain't her thing, man."

"Eating corn muffins and drinking coffee?"

"Squeezing Petey the Perv."

"Ah."

"You sure he's back in town?"

I cut my eyes over at him and finished my corn muffin. I was holding at two, but I'd bought a half-dozen. That meant, in fairness, I had the option of taking another. But if I had another, it might negate the last hour at the Harbor Health Club.

"Does he travel with people?"

"He has a driver," I said. "Sizable guy."

"How sizable?"

"Remember Refrigerator Perry?"

"Sure."

"This guy looks like the walk-in version."

"Fat ain't muscle."

I nodded, sipping more coffee. A cool morning breeze blowing through the open windows. "Guess we'll find out."

We had parked on the street a block from Steiner's place, having a view of his front entrance and the service alley. Hawk and I waited a short twenty minutes before we saw Steiner's light blue Rolls-Royce Phantom wheel out from the alley and approach Comm Ave.

"That him?" Hawk said.

"That's him," I said. "Unless there are two light blue Rolls-Royce Phantoms parked in that alley."

"I pull alongside him," Hawk said. "And you roll down the window. Ask that motherfucker if he got any Grey Poupon."

"I was thinking the exact same thing," I said. "Or perhaps we discreetly tail him hither and yon to find a good place for a proper introduction."

"Hither and yon."

Hawk started the Jag, the motor purring, and waited a beat before following the Rolls across the Commonwealth Mall and heading back toward downtown. He slowed as we got close to the Public Garden, waiting for the Rolls to turn and then shoot up Boylston by the Four Seasons. Traffic had grown tight, and we almost got stuck at a light.

"I think I know where he's going," I said.

"Do tell."

"Ever been to the Blackstone Club?"

"*Black*-stone?"

"Yeah," I said. "I'm sure you'll fit right in," I said. "It's just the kind of place that celebrates its diversity."

As we edged the Common, Hawk slowed down, the cab of the Rolls a shiny beacon in the sunlight. We caught up with the car as it headed toward Chinatown and turned onto Washington. Soon the Rolls slowed to the curb and an XXL chauffeur climbed out to get Steiner's door.

"Goddamn," Hawk said. "What they feed him?"

"Anyone who annoys his boss."

The bald guy who'd followed Mattie through the Common appeared outside the nondescript entrance for the club. He exchanged some kind of pleasantries with Steiner, and Steiner palmed him a tip.

Steiner was dressed in a pinkish seersucker suit with white buckskin shoes. He'd gotten even more tan from his recent visit to Florida, and his silver hair was combed straight back from his broad face.

"Never cared for seersucker," Hawk said.

"White people love it."

"Never seen you in it."

"On me, it would look like I was wearing a circus tent."

Hawk switched off the ignition. The inside of the Jag grew silent and still. I could hear the creaking of the leather as I shifted in the passenger seat. The city bustled about us. People hustling up and down the street, traffic backed up into the Financial District. A few horns honked in frustration.

"Shall we?" Hawk said.

"Will you get the door, Rochester?"

"Never have," Hawk said. "Never will."

"Will you still ask Steiner about that Grey Poupon?"

"Sure," Hawk said. "While you play patty-cake with André the Giant."

I smiled and reached for the door. "Don't embarrass me," I said. "I have standards among the Brahmin."

"Me, too," Hawk said. "Better wipe those muffin crumbs off your T-shirt."

I got out and brushed them away before Hawk and I crossed the street to the Blackstone Club.

42

I RANG THE BUZZER.

The bald guy who'd tailed Mattie opened the door. He seemed to remember me from our meeting on Marlborough Street and didn't seem pleased to see me again.

As he opened his mouth to voice his displeasure, I grabbed him by the throat and marched him into the vestibule. Hawk followed, strolling, removing his sunglasses, and taking in the Blackstone Club. The patterned marble floor, the wood-paneled walls, the oil portraits of distinguished members of yesteryear.

"Always wanted a painting of an old dead white man," Hawk said.

"So many to choose from."

I checked the guy for a gun, found the same one I'd taken away before, and slid it into my belt. I tossed him into a nearby coat closet and stuck a chair under the knob. As he began to hammer from the inside, my old friend T. W. Shaw waddled up, nervous and mopping his face with a silk hankie.

"What on earth is going on here?" he said. "I must inform you, Mr. Spenser, you've been banned from the club."

"I don't want to be part of any club that would accept me as a member."

"Cute," Shaw said, making a distasteful face. Shaw had on a black double-breasted suit today, along with a black bow tie. He looked very much like a fat little penguin with his beady eyes and sharp nose.

"How about me?" Hawk said. "I can't wait to meet all these fine folk. Maybe even bring some of my friends next time. Put on some Z. Z. Hill records and kick back."

The pounding on the coat closet continued.

Shaw fingered his jet-black mustache. "Have you locked someone in there?"

"No," I said. "Why?"

"Well," he said. "Because."

I turned to Hawk. "Do you hear something?"

"See no evil," Hawk said. "Hear no evil."

Shaw's brain seemed to be stuck in civility mode, open-mouthed about the ruckus in the foyer of such a fine joint as the Blackstone Club. We left him there considering the situation and headed on into the big study, where we found Peter Steiner on a leather couch smoking a big cigar and speaking in low tones with a man hidden by a high-backed chair.

Steiner wore a white oxford cloth shirt open at the neck under the pink seersucker suit jacket. He studied me and Hawk with a lot of amusement before taking another puff on his cigar.

"Sometimes a cigar is just a cigar," I said.

"And sometimes it's a big black ding-dong," Hawk said. "Right, Petey?"

Steiner smiled wide, crinkles around his brown eyes. He

elevated the cigar in his hand, smoke trailing up to the second-floor balcony of leather-bound books. The other man hadn't made himself known, staying silent and still in the high-backed chair.

"We came to clarify the situation," I said. "Leave the girls alone. Or else you'll be seeing a lot more of us."

Steiner tilted his head and drew again on the cigar.

"In other words," Hawk said, "keep that crooked old pee-pee to yourself."

The hidden man stood up from the chair and took a seat with Steiner on the couch. I felt a chill in my blood, tension bunching up in my trapezius muscles. It was Ruger.

He was dressed in gray as always—gray linen suit, gray shirt, and gray tie. Color coordination must never be a problem.

I looked to him. I nodded.

"You two have met," Steiner said.

No one said a word.

"And you as well, Mister—"

"Tibbs," Hawk said. "They call me Mr. Tibbs."

Ruger's bloodless face twitched in what might have been a smile.

"As I was saying," I said.

Steiner's eyes actually twinkled as his extra-large chauffeur rushed into the library, out of breath and his face covered in sweat. Ruger leaned back in the rich leather and pulled a cigar from his jacket. Steiner passed a silver lighter, and Ruger burned the tip with a large flame.

Ruger blew a plume of smoke at me. Steiner nodded toward me and Hawk.

The chauffeur towered above both of us and reached out with his huge hand to grab Hawk by the upper arm.

Hawk landed a series of very fast and very focused blows to the big man's gut. The big man started to make croaking sounds, gasping for air, until Hawk kicked hard against the man's right knee and toppled him into a massive heap on the fine Oriental carpets. The sound wasn't unlike a redwood landing in Muir Woods.

Steiner leaned forward and set the cigar in a very fine china tray. Ruger had yet to move, watching the show, puffing on the cigar again and blowing out another large cloud of smoke.

"I've heard you're a reasonable man," Steiner said.

"You must've spoken with the wrong people," I said.

"I can pay you for your time," Steiner said. "Or I can let my friend here deal with you. Again."

"There have been other times," I said. "I believed we had an agreement."

"Amongst gentlemen?" Steiner said. "How old-fashioned."

Hawk stared hard at Ruger. Ruger met his gaze and never blinked. There was an electric stillness in the air, and I waited for something ugly to happen very quickly.

"Where is Carly Ly?" I said.

Steiner shook his head, reaching for the cigar and ashing it onto the edge of the tray. He took a long pull and then rested his arm against his right knee.

"How 'bout we shake loose an answer," Hawk said. "You won't mind, will you, Ruger?"

Steiner's chauffeur was on his hands and knees and attempted to hold on to the couch to lift up his big frame.

Hawk didn't give him a chance, kicking out his arms and legs from under him.

"I heard you nearly bled out before they found you in the snow," Steiner said. "A man doesn't often come back from something like that. And rarely gets a second chance."

I looked to Ruger. He held his cigar high in two fingers like Sydney Greenstreet often did.

"Ruger knows where to find me," I said.

Ruger did not move. With the gray suit and sallow complexion, he appeared to be carved from granite.

"Now we have that straight," Steiner said.

"And the police know where to find you," I said. "Nothing happens to any of those kids. And Carly Ly comes home. Now."

Hawk had his cowboy boot on top of the chauffeur's back, saying in soft tones for the man to be quiet and stay down. Hawk turned to Steiner. "My .44 Magnum got a range of about three hundred yards," he said. "You whip that thing out to a kid again, and I'll shoot it clean off."

Steiner shrugged and blew out a lot of smoke. "I don't know where Carly is," he said. "She's a very hot-tempered young woman. With many friends. She could be anywhere."

"You better find her, Petey," Hawk said.

"I'm so glad to be visited by such Puritans," Steiner said. "I'm a man of means who enjoys the company of young women. So what? If we were in France, no one would say a word or lift an eyebrow. The Greeks were with young boys. The Romans with everyone. All civilized societies have done the same. We put all these hang-ups and taboos on something that all men want and desire. Are you telling me you don't find young girls pleasing?"

"I prefer the company of women," I said. "Not children. I heard Poppy has procured twelve-year-olds for you."

"Really," Steiner said. "That young? Very interesting."

I stared at Ruger. Ruger stared back. No one said a word for a good sixty seconds, but I knew we were being watched from the wings.

"Spenser," Ruger said. He made a motion, cigar in hand, of saluting me.

"Glad to know you're a man of his word."

"All is fair in love and war," Ruger said.

"And you understand who you are protecting and what he does to children?" I said.

Ruger just drew on the cigar, legs crossed, his soft, lazy gray eyes on mine. Something about him had changed. He looked skinnier and even more gray, like a man who'd been locked away for a very long time and had just experienced daylight again.

"Always knew I'd have to kill your ass," Hawk said.

Ruger's cheek twitched again. He sat still and quiet.

"If you're going to threaten me," Ruger said, "how about you try to speak like a white man."

"Wow," I said. "So many reasons to hate this guy."

"Long list," Hawk said.

"Two assholes for the price of one."

"Hot damn."

We walked out of the Blackstone Club, passing T. W. Shaw and the bald guy I'd locked in the closet. No one offered to hold the door.

Some club.

43

THAT AFTERNOON, Pearl was a welcome diversion from time ill spent with Peter Steiner and the Gray Man.

I sat alone in my darkened office, slumped into one of my client chairs and tossing a tennis ball into the empty anteroom over and over. Pearl and I made a great team, a resounding *thud, thud* rhythm like McQueen got going while stuck in the POW cooler. Pearl would catch the ball on the second bounce off the wall. Her hunting and retrieving instincts as deeply ingrained as mine to snoop and eat.

I tossed the ball through my office door to the outer door again, the repetition helping me unwind and focus, to practice what Susan called non-emotional, tactical thinking. I mulled over how to tactically eliminate the Gray Man from the equation and deliver the goods on Steiner.

On what I guessed to be my fiftieth throw, Pearl figured she'd had enough and bypassed me for the couch. She jumped up onto the cushions and began to work out the ball with her tiny teeth.

"Any ideas?" I said.

Pearl continued to chew.

"They won't hesitate," I said. "It will be quick and unexpected."

Pearl chewed hard enough that the ball squeaked. The squeak seemed to surprise her, stopping her chewing, and then she resumed the activity with a squeak every few seconds.

"Lee Farrell is a great cop," I said. "But his work might take months."

Squeak. Squeak.

"We don't have months," I said. "These young women need to be heard. Carly Ly needs to be found. Investigations, civil suits, the Feds. Too much time."

Squeak.

"It's not what you look at," I said. "It's what you see."

Pearl continued to chew but stopped momentarily to stare. Her skinny tail wagging back and forth. She looked content lying on her belly with her back legs spread out and her front paws holding the ball.

"I have to draw them out," I said. "And the only way to do that is to keep annoying Steiner. Fortunately, being annoying is my skill set."

Pearl dropped the ball, and it bounced onto the floor. She looked up at me with her brown eyes and yipped. She wanted me to retrieve it for her.

"We know Ruger will come for me," I said. "It's the waiting. Waiting is such hell."

I reached down and grabbed the ball. She snatched it from my hand and started to squeak with even more fervor. I rubbed her back and her ears and thought about what Susan had said, about not saddling her with a puppy.

Pearl looked up at me, panting, with an immediate and

familiar stare. I knew that look, had known it since I was a kid in Wyoming to that time I'd been ambushed in the woods by Gerry Broz and his men in Stockbridge. We'd been through much together.

"Me and you," I said. "Always."

I heard Mattie's familiar triple knock on the door. Pearl jumped off my lap and bounded through my office and into the anteroom.

"I heard voices," Mattie said.

"I was talking to Pearl."

"Did she talk back?"

"Not yet."

"Oh, thank God," Mattie said.

I asked her to sit, and she did so in my chair. Mattie Sullivan looked completely at home with her Chuck Taylors kicked up at the edge of my desk.

"It's a good idea for you to stay away for a few days," I said.

I told her about Hawk and me meeting with Peter Steiner and his surprise very special guest. Mattie listened and for once didn't speak until I was done.

"Nope."

"They'll kill me and you without giving it a second thought," I said. "When this is settled, we can go back to our agreement. Okay?"

"Nope," Mattie said again.

"This man doesn't care about you," I said. "He's been paid to get rid of me."

Pearl brought Mattie her ball. Mattie tossed it into the

other room, but it didn't have the elegant double bounce I'd perfected.

"Ever hear that discretion is the better part of valor?" I said.

"Is that an old saying where you come from?"

I nodded.

"We have an old saying in Southie, too," Mattie said. "And Peter Steiner and Poppy Palmer can go royally fuck themselves."

"Would you consider staying with Susan until things are settled?"

"I dunno," she said. "Maybe."

"She might need a little help with Pearl."

"Planning on going somewhere?"

I walked over to the right-hand drawer of my desk for the .357 and a box of ammo. "Not a chance."

44

TWO DAYS LATER, Mattie and I waited on the narrow front porch of a sagging duplex facing Blue Hill Ave in Roxbury. Grace Bennett's little sister had finally agreed to meet with us.

I'd picked up Mattie at Susan's that morning and was looking sharp and polished in a black polo, crisp khakis, and dark suede desert boots. I'd dusted off my Braves cap and gargled twice. But Grace and Bri's mother wasn't taken by my looks and charm. When she'd opened the door, she'd promptly closed it, and it took a full five minutes before Bri let us inside.

"She doesn't want me to talk about any of this," Bri said. "Ever."

The air inside the duplex was nearly as warm as outside, smelling of rich spices and cooking onions. Bri resembled her older sister, just as pretty, but a little shorter and heavier. She had on a long linen blouse with extra-wide sleeves that looked like wings when she stretched out her arms.

"You're the girl who started this up again," Bri said. "Right?"

Mattie looked to me. For the first time, she appeared to be at a loss for words. Her freckled face colored a bit.

"My friend's little sister," Mattie said. "Steiner tried something on her and took something that wasn't his. We got it back, and she told me about the other girls."

"A lot of girls," Bri said. "So many of them."

"Too many," I said. "We've nearly lost count."

She invited us to sit down in their small living room. The mother was back in the kitchen, rattling lots of pots and pans. Just in case we got too comfortable.

I recognized two of Grace's paintings on the wall, big, bold tropical landscapes and religious allegory, along with many framed family photos and diplomas and two tall bookshelves stocked with old paperbacks. The television was playing a soap opera without sound, a man and a woman in a heated discussion in the lobby of a hospital. The woman slapped the man hard across the face.

"My mother thinks I should be quiet," Bri said. "Keep the worst of it to myself."

"And what do you think?" I said.

Mattie nodded across from me, her lanky arms draped over her knees. She borrowed one of Susan's fancy tank tops, black with some embroidery, and a pair of jeans. She'd ditched the ball cap but still had on her Chucks, chewing gum while Bri spoke.

"I think that way of thinking nearly destroyed me," Bri said. "My mother blames herself. She believed in Peter Steiner, too. She fell for his flattery and all his talk about loving Jamaica. He talked about old ska music he listened to and knew a lot about politics back home. The PNP vs. the

JLP and all that. He's very charming. She thought he could help our family."

"Maybe I should tell her I own a nice collection of original Toots and the Maytals records."

"Tell her you can get me into Harvard, and she might listen," Bri said.

"My girlfriend went to Harvard," I said. "Does that count for something?"

Bri smiled. She had a very pretty smile and lovely hair woven into cornrows. Her skin was a light copper, and she had golden-colored eyes.

"Your sister said you'd been on his island," Mattie said.

Mattie reminded me of Frank Belson. His idea of a polite interview was not blowing smoke in his subject's face. Subtlety and smoothness weren't part of Mattie's process.

"Yes," Bri said. "Many times. I was on the island maybe three, four times before I even told Grace. It's a pretty amazing place. I never knew you could own an entire island. But that's Peter Steiner. There was one big main house topped with a blue dome, like a mosque, and several little cottages across the estate. He had a saltwater pool made of mosaic tile and a private lagoon. We would fly into Nassau and then take a boat to the island. It was about an hour away."

"And what did you see?" Mattie said.

I motioned my head back toward the kitchen, where it sounded like Mrs. Bennett was kicking a very large can down the road. The heavyset woman, in an ankle-length dress, blue, with tropical flowers, looked through the kitchen doorway. I smiled at her, and she quickly disappeared.

"Don't worry," Bri said. "My mother knows everything.

She's been to therapy with me and had to hear the worst of it."

Mattie spread her feet out and rested her elbows on her thighs. She looked a bit like Carlton Fisk ready to give me a signal for a slider. I waited for the sign but received none.

"Mr. Steiner had a private plane," she said. "He flew me and two other girls from Boston there. It was supposed to be a strategy session for our future. He and Poppy said we'd meet some of the brightest and most influential minds in the world."

"And did you?" I said.

"We met a lot of creepy old men," she said. "The first time I had no idea what to expect."

"And the next times?"

"He told me he'd punish Grace," she said. "If I told anyone about what I'd seen. Or, later, what I'd done."

I felt all the air escape my chest. Mattie clenched her teeth, her face turning a deeper shade of red. It was a little like attending a sex education course with your daughter.

"Did he assault you?" Mattie said.

"On the first trip, he crawled into bed with me," Bri said. "He told me that I reminded him of his sister. He said he only wanted to cuddle, but I knew what he was trying to do. And I knew it was wrong. I got away from him and stayed away from him the whole time. I took long walks and tried to stay around the help. On the flight back from the Bahamas and then Miami, Poppy wouldn't speak to me. She told me I'd hurt his feelings and humiliated Peter."

"What did you see on the island?" I said.

"Sex," she said.

"Just out in the open?" I said. "Like *National Geographic?*"

"By the pool, in the pool, and in cabanas on the beach," she said. "There were a dozen or so girls there. Most of them didn't speak English."

"Where were they from?" Mattie said.

"They were mostly Eastern European," Bri said. "I don't know from where or how old they were. But they looked very, very young. Even to me, at that age, I knew they were just kids. It's really hard to explain how Peter and Poppy made me feel. They made me feel important but disposable at the same time. I thought if I didn't do this, if I didn't act like I was older than I really was, I'd hurt my sister and my family. So I put on the makeup, the sexy clothes, the bikinis. I laughed at their jokes and did everything Poppy told me to do. I told myself this wasn't forever. This was just something to get ahead."

A large clanging came from the back of the kitchen. And then a steady string of curse words. Mother Bennett wasn't pleased with the direction of the conversation.

"Poppy heard me singing once and told me I had a lovely voice," she said. "She told me that I could be the next Rihanna and she knew people who could make it happen. I believed it. I believed all of it."

"A promoter once told me I had a bright future as a boxer."

"And what happened?" Bri said.

"He dropped me after my first loss."

Mattie glanced over at me. "I thought you said you were undefeated?"

"Only spiritually," I said.

"Did young women live there or just visit?" Mattie said.

"Both," she said. "Why?"

Mattie told her about Carly Ly and that she'd been missing for several weeks.

"Sounds like the kind of girl Peter and Poppy would groom," she said. "They knew the ambition of immigrant parents. I'm sure he promised her the world. My mother didn't know any better. My father was alive back then. My father even dropped me off at Peter's home. Poppy would greet him and speak with him like an old friend. She gave everyone the feeling of respectability, like she would be a chaperone."

"How did you finally get away from them?" I said.

"Grace," she said. "When Grace found out, she went after them. She made me promise to never see them again. She told me how dangerous they were and made me go with her to the police. But none of that mattered. No one cared about two girls from Roxbury. I hate to say this, Mr. Spenser, but you're both wasting your time. Do you know how connected this guy is?"

I shrugged. Mattie shrugged.

"Don't care?" she said.

"Nope," Mattie and I said at the same time. I tipped my hat to Mattie.

"Poppy told me I was a special girl," Bri said. "An exotic flower from the Caribbean. She paid me extra when I performed special massages on her friends. She said it was all normal and natural. I was only fourteen. I thought this was how adults acted."

"Do you remember names of those special friends?" I said.

"Some," she said. "Most all of that time is a complete blur."

She gave us a few names I didn't know, but one I recognized from many stories in *The Globe*. A recent U.S. senator who had been mentioned as a possible presidential candidate. The politician was often shown in the company of his wife discussing family values and his tough stance against crime. Bri Bennett's explanation of her duties to the senator seemed contrary to both.

"Nobody will ever let us talk," she said. "Too many people in the government and the police will stop it. They did this to us before and will do it again. I've come to the place where I can forgive people and make amends for my own decisions."

"You were a kid," Mattie said.

"I'm not a kid now," she said. "Spending time with hate, waiting for revenge, is no way to live. I understand that now. Peter Steiner has too much money and power."

"It's different now," I said. "I promise you'll be heard."

"I don't know."

"If you don't," Mattie said, "he'll just keep on doing it. They kick out the old girls and bring in new ones. You can help them. Stop this sick bastard."

Bri looked back at the kitchen. Her mother stood there in her tropical frock, hands on her hips. The older woman looked to Bri and nodded. Bri nodded back.

"Okay," she said. "I'll do it."

45

I SPOTTED A CREW from Cerberus the following night.

Susan and I had just left Henrietta's Table inside the Charles Hotel and were walking back to Harvard Square. I was extolling the many virtues of their Yankee pot roast while still lamenting the loss of Rialto. Susan and I both very much missed our after-dinner conversations with Chef Jody Adams.

"Is there a game afoot?" Susan said.

"Perhaps."

"Someone following us?"

"Two men," I said. "One followed us from the Charles. The other joined him at the bus stop. They're both following us now."

"Are you sure?"

"Does a one-legged duck swim in circles?"

"I don't know," she said. "I don't know any one-legged ducks."

We passed Charlie's Kitchen and walked on toward Brattle Square. A classical trio had set up by the T station, students playing a violin, a cello, and an electric keyboard. The music was lively and feverish and added much to the pursuit.

"I've never beaten anyone up to Mozart," I said.

"Is that what you plan to do?"

"I would like you to walk into the Coop and order us two coffees," I said. "I will join you in just a moment."

"I'd rather not leave you."

"If they wanted to shoot me, it wouldn't be in plain sight on the Harvard Square," I said. "I promise."

"Then what are they doing?"

"Keeping tabs," I said. "And reporting in."

"And you want to give them a little reminder before they do so?"

"Probably."

"As a trained therapist, might I suggest joint counseling?"

"You may."

Susan had her arm hooked in mine, both of us strolling and window shopping. We took our time, making our way to the Coop. We stopped in front of the Ray-Ban store and Rebekah Brooks jewelry. Susan admired an antique pearl necklace on display. We continued on past the Beat Hotel and then the Coop, where we parted ways. I kissed her on the cheek as if we were saying good night, and I continued down Brattle Street toward the T station. I took my time, stopping off at the newsstand and catching a glimpse of one of the men following me.

It was one of the same men I'd met with Poppy Palmer in Boca. He'd ditched the pastel colors for a summer-weight blue jacket, presumably to hide his gun. He was a young and fit Latin man with a neatly trimmed mustache and goatee, wearing sunglasses even though it was past nine o'clock.

I purchased a copy of *Sports Illustrated* and continued down the steps and into the T station, bustling with passengers headed back south and into Boston. I took my time at the foot of the stairs, looking down into the river of people flowing to the trains. I waited a beat, making sure I was spotted, and then strolled into the bathroom.

As I walked, I rolled up my copy of *SI* into a nice tidy tube.

Inside the small bathroom, a young white kid was combing his hair in the mirror. He had on a crimson Harvard T-shirt just in case anyone might mistake him for the great unwashed.

"I know this sounds strange," I said. "Perhaps even offputting. But I'll pay you ten bucks to tell a guy outside that you saw me leave through the back door."

"We're down in the station," he said, smirking. "There is no back door."

"Ah, you *are* a Harvard student," I said. "But he isn't. He's from Miami."

"Miami?"

I might as well have said Timbuktu. I reached into my wallet and pulled out two fives.

"Is this some kind of kinky game?" the kid said.

"What if I told you I was a private investigator and this man was part of a multinational security company with ties to some really bad people?"

The kid shook his head and took my money. I walked

into a stall and unrolled the *Sports Illustrated*. There was a cover story on the Women's World Cup. I read about the USA's victory over the Netherlands until I heard the door open and shoes upon the dirty tile floor. I closed the issue and again rolled it back up tightly.

I heard the man kick in the first stall and then walk in front of mine. I snatched open the door fast and smacked him three times across the face with the magazine.

"Bad doggie."

He wasn't expecting it.

"Sit."

The man fought back.

I dropped the magazine and punched him twice in the gut, reaching for the lapels on his crisp summer jacket and launching him at the sinks. He landed hard against his back, all the wind going out of him, and stuck his hand into his jacket for his gun.

The bathroom was very small, and I stopped him before he found it. I tossed the gun onto the floor, grabbed up a good bit of his hair, and dragged him into one of the stalls. I dunked his head over and over into the toilet until the fight was gone in him.

I left him there, hands on each side of the rim, trying to get to his feet.

I reached down and pocketed his little automatic, washed my hands in the sink, and reached for a paper towel.

I didn't look back until I was aboveground again. I didn't see the second man anywhere.

I crossed the street and headed upstairs at the Coop. Susan was seated by the elevators, perusing a copy of *Raising*

Boys to Be Good Men by Aaron Gouveia. Two coffees in the center of the table.

"Should I ask?" Susan said.

"Nope."

"Has it started raining?"

I looked at the water across the front of my shirt and then reached for the coffee. I removed the lid. "Just a sprinkle."

"Sugar?" I said.

"Of course."

"How's the book?"

"The author says young boys are seeing too much anger, dysfunction, and violence and are being suffocated by their social codes."

"Do tell."

"The author says showing your emotions and being physically demonstrative is a good thing."

"Would you be okay with me saying I stuck a man's head in a toilet but feel bad about it?"

"Was he working for Steiner?"

I blew across the coffee even though I knew it had grown cold. Habits were hard to break.

I nodded.

"Then yes," Susan said, putting the book onto the table and reaching for the coffee. "I'd be fine with that."

"We won't be bothered any more tonight."

Susan lifted her coffee cup, and we touched the rims.

"I wish I could reward you," Susan said. "But we have a full house."

"Plus two cops watching the street."

"Maybe the pup can sleep with us tonight."

I looked up from my coffee and raised my eyebrows, as this was a new development.

"But don't get any ideas," she said. "I think she's been lonely and confused. I'm just trying to be responsible and ethical."

"Of course," I said.

"Why are you smiling?"

"No reason at all."

46

I MET LEE FARRELL and Rita Fiore at the Bostonian for break-fast. I would've preferred getting a bagel sandwich across the street at the Quincy Market, but Rita didn't like to eat with her hands or standing up. She looked at home in a booth by the window, sipping from a ceramic cup while Farrell ran down what he'd learned about Carly Ly.

"She was on a flight log two weeks ago," Farrell said. "On a private plane to Boca."

"And then?" I said.

"And then nothing," Farrell said. "That plane returned three days later, and she wasn't on it."

"Have you contacted Steiner?" Rita said.

"We're trying," Farrell said. "We've heard from his attorney, guy named Greebel."

"I know Greebel," Rita said. "A creep that specializes in creeps."

"We've met," I said. "I was dazzled by his dentistry."

"He can't jam us up forever," Farrell said. "Carly Ly is a

missing person right now. Since her flight originated in Boston, that'll give us room to work."

My plate had been cleaned of the ham and eggs with rye toast. Rita had picked at her lox and bagel, and Farrell was still working on an egg-white veggie omelet. He told me his much younger partner had gotten him training for the marathon next year.

"When can I speak to the girls?" Farrell said.

"I'd insist on being present," Rita said.

"Of course," Farrell said. "And we'll keep everything between me, the captain, and Quirk. When we're ready for the grand jury, that will all change. But you know how that works better than anyone."

Rita agreed while the waitress returned to refill our coffee. I watched her pour a little cream in her coffee and add two lumps of sugar.

"Are you staring at my lumps?" Rita said.

"Yikes," I said. "Are you harassing me?"

"You bet, sweet cheeks," Rita said.

"I would never stare at your lumps," Farrell said.

Rita wore a very low-cut summer dress with her assets on full display. She looked down at her chest and then back at Farrell. "Really?"

"Sorry," Farrell said. "Boobs aren't my thing."

I tapped at my water glass with a spoon and cleared my throat. "So glad we've been able to establish our personal parameters."

Rita smiled and cut off one more piece of bagel and lox. She chewed thoughtfully and then leaned in, resting her chin on the tips of her fingers. "Well," she said. "We may be fucked. Chloe Turner's mother says they're dropping out of the suit. Someone got to her."

"They know Chloe Turner because of what happened at the Blackstone," Farrell said. "But how'd they know you'd spoken to Grace Bennett?"

"I must've been followed."

"You?" Rita said.

"I know," I said. "Even the pros make an error. From time to time."

"Whatever happens, I don't want the DA involved yet," Rita said. "The Bennett sisters went through hell with my previous employer. What a creep. I like our new DA but don't trust him any farther than I can toss him. Not with this much money and power involved."

Farrell nodded. My phone buzzed, and I saw Mattie's name. I turned off the ringer and set it aside. If it were an emergency, she'd call back.

"Is it true about the good senator?" Rita said. "And possibly our president one day?"

"Family values," I said. "Law and order."

"That's probably what he shouts when he climaxes."

"Thanks for that mental image."

"Cerberus is the absolute best at discrediting witnesses," Rita said. "They'll be scouring every social media post, interviewing friends of these girls, talking with teachers. Any missteps, however tiny, will be amplified. Same for you, Spenser, and you, Lee."

"But my heart is pure," I said.

"Your heart may be pure, but your record looks like shit," she said. "Do I need to remind you that you've made a goddamn encyclopedia of enemies over the years?"

I clutched my imaginary pearls and offered a surprised expression.

"I've worked with these guys before," she said. "I don't want to shock you, but sometimes I work for some really awful people."

"Everyone deserves a good defense," Farrell said.

"Even Peter Steiner?" I said.

"Most everyone," Rita said.

"Looks like our best bet is going to be the Feds," I said.

"Unfortunately," Farrell said. "I had to reach out to them about the flights."

"Anything new?" I said.

"Seems your man in Miami is on to something," he said. "But you know the Feds work in strange and mysterious ways."

"Mainly strange," I said.

"Billionaires, athletes, and politicians," Rita said.

"Oh, my," Farrell said.

Rita rolled her eyes and leaned in to the table. She looked back behind her and over to two men seated at the bar drinking Bloody Marys. "Those two?"

"Maybe," I said.

Farrell lifted his chin to the door, at a guy in a navy suit scrolling through his phone. "Or him?"

I shrugged.

"How's the kid?" Rita said.

"Staying with Susan," I said.

"And we're watching Susan," Farrell said.

"If Susan is watching the kid and the police are watching Susan, who is watching Spenser?"

"Spenser," I said.

"And Hawk?" she said.

"Thinking of taking another little trip," I said.

"An exotic port of call?" Farrell said.

I placed a finger to my lips and winked.

47

MATTIE HAD TAKEN the Red Line back down to Southie.

Or so she said in her voicemail. I tried her back several times without luck.

After leaving Rita and Farrell, I picked up Hawk at the Harbor Health Club. Hawk was still dressed for exercise in black silk pants, a gray sweatshirt with cutoff sleeves, and black Nikes that appeared fresh from the box. I detected the heavy item in his black gym bag wasn't a kettlebell.

"Moakley Park," I said. "It's where we first met Chloe Turner."

"Mattie's trying to get Chloe to change her mind about saying what she saw?"

"Precisely, Watson."

"Only Watson I know played for the Astros."

"Bob Watson," I said. "Also played for the Yankees."

"Every man has his faults," Hawk said.

We parked by the stadium and walked around to the bleachers. One man jogged around the rubberized track as we looked around for Mattie. Hawk saw her first, up in the top row of the aluminum bleachers, talking with Chloe. They were alone.

"I'm gonna get in a few laps," Hawk said. "Whistle if you need me."

"Can you run with a .44 strapped under your shoulder?"

"Easier than strapped between my legs."

I continued across the AstroTurf to the bleachers. The field was littered with crushed Gatorade cups and forgotten chin straps. It reminded me of being back at practice when I played strong safety at Holy Cross. Back then we still had leather helmets and kept up with the exploits of Red Grange. Simpler times.

Mattie noticed me but continued talking with Chloe. They sat close together, Chloe bent at the waist, elbows on her knees and hands over her face. It appeared she was crying.

Leave it to ole Spenser to break up a heart-to-heart between two women and offer my manly advice.

I hotfooted it up the bleachers and crossed over the rows to where they sat in a far corner. Chloe wiped her face. Mattie squinted up at me, the sun behind my back.

"Something's a matter."

"You might have told Susan you were leaving," I said.

"Wasn't time," Mattie said. "Those people from Miami have been following Chloe the last few days. They won't leave her alone. They've been asking around the neighborhood, wanting to know if she was some kind of slut. And then they gave her mom some money. Chloe doesn't know how much. But now her mom wants her to stay away from us and Rita Fiore."

"Could they have followed you here?"

Chloe didn't answer. She wiped her face with her shoulder. Mattie was right. Something was a matter. Chloe was shaking as though we were in the midst of a Boston winter.

"How many of them?" I said.

Chloe didn't answer. Mattie stared at me.

"Did they want you to bring Mattie here?" I said.

Chloe nodded. "My mom said I had to listen to them," she said. "She told me this was all my fault and I was a whore for taking that five hundred bucks."

I looked around the field, noting the same jogger but not seeing Hawk. The field was empty, and the bleachers empty except for us.

I had on my ball cap and sunglasses, watching for the different paths into the stadium. Behind the chain-link fence and by a trailer field house I spotted two of them. I couldn't tell if they were the same men from Cambridge, but whoever they were, they weren't dressed for a midday workout. They wore light-colored suits and sunglasses and appeared to be splitting up and walking into the stadium in two different directions.

I nodded to Mattie. She saw them, too.

"Shit," she said.

"Maybe not," I said.

A man I hadn't seen yet entered the stadium from behind the bleachers and began to mount the steps. Soon another one followed. I didn't see the third but hoped Hawk had.

"Shit," Mattie said again.

I stood up. I had my .357 worn on my right hip under my T-shirt. My .38 on my ankle.

"Good morning," I said. "Came to take in some exercise?"

One of the men was the guy whose head I had left in the T station toilet. He appeared to still hold a grudge. The other man was roughly the same age, a younger black man in a light blue linen suit. The Latin man from the other night had on a khaki suit so light it appeared white in the noonday sun.

"Crockett and Tubbs," I said.

"Who the fuck are Crockett and Tubbs?" Mattie said, whispering.

"I'll explain it later," I said.

"Okay, asshole," the black man said. "No tricks today. These girls are coming with us."

"A fellow of infinite jest," I said.

"Hands up, dickhead."

"And of most excellent fancy."

"I said 'hands up,'" the Latin man said. "Now."

He fell first, very hard and very fast, his legs seeming to go out from under him. He landed with a mighty clang on his back. The black man with him jerked his head back and then looked down at his feet. He fell hard and fast, too. His gun clattered down into the bleachers.

I was on both before they even looked up, holding them with my gun.

"Cerberus?" I said. "More like Pinky the poodle."

"Got 'em?" Hawk said, down below the bleachers.

"Yep."

The first shot came close, pinging off the aluminum. I yelled for the girls to get down. Mattie and Chloe scrambled down into the bleachers. I got onto my stomach, seeking cover, and tried to see up under the seats. The two men ran off, down the bleachers and onto the track.

It was quiet and still. The jogger scattered, running away from the track. He hopped the chain-link fence and ran into the park.

"You okay?" I said.

"Fine," Mattie said.

I peered over the seats, and the Latin man fired two shots at me from the base of the bleachers. I ducked down and returned fire. My .357 was a newer model and held eight shots. I was lucky to have an extra two, although I also had the .38 on my ankle. My gun was heavy chrome and felt substantial as I fired off another shot.

From below the bleachers, I heard a quick double shot that sounded like small cannon fire.

The third man fell by the chain-link fence.

Two more fast shots.

I looked over the aluminum seats, my ears ringing hard.

The man from Miami couldn't help himself and popped up again. I took the shot. The bullet ripped into his shoulder, and he fell backward, dropping from view. I heard the squeal of a car, the white Charger that had taken a run at me and Pearl, now heading over to the man lying by the fence. The car swerved onto the grass. The black man who I'd just met jumped out from behind the wheel and pulled the wounded man into the backseat.

The car sped away.

I stood up, watching the base of the bleachers. The sun high and hot over us. Heat and light radiating off the aluminum. It was quiet now, a low ringing in my ears. I told Mattie and Chloe to stay put.

I moved slow, gun in hand, down the steps. I waited for the man from Miami to pop up again. He didn't.

Hawk met me down on the track. The man was on his back, bleeding profusely from his shoulder, squirming and in a lot of pain.

"Shame," Hawk said. "Damn nice suit."

"What do we do with him?"

"Put one in the head," Hawk said. "Dumpster out back."

"Oh, God," the man said. "Please."

"You get your rocks off picking on two little girls?" Hawk said. "And working for a child molester?"

The man gritted his teeth, writhing in pain, the warm blood streaking across the rubberized track.

"I'll call Quirk."

"When the shit goes down," Hawk said. "Ain't nobody wants to be the last black man in Southie."

I pitched Hawk my keys and dialed Quirk's number as I watched him leave. I told Quirk to send an ambulance, too.

48

"THAT WAS FUN," Mattie said.

"Always a pleasure sitting around a crime scene in the hot sun."

I had popped two cold beers from the mini-fridge in my office. We drank them in the air-conditioning early that evening and discussed how little we'd learned from the man I'd shot.

"You'd think he'd be more helpful," Mattie said. "Bleeding on the ground like that."

"I know," I said. "The nerve."

"What do we do next?"

"Sit around and wait for the guy to confess," I said. "Quirk will call to tell us Steiner and Poppy Palmer have been arrested and all will be right in the world."

"Bullshit."

"Agreed," I said.

"Guys like that never talk," she said. "They lawyer up. I don't care how they dress or where they're from. They're the same as Jack Flynn and Gerry Broz. A bunch of bozos with guns."

"I like to consider myself a well-armed Emmett Kelly."

"And who is Emmett Kelly?"

"The kind of guy who'd smash a peanut with a sledge-hammer."

"And in this scenario, Steiner is the peanut?"

"Listening to Susan theorize Steiner's anatomical situation, most definitely."

Mattie drank a little beer. And I realized this was the first time we'd shared a beer together. It reminded me of when I'd first shared a beer with Paul Giacomin. That seemed a long time ago, and Susan and I both missed him. Since he'd gotten married and moved to San Francisco, we didn't talk as much as we once did.

I tried to make the beer go slowly. Somehow, no matter the substance, I drank all liquids at the same rate of speed. Be it brown liquor, cold beer, or ice-cold lemonade. It was my cross to bear.

"Chloe is scared shitless."

"As she should be."

"And her mother is a bitch," she said. "Calling her own daughter a whore. Who does that?"

"How does she know her mom took a payoff?"

"She saw those guys at her house and heard them talking," Mattie said. "Wasn't even a lot. It was like two thousand bucks. Rita said they were talking millions in a lawsuit."

"A bird in the hand."

"Now we're down to Amelia Lynch, Maria Tran, Haley Lagrasso, and the Bennett sisters."

"And Carly Ly if we can find her," I said. "Maybe Debbie Delgado?"

"Not a chance," Mattie said. "She's Poppy's pimp."

"Nice alliteration."

I drank some beer, trying to be conscious to conserve. I drank a little more, the patterns of light from the bay window diminishing across the office floor. A slash of light across my Vermeer print, the girl at the piano taking the lesson.

"I'm sorry I ran out on Susan," Mattie said. "I didn't mean any disrespect."

"None taken," I said. "But I'm glad you called me."

Mattie held her beer, touching the cold glass to her cheek. She seemed lost in thought, her Sox cap on the chair beside her, long red hair pulled back into a ponytail. Her pale freckled face fresh and eager but with much older and wiser green eyes.

"What does it feel like?" she said.

I waited. I drank some more beer and contemplated another. We had skipped lunch and by now nearly skipped dinner. It felt as if I'd been sitting around the stadium at Moakley Park for an eternity, taking questions from patrol officers and medics. At one point, some reporters arrived and set up their trucks and cameras. But they left soon after, disappointed there wasn't a body under a sheet.

"To shoot someone."

"If I were a carpenter, it would feel like swinging a hammer," I said. "I don't take pleasure in it. But I don't brood on it, either."

"Because they would have killed you."

"And possibly you and Chloe."

"That's desperate," Mattie said. "Steiner is crapping his pants."

"It certainly appears that way," I said. "He has much to lose. As do his many friends."

I finished the beer and retrieved another. Mattie hadn't had but two sips of her first. She'd spoken to me in the past about her mother and her mother's mother and how alcohol had consumed them. Mattie said she loved her mother but never wanted to be like her.

The sunlight was gone. Berkeley Street was alive to unlucky folks just leaving their offices and lucky people headed out to dinner. I checked my watch, ready for us to drive back to Susan's.

The phone rang. Not my cell but the old-fashioned landline that I just couldn't quit.

"Where the hell have you been?" Rita said.

"At the track."

"I've been calling you for the last two hours."

I checked my cell. The ringer was off, and Rita spoke the truth.

"Maria Tran," she said. "Remember her?"

"Carly Ly's friend."

"She showed up at my office," she said. "I was in the middle of a major deposition. I guess she got bored and left. But she left me a note."

"And?"

"She's heard from Carly Ly," Rita said.

49

MARIA TRAN WORKED at her parents' nail salon in China-town but agreed to meet us at the Starbucks on Charles Street, just off the Common. Mattie and I walked from my office, watchful of anyone following us, through the Public Garden and over Beacon.

Maria stood up as we entered and waved to us from a small back table. She looked even younger than when I'd first met her at Rita's office. She wore no makeup, her straight black hair down across her shoulders, and had on a red summer dress overlaid with a white cardigan. She looked like she should be skipping through the forest with a picnic basket.

We joined her at the table. She told us she didn't have much time.

"Carly emailed me," she said. "She's on that island, and they won't let her leave."

"Holy Christ," Mattie said. "Those assholes."

"Peter and Poppy are flying back there tomorrow," Maria said. "She was told she had to stay and work at another party. She begged for them to let her leave, but they won't."

"Did she call her father?" I said.

"No," Maria said. "Her phone doesn't work there. I think she reached out to her sister, too. I'm scared for her. Do you think they'll hurt her?"

Mattie shook her head and said no, lying through her teeth. I did the same.

"Can you tell the police?" Maria said.

"Sure," I said. "But they can't do much. Boston police are pretty much limited to Boston."

"What about your friend in Miami?" Mattie said.

"Pretty much limited to the U.S.," I said. "The exact reason Steiner parties offshore."

"They can't do that," Maria said. "They can't keep her locked up. Forcing her to work. I told her I would come for her. I've already checked in to flights. I can find her. I can help her get free."

"And then you'll get stuck like Carly," Mattie said. "Or worse."

Despite the conversation, it was still and pleasant inside the Beacon Hill Starbucks. They played Louis and Ella doing "I'll Never Be Free." I tapped my fingers on the small table, the flat top wobbly. I thought about the many limitations of American law enforcement and the many possibilities of being a hot dog freelancer.

"But I can," I said.

Mattie shook her head. "This is what they want."

"I know."

"The Gray Man will be there, and he'll try and kill you."

"*Try* being the operative word."

"It's almost like you want to face him," she said. "Like some kind of duel?"

I thought about it. I nodded.

"I want to go with you," she said. "I can help."

"Not with this."

Mattie gritted her teeth and crossed her arms across her chest. "God."

"What exactly did Carly say?" I said.

Maria pulled out her phone, tapped at the screen, and showed me the message. I read through it and scrolled through the thread. The thought did occur to me that she had been coerced like Chloe. You can take Spenser out of Boston, but not Boston out of Spenser.

I tapped along with the song, like I was playing the piano. Ella hitting that last wonderful plaintive note. "Hmm," I said.

"They're calling you out," Mattie said. "Goddamn, don't you see it?"

"Toss me in the briar patch."

"Better not talk that way around Hawk."

"Why not?" I said. "He's going with me."

"Thank you," Maria said. "Thank you."

"Hawk knows people there," I said.

"Hawk knows people everywhere," Mattie said.

50

I WAS PACKED, with tickets for me and Hawk on a morning flight to Miami and from Miami to Exuma International Airport in the Bahamas. I'd made arrangements with Quirk to have Cambridge PD watch Susan's house while we were away. Earlier that night, I'd cooked filets and asparagus wrapped in bacon for Susan and Mattie. After Mattie had gone off to sleep with Pearl, Susan and I made love quietly but with no less intensity.

"Wow," I said.

"Back at you, cowboy," Susan said.

"I think you have that backward," I said.

"You know," she said, "I think you're right."

We were naked and under the sheets, the window cracked and letting in cool night air off Linnaean Street. It was past midnight, and I had to be up at five to meet Hawk at Logan.

"What does Hawk think?" Susan said.

"He believes he's the perfect human specimen," I said.

"About this trip."

"Did you know he's a frequent visitor to one of the outer islands?"

"He never mentioned that before."

"There are many things Hawk hasn't mentioned."

Susan was quiet. She turned to me and rested her head on her forearm. Her dark hair was wild and loose, splayed against her bare back. I reached to lift up the sheet for a better view, and she swatted my hand away.

"Does he think it's a setup?" she said.

"All we know is that we don't know."

"But it's worth a try."

"I believe that Carly Ly is there," I said. "I believe Peter Steiner and Poppy Palmer are there. And I believe there may be other girls he's hoarding on his little island."

"Can you imagine?" she said. "Owning an island?"

"I once bought a square foot of land in Ireland," I said. "I was told it would make me a lord."

Susan was quiet again, and I reached over to brush the hair from her eyes. The overhead fan was on, and the sweat began to cool from our bodies.

"I was thinking about that hill in Santa Barbara," she said. "Where you and Hawk would go every day. You had to drag your leg up. I wasn't sure if you'd ever make it to the top."

"But I did."

"You did."

"Hawk wouldn't let you do this if he thought you were outmatched."

"Nope."

"He has friends there."

"It is home away from home."

"And where is his home in Boston?"

"I have absolutely no idea," I said.

"You had to keep squeezing that rubber ball in your hand," she said. "You had to weave back your nerve endings that were separated by the bullets."

"I was there," I said. "I remember."

"Six months," she said. "We nearly lost everything. My practice. You."

"I'll bring you back a straw hat," I said.

"And what about the baby?"

"Is she the baby now?" I said. "Again?"

Susan didn't answer. She tugged the sheet up to her chin, changing from exhibitionist to prude in a matter of minutes.

"If something happens," she said, "I will take care of her. I will love her. But be very angry at you."

"Thank you."

"Because if you believe she's Pearl, then she's Pearl."

"I came to the same decision just the other day," I said. "It's what you shrinky types call an epiphany."

"It's called love, dumb-dumb," she said. "If you love her, I will, too."

"Even if it hurts to remind you of our other baby?"

"Even then," Susan said.

I slowly peeled the cotton sheet from her nude body and surveyed the landscape. It was quite impressive. Susan didn't try and stop me. She turned onto her side and held her head up with her hand. I traced over her thigh and hip and curved my fingers over her breast.

"You have to be up early," she said. "I don't want to wear you out."

"Dear love, for nothing less than thee."

"Does that mean you're not tired?"

"My strength is the strength of ten."

"Okay," she said. "Saddle up, Lord Spenser."

"Yee-haw."

51

HAWK HAD TAKEN the rental car to do whatever Hawk does. And I'd been left on Cat Island in a small bungalow facing a private beach. The house was small, stucco, with jalousie windows and exposed wooden beams. As promised, Hawk's friend had left a key under a certain rock, and we made ourselves at home. I was delighted to learn the refrigerator was stocked with not only bread, eggs, and milk, but a six-pack of Kalik beer. I helped myself.

We'd been traveling for most of the day and I didn't un-pack, as I wasn't sure what the night or the next day would hold. Instead, I changed into a pair of swim trunks and walked the short distance from the back porch to the beach. I stood at the water's edge, waves lapping on my feet, taking in the sunset. It might have been relaxing if we didn't have an ugly job to perform.

The island was narrow and unspoiled, without all-inclusive resorts and tacky mansions. No cruise ships or yachts, just small crafts, fishing boats, and cottages. A one-lane road en-circled the entire island. There was a lot of pine and sea grape, and coconut trees swayed in the wind. Hawk told me he'd been on the island many times as a guest and had made certain friends. We hoped those friends might arrange transportation to Steiner's private island across the channel and perhaps loan us some guns.

We could show up on Steiner's island with knives in our teeth, flying the Jolly Roger. But guns would get the message across much better.

I walked north along the beach, seeing similarly built houses and colorful cottages that looked as if they'd been there for years. On the flight in, the pilot told us the highest point in all of the Bahamas was on Cat Island and on top you'd find the relics of an old monastery.

The beach was still and quiet. Farther north I watched the shadows of paddleboarders off the coast, a hard gold light shining off the water. There was the faintest ripple of wind across the surface.

The three plane rides hadn't been kind to me. I could feel every old break, bruise, and irregularity in my body. It had been eight years since I'd first met Mattie. Now she was a grown, successful person. And I was still doing what I do, none the wiser, not finding a better line of work. Maybe someday I'd retire to a place like this.

The idea that Hawk found solace on this island and had returned many times wasn't lost on me. Few get out of our livelihood by being politely asked. One day all the push-ups, wind sprints, and sparring wouldn't save us. At this point in my life, I'd been doing this for many more years than I had not.

I stretched my arms over my head and could feel where

the Gray Man had shot me. I recalled some of that day. The pieces of ice floating in the river, the skies spitting snow, the way he coolly raised the gun and shot me three times. Lately I'd been revisiting that time way too often. Hawk pushing me up that hill, me dragging my leg, by mind willing but my body failing me.

Somewhere, roughly forty miles away, was Steiner's island, Bonnet's Cut.

We would need to plan, we would need to reconnoiter, and we would need to execute our plan faster than Speedy Gonzales after two espressos.

"Something on your mind?" Hawk said.

I hadn't heard him. And I didn't turn around.

"Reconnoitering," I said.

"Anything else?"

"That I like Bahamian beer," I said.

"Welcome to my home away from home."

"You told me," I said. "Would've been easier back in Boston."

"Oh, yeah?" Hawk said. "Found us a boat. Maybe some guns."

"That fast?"

"Place belongs to an old friend from my days in the Legion."

"You're a better man than I am, Gunga Din."

"French Foreign Legion," Hawk said. "Not British Army."

"Excuse moi."

"Name's Godfrey," Hawk said. "Grew up here. He's good. One of the best I've ever known."

"Better than me?" I said.

Hawk waffled his hand.

"My Man Godfrey," I said. I couldn't resist.

"Godfrey's his own man," Hawk said. "And he'll see to it we get on and off that goddamn island."

"I like him already."

52

WE MET GODFREY at a restaurant called the Hot Spot in Arthur's Town.

He sat in a back booth sipping some rum from a jelly jar. I assumed it was rum, but it might've been Gautier cognac for all I knew. He was a thin, hard-looking black man of indeterminate age. He had dark eyes and a short Afro with a substantial beard. There were the faintest traces of gray in the beard.

Hawk introduced us. Godfrey, much taller than I expected, stood up and wrapped Hawk in a bear hug. He had on khaki cargo shorts and a loose blue Hawaiian shirt.

"It's good to see you, my friend."

Godfrey offered a hand. It overlapped mine with a grip that could crack walnuts. The room was cool and quiet. Twinkling white lights crisscrossed lattice that stood in place of walls. Both a front and back door were wide open, offering a little light into the darkened space. A big poster for something called the Rake and Scrape Festival hung by the bathrooms.

"This him?" Godfrey said.

Hawk nodded.

"Heard about you, Spenser," Godfrey said. "Hawk said one day you'd come to Cat Island."

"I wish it were under more leisurely circumstances."

Hawk joined Godfrey in the booth, and I found a nearby chair to sit. The booth wasn't meant for three men of our size. A woman walked up to the table, bringing two more glasses of the dark liquid. Godfrey smiled at her.

The woman was very beautiful, with sleepy eyes and full lips. Her nails were long enough to help us dig a tunnel down to China. She smiled at Godfrey and then Hawk and wandered back wordlessly to the bar.

Godfrey lifted the glass. We clinked them together, and I took a drink.

I was right. It was dark, very good, sweet rum.

"Relax, gentlemen," Godfrey said. "We have you covered."

I thanked him for his hospitality. For the car, the cottage, and the good rum.

"I've heard of this man, Steiner," Godfrey said. "And I've made some inquiries. I know some people who've been on his cay and seen many things."

I liked the small restaurant made of clapboard, tin, and concrete block. The daily specials were listed on a chalkboard. Conch burgers, cracked conch, cracked lobster, conch fritters, and conch salad. Godfrey caught me staring at the menu.

"I wonder if they have any conch?" I said.

Godfrey smiled and motioned to the waitress. Hawk ordered two lobster tails with black beans and rice and plantains. I ordered one of everything and two beers.

"Beer for me, too," Hawk said.

The woman looked back at me.

"Planning ahead," I said.

Hawk and I finished the rum at the same time and placed the jelly jars onto the center of the table. Godfrey leaned forward, looking up at us and nodding. "I know some people who'd worked for this man," he said. "It's not a large island. But big enough to employ security. I heard there are cameras everywhere. Even the beaches."

"Can you get us ashore at night?" I said.

"Of course," he said. "No problem."

"Can you get us guns?" Hawk said.

Godfrey just smiled. "Already waiting for you back at the cottage."

Hawk nodded his approval.

"Do you mind telling me the purpose of your visit there?" Godfrey said.

The waitress returned with three beers. Hawk tried to take two. I intercepted them both. He again smiled at the woman. She smiled back and went away. Something personal and intense passed between them.

"Karena hasn't forgotten about you," Godfrey said.

"Or I her," Hawk said.

I drank some of the beer. More Kalik. I wondered if there were any more breweries in the Bahamas or if rival beers were outlawed.

"We're looking for a young woman," I said. "Her name is Carly Ly. She's from Boston, of Asian descent, and fifteen years old."

"I know about the girls," Godfrey said. "Some people call it Pedo Island. It's an island of pleasure for old men. All the workers must sign an agreement. If they talk too much, they're fired. Or worse."

"What's worse?" I said, already knowing the answer but wanting to know more.

"There was a cook," Godfrey said, scratching at his beard. He leaned back into the ragged vinyl booth. "Some years ago. He took some photographs. Possibly tried to sell them."

"And then?" I said.

Godfrey threw up his hands. "No one knows," he said. "One day he went to work. And never came home."

"Do you know someone there now?" Hawk said.

Godfrey nodded.

"We will need to speak with them," he said.

"I don't know what they'll tell you," Godfrey said. "But I do know you will need more men."

"You've never seen me and Hawk in action."

"I have seen Hawk," Godfrey said. "And even if you are half as good, you will need at least two others."

"Half as good?" I said, pointing at myself.

"Maybe a quarter," Hawk said.

Soon the food arrived, and we took a break to eat. Mine was served on a platter the size of a manhole, with both cracked conch and cracked lobster with sides of beans and rice and plantains. I ordered another beer.

When we finished, Godfrey and I walked out to an open courtyard where people had started to gather for a karaoke night. Hawk had wandered up to the bar to chat with Karena.

"Hawk is a brother to me," he said.

"And to me as well," I said.

"You shall have whatever you need," he said. "Guns, assistance. People like Peter Steiner are like a cancer on our islands. They are no different than the plantation owners from a hundred years ago. They destroy the natural beauty and use our people to do it."

I watched as he pulled a very large cigar from his Hawaiian shirt and set fire to it with a lighter that resembled a grenade. The cigar had a big fancy band on it that looked expensive. I waited until he had it going.

"There's another man who may be there," I said. "I don't know his real name, but he often goes by Ruger. He has gray hair and gray eyes. He only wears gray clothing."

"Sounds like a very strange man."

"If he's there," I said. "I would like to know."

"Of course," Godfrey said. "Anything. Anything at all."

Hawk walked out and clasped Godfrey on the shoulder. He looked at me and said he'd be back to the cottage by midnight.

"Some unfinished business?" I said.

"Don't wait up," Hawk said.

53

THE NEXT MORNING, we were on a fishing boat captained by a very large man named Rex. I learned that ten years ago, he had been the strongest man in the Bahamas and had twice competed in the Olympics.

Watching him pilot the Hatteras named *The Dead Reckoning* with arms the size of howitzers, I decided against a mutiny.

The sky was a light blue and nearly cloudless. I considered the subtleness of the sea, knowing there was treachery hidden beneath the loveliest tints of azure.

We were more than halfway to the Exumas, the ship making good time at forty knots an hour, which I understood meant fifty miles. Hawk and I had taken a run on the beach that morning. He didn't mention his night, and I didn't ask. We did one hundred push-ups, sit-ups, and a series of squat jumps on and off a concrete piling. We finished with a fast three-mile jog along the beach and back along the one-lane road. Stay sharp. Be sharp.

I cooked us bacon and eggs with black coffee before we

met up with Godfrey and Rex. Rex wasn't much of a talker, more of a grunter, as I assisted untying the ropes from the moorings and pushed us off. Hawk went below, where we'd stowed our guns, and returned, handing me a Browning nine-millimeter. It was nearly identical to the one I had back home, although this one didn't appear to have ever been fired. Hawk had a Smith & Wesson .500 Magnum pistol slung over his shoulder.

"Any grizzlies on these islands?" I said.

"Never know."

"Steiner better not whip it out," I said. "Only a smoking crater would be left."

"Damn shame."

"Think we'll learn anything today?"

"Nope," Hawk said. "Big house. Nice beach. We shouldn't get too close."

"I'd hate to ruin the surprise."

"Ain't no surprise," Hawk said. "Me and you know that. Only surprise is us showing up with Godfrey and his people."

"How good is Godfrey?"

"Remember me telling you about the Sudan?"

I nodded. Hawk rarely shared details of what he did outside Boston.

"Godfrey was there," Hawk said.

"What about Rex?"

"Don't know about Captain Rex," Hawk said, looking up to the pilothouse. "I heard he could bench-press this boat."

"Might be useful," I said.

"No doubt," Hawk said.

I ejected the magazine from the Browning. I checked the rounds, slammed it home, and racked the slide to chamber a round, then placed it into a side compartment in my shorts. Susan had always hated the shorts, saying I looked like a suburban dad. I always told her only if suburban dads were holding extra bullets.

The closer we got to Bonnet's Cut, AKA Pedo Island, the choppiness intensified. It reminded me of why after I left Holy Cross, I'd enlisted in the Army and not the Navy. Seated across from me, Hawk grinned as my face possibly turned green.

I held firm and tried to find land. If I could see land, I knew my stomach would settle.

"Godfrey packed us some sandwiches," he said.

"No, thanks."

"Nice and calm out here," Hawk said. "Barely feel a thing."

The bow cut into the waves, rocking the ship up and down. Hawk continued to smile.

I saw land. My stomach settled. Twenty minutes later, Godfrey appeared from belowdeck and handed me a pair of binoculars.

"Rex will get as close as he can," he said. "There's a long pier and a small marina for pleasure crafts. Steiner keeps a yacht in Nassau. He brings his guests in from there."

"Do you know if he's back now?" I said.

Godfrey nodded. "He's back," Godfrey said. "With a white woman with short black hair."

"Poppy," Hawk said.

Rex slowed the engines to a chug, maybe three or four hundred meters from shore. The beach stretched the entire length of the skinny cay. The cay had a humped back full of vegetation and the round house on top with a blue dome, as we'd been told. I could see the shimmer off a large oval-shaped pool and four smaller houses descending from the main house. All of them fashioned of stucco and mosaic tile, appearing more Greek than Caribbean. We continued south along the western shore and away from the island for thirty minutes before cutting through another string of small islands and doubling back.

Rex kept the Hatteras moving slow and easy, just some businessmen from Milwaukee out for a nice day of fishing, as we headed north again, this time along the eastern shore of Bonnet's Cut. On this side of the island, we got within a few hundred yards of the long wooden pier and four boat slips. There was a stone staircase with several terraced gardens on the way up to the main house. From this side, I saw two more outbuildings, making six in total.

I didn't use the binoculars until we'd gone well past. Godfrey pointed out the rocky tip that would make the best landing. It was a jagged jetty of sharp rocks but far enough from the pier and main house to slip onto the grounds.

"You can take a dinghy ashore and stow it just beyond the rocks," Godfrey said. "I'm also working on getting us some help on the island."

"What's the layout inside the house and the outbuildings?" I said. "Where are the guards?"

"Patience, my friend," Godfrey said. "Have someone for you to meet tonight."

I looked to Hawk. He nodded.

Godfrey waved to Rex, and he pulled hard on the throttle.

The engines whined and hummed as we headed from whence we came.

"You in a rush to get back to Cat Island?" I said.

"I always take my time," Hawk said.

"If Ruger's there," I said. "He's mine. Okay?"

Hawk grinned. The boat rocked up at time. "Wouldn't have it no other way."

54

BACK AT THE COTTAGE and lying in bed, I still felt the rocking of the boat.

Hawk was off reconnoitering with Karena while I rested and checked in with Susan. The jalousie windows were cranked open and the back door ajar. You could hear the ebb and flow of the surf. Wind chimes tinkled from the back porch.

"Your dog ate another shoe," Susan said.

"Was it a good one?"

"All my shoes are good ones," she said. "This one was a Jimmy Choo."

"Thank God she didn't get both."

"Yes," Susan said. "I can't wait to hobble out to an expensive dinner when you get home."

"Just hold on to my arm," I said. "No one will notice."

"Other than her appetite for fashion, Pearl's been a sweetheart," she said. "She whines and whimpers, keeps walking to the door waiting for your return."

"The sound of her master's voice."

"Or maybe it's because you feed her while you cook."

"Just a nibble here and there."

We were set to meet Godfrey and his contact late that afternoon. I planned to spend the hours in between on a towel by the water's edge. I had found a Styrofoam cooler under the sink and packed it with ice and a six-pack of Kalik. There was no reason Hawk should have all the fun.

"Any luck?" Susan said.

I told her about meeting up with Godfrey and the stout Captain Rex, who may or may not be able to bend metal bars in his teeth. I left out the part about me getting seasick. I didn't wish to burden her with my maladies.

"When will you go?"

"Soon," I said. "I hope. Until then I plan to rest and drink beer."

"That's very selfless of you."

Susan was quiet for a moment. I closed my eyes and the bed stopped moving up and down.

"I hope this doesn't cross any boundaries," she said. "But in your absence, Mattie and I did some further checking into Steiner's friend, Poppy Palmer."

"And you learned she's actually a kind and giving person."

"Um, no," Susan said. "She seems to be a fucking train wreck."

"Was that a headline in *Psychology Today*?"

"Did you know her father committed suicide?"

"No," I said. "I did not."

"He was a self-made man," she said. "Born to an impoverished family in London, he made his fortune in real estate but ended up losing it all. Owned a string of resorts in

Portugal and a professional football club. That's soccer to the ugly American. Oh, and he also hung himself at their country estate at Christmas. Poppy was there. She was thirteen."

"And that made her susceptible to Steiner?"

"No," Susan said. "I think that made Steiner susceptible to her."

"Come again?"

"After I read about her father, I went to a message board and reached out to some therapists in Boston," she said. "This is sometimes done in cases of someone being a threat to themselves or others."

"And what did you find?"

"I heard back from a therapist who would not confirm or deny she worked with Poppy," Susan said. "But apparently, if we were talking about Poppy, there was an indication of years of physical and sexual abuse by the father. This goes back to what we've already discussed."

"Poppy wants to master that time," I said. "By creating it again and again."

"Wow," Susan said. "You were paying attention."

"And what about Peter Steiner?" I said. "What makes him do what he does?"

"Oh," Susan said. "I just think he's plainly fucked up."

"Do you mind speaking slower?" I said. "Your fancy terminology confuses me."

"Of course it does."

"Did the therapist think that's why Poppy's father killed himself?"

There was silence between Cat Island and Cambridge.

A small yip on the other end of the line. And then more barking.

"No," Susan said. "She thinks Poppy may have had something to do with it."

"At thirteen?" I said.

"Never too young to kill your sexually abusive father."

We spoke for another minute or so or until Pearl insisted on getting one of her many daily walks. I hung up, changed into my swim trunks, grabbed the cooler and a pair of sunglasses, and walked to the small back porch.

I looked out at the cool blue ocean and dialed Epstein's number in Miami. After two rings, he picked up.

"I have a theoretical question for you," I said.

"For which I will give you a theoretical reply."

"If I happened to help free an American citizen in a foreign land, would Uncle Sam assist me with the paperwork needed to get her home?"

"Does this theoretical person have a passport?"

"She may," I said. "But she may have to leave in a hurry."

"I don't see that being a problem."

"And there might be others with her."

"How many?"

"I don't know."

"What do you know?"

"That when she returns home, she'll have a wild story to tell."

"She a kid?"

"Fifteen."

Epstein let out a lot of air.

"International travel with a minor for sexual purposes?" Epstein said. "Yeah. I'd be interested in hearing her story. Will you be flying back through Miami?"

"I can."

"See that you do."

55

HAWK AND I drove to the southern tip of Cat Island early that evening, the windows down in the aging rental, pulsing electric dance music on the radio. Hawk seemed to be enjoying it, tapping out the rhythm on the steering wheel.

"Whatever happened to the Montagu Three?" I said.

"Coconut water with rum, tastes like candy."

"Makes you feel so dandy."

The single-lane road curved and twisted along the beach, the palm and coconut trees whizzing past the windows. The little houses along the beach were bright blues, yellows, and greens. The sand blinding white in the late-afternoon sun, the ocean going from a sky blue to a deep navy. Cat Island sure beat summering in Chelsea.

"What a horrible place to spend time."

"Good place to shake loose those cobwebs," Hawk said.

"You want to tell me where we're headed?" I said. "Or just taking in the sights?"

"Godfrey brought in a woman works for Steiner," Hawk said.

"How recently?"

"Today too soon?"

"Today works."

We made our way down to the same marina where we'd left that morning. I followed Hawk across a crushed-shell lot and up to a bright yellow clapboard building on stilts. He knocked on the door and Rex answered, ushering us inside.

Godfrey sat at a small table playing dominoes with a woman wearing a blue utility dress. She was of a plus size, with thick arms and thighs. Her face was broad and pleasant, and she made jokes with Godfrey as she carefully placed her domino against the pattern on the table. She had a large rose tattoo on her left arm and wore a golden chain with a cross around her neck.

"Sit," Godfrey said. "We're about done here."

"Not so fast," the woman said. "Godfrey boy." She had a big, infectious laugh.

I took a seat in a metal-and-vinyl chair like you'd find in a motel conference room. Hawk stood by the door, watching the game being played and checking the window that looked out onto the small marina. The walls were cheap wood paneling, buckling from the studs, tacked with fishing charts, islands maps, and posters from past marlin tournaments. It was the kind of place that would've made Papa proud.

Rex kept a small cluttered desk opposite Godfrey and the woman. His metal desk overflowed with empty cups, foam plates, and an old fan rotating back and forth. He hunched over a laptop computer, typing with massive index fingers.

Rex looked like he could deadlift two-fifty using only his pinkies.

"Don't you ever count me out, Mr. Godfrey," the woman said. She laughed more.

Godfrey pushed his dominoes into the center pile and shook his head.

"Too much, Shona," he said. "Too much for me."

Godfrey looked over to me and Hawk and ushered us closer to the table. I brought the chair with me. Hawk stood while Godfrey introduced us to Shona.

"I don't want no trouble," she said.

"For your trouble," Godfrey said, passing along a thick wad of bills across the table.

I reached for my wallet, but Godfrey held up his hand and shook me off. I looked over to Hawk and he nodded.

"You were there today?" I said.

"Yes, sir," she said. "I work four days on Bonnet's Cut and two days off. I cook, I clean, I take care of the island business."

"Mr. Steiner is on the island now?" I said.

She nodded. "Arrived two days ago," she said. "With Miss Palmer. They're planning a party for the weekend. VIPs, we're told. Flying into Nassau."

I grabbed my phone and showed her a photo of Carly Ly.

"Yes," she said. "She's there. With five other young ladies. Special guests of Mr. Peter who perform special duties for the VIPs."

Shona appeared to have lots of distaste for those special duties. She shook her head and closed her eyes, taking in a deep breath.

"And what are those duties, Shona?" Hawk said.

"We are not permitted to say," Shona said. "It's in our

agreement with Mr. Peter. But I can say, what else would an old man want of women so young? Yes, I have seen things. Things that I wish I could wash from my mind. Where are these girls' parents? Why would they come to such a place and be able to stay so long? Many don't speak English. But this girl, the one you showed me, is American."

"She's from Boston," Hawk said. "Needs to get back to Boston."

"Are you going to hurt Mr. Peter?" Shona said. "Whatever his personal tastes, he is good to us. I'm paid and treated well. Not like Miss Palmer. I think she enjoys screaming at the staff. Throwing things. I saw her once slap a guard for moving too slowly on the dock."

"What happens to Mr. Peter is up to Mr. Peter," I said. "How many guards?"

"Five," Shona said. "Plus a new man. A white man who works very closely with Mr. Peter."

"Does he have gray hair and wear gray clothes?" I said. "Goes by the name Ruger."

"The man I'm speaking of is called Mr. Grey."

"Cute," Hawk said.

"As a button," I said.

"He arrived with Mr. Peter and Miss Palmer," Shona said. "He has a cold face, as if it's never seen the sun."

"What about the staff?" I said.

"Eight," she said. "Many more on Friday to set up for the weekend party."

Godfrey walked over to Rex's cluttered desk and found a yellow legal pad. He swept away the dominoes and set it in front of Shona. "Draw us the rooms in the main house," he said. "Show us where this man Steiner eats, sleeps, and stays. And this Gray Man, too."

"He carries a gun," she said. "All the guards have guns. They speak as if someone might be coming."

"And they'd be right," Hawk said.

Godfrey looked to us over the table as Shona began to sketch off squares with notes on the legal pad. He reached into his pocket for more cash and set it in front of her. "Take off the next few nights," he said. "You have a cold. You got hurt. A family member is sick."

"Yes, sir," she said. "You'll be coming to the party?"

"Always enjoy me a good party," Hawk said.

Godfrey walked out the front door. Hawk and I followed. Godfrey picked up a half-burned cigar and lit it again. The sun was going down over the marina, twenty or more fishing boats and pleasure boats huddling into their narrow slots. Godfrey blew smoke in the wind. The sun big and shimmering over the ocean and Bonnet's Cut, forty miles away.

"When?" Godfrey said.

Hawk looked to me. I nodded back.

"Can you be ready to go after midnight?" Hawk said.

Godfrey nodded. They pounded fists.

We walked down the steps and back to the rental. The skies were darkening with a slate-black line of clouds approaching from the south. Hawk shielded his eyes with the flats of his hands.

"Hmm," Hawk said. "Red skies this morning."

"Remind me to skip dinner."

56

IT DIDN'T START TO RAIN until we got halfway to Bonnet's Cut. I again contemplated the subtleness of the sea and how its most dreaded creatures glide under the water. My stomach undulating along with my thoughts.

"You take those pills?" Hawk said.

"Two."

"Don't throw up on my shoes," Hawk said. "I like these shoes."

He was dressed in black military pants and a black T-shirt. Rain beaded off the top of his bald head. He had the .50-cal Magnum strapped over one shoulder, the gun tightly wrapped in a garbage bag with string.

"Wouldn't dream of it," I said.

Hawk and Godfrey inflated a small dinghy with an air pump. Rex would drop us as close as possible to the jetty and then Godfrey on the opposite side. Godfrey would swim his way onto the beach.

As Godfrey was a native of the islands with much more practice, I didn't argue with the plan.

I wore a navy shirt, navy pants with side compartments

for ammo, and a pair of dark running shoes. I didn't think running around the islands in flip-flops would be practical. Although I might as well have dressed in a neon tuxedo and carried an ooga-ooga horn. According to what Shona told Godfrey, cameras were everywhere.

At least we knew where the guards slept and their routines. And we knew the small cottage where the young girls, including Carly Ly, slept.

I held on to the railing as the boat sliced through a large black wave, taking us up high and then crashing us back down hard. I could barely make out Rex inside the pilothouse, a lump of dark shadow in a trucker's cap, the glowing tip of a cigar clamped in his teeth.

"What about those other girls?" Hawk said.

I looked around the boat and nodded to the quarters belowdeck.

"You talk to Godfrey about this?"

I shook my head.

"Want me to talk to Godfrey?"

"Better to ask forgiveness than permission."

"After we lock down that main house and account for the guards," Hawk said. "Bring the girls down to the docks. Ain't no time to be rowing."

"Great minds."

"Be crazy as hell," Hawk said.

The rain started to fall harder, stinging my face, and we went inside. Godfrey was there filling a coffee cup, half a sandwich in hand.

"Hungry?"

"He already ate," Hawk said.

We sat in a little nook by a window, the sky and seas equally black. A row of colorful bottles behind Hawk's head rattled and shook. A nice collection of whiskeys and rum. The thought of each of them made me sick. I excused myself to the head, threw up, and then ran a trickle of cold water in my hand. I cupped my hand for the water and washed out my mouth.

I soon made my way to the wheelhouse, where Rex checked a computer screen displaying the water currents and patterns of other boats. In the darkness, he pointed to the island and showed we had a clear path that night.

Rex looked at his big diver's watch and then back to me, grunting and pointing back to where Godfrey and Hawk stood in the rain.

I could barely make out the island as we chugged along, illuminated in cracks of lightning, the rain driving in sheets across the black water. Rex got us closer and then cut the engines, and we bobbed up and down silently.

I could make out the shore better now as Hawk set the dinghy into the water.

Godfrey handed him the oars. I handed Godfrey the rope and set down the ladder onto the dinghy.

"Would you like me to whistle 'Secret Agent Man'?" I said.

"Will it help keep down your lunch?"

"It just might."

Hawk nodded and began to row toward the jetty.

57

WE MADE OUR WAY onto the jetty, pulling the dinghy up onto the rocks before Hawk punctured it with a long knife and kicked it into the water. We kept to the western side of the jagged rocks, crouching in shadows until we dashed into a thick patch of foliage at the southern tip of Bonnet's Cut.

I was so glad to be off the boat that I nearly kissed solid ground. Moving into a thick patch of coconut trees and saltwater bush, we kept low and away from the security lights mounted on palms rocking in the wind. Beyond the trees, a concrete path snaked up to the big house. I pointed to the blue dome as Hawk unwrapped the .500 Magnum, his pockets bulging with more rounds.

We followed the path from behind row after row of blooming hibiscus and birds-of-paradise. The air was wet and smelled of citrus. We would meet up with Godfrey at the house. In twenty minutes, Rex would circle back and idle at the pier.

As we got closer to the big round house, we saw more lights and cameras high in the trees and trained on the grounds. Anyone who was watching at three a.m. would know we'd arrived. I carried the gun in my right hand.

The closer we got to the big house, we heard music and laughter. Splashing.

"Sound like the party started without us," Hawk said.

"The nerve."

Bougainvillea bloomed bright red, covering most of a stucco wall. The pool sat directly below the main house, facing west. We darted out of the thick shrubs and up the hill to get a view over the wall.

It was a small party. But I could clearly see Peter Steiner in what could politely be called a blue banana hammock. A topless Poppy Palmer sat alongside him, reclining in a lounge chair. They seemed to be delighted with the rain.

"Poppy?" Hawk said, whispering.

I nodded.

"Sounds right," he said. "Woman could pop a damn eye out with those things."

Three young women frolicked in the pool, ducking under the water and swimming to the other side, where they would suddenly reappear. They chirped and laughed in high voices, calling out to Poppy. Finally, Poppy jumped off the chair and dove into the pool with them.

There was much frivolity and laugher to the beat of electric dance music. An Asian girl emerged from the pool in a teeny-weenie pink bikini.

"Carly?" Hawk said.

I shook my head.

Hawk pointed to the cottage across the way. I nodded.

He ran off into the darkness to connect with Godfrey. I jogged down the hill, through row after row of tropical flowers and plants, the rain falling harder now. This close to the main house, there was enough light to plainly see where I was going. My stomach felt hollow and my shoulders tight. I knew they were with us now, watching, making me an easy target for Ruger.

I found another path snaking from the northern side of the pool. The layout was exactly as Shona had drawn it, down to the wooden carving of a mermaid on the wall of the cottage. It looked like a replica fashioned from an old whaling ship. A light was on by the front door.

I flicked on a small flashlight I'd brought, opened the unlocked door, and walked inside. It was cool and quiet inside the cottage, with only the hum of the air conditioner. I pressed into the first door to the left, where I found two girls asleep in two small beds.

Both girls, very young, with platinum-blond hair, shot upright in the bed, shielding their blue eyes and speaking to me in what sounded like Russian. I asked them three times for Carly Ly. When they didn't answer, I showed them the photo on my phone.

One of the girls, who looked all of twelve, pointed back into the hall. I smiled, put a finger to my lips, and moved farther into the cottage. Two bedrooms, two baths, a kitchen, and a common area.

Carly slept on a couch in the common area. I shook her awake.

She woke up with a scream and tried to bite my hand. I covered her mouth.

"I came from Boston," I said. "Maria Tran got your email."

She stopped screaming. I let go slowly, careful she didn't bite into one of my fingers.

"You know Maria?" she said.

I told her that I'd met her father and sister at their family restaurant on Revere Beach. The more I spoke, the more she seemed to believe me. I tried to appear as cool and trustworthy as possible, as armed men were probably coming for us.

"But I never sent Maria an email," she said.

My stomach tightened as I gripped the handle of my gun. I understood now and nodded to the sliding glass doors. "Leave everything and come with me."

She was dressed only in a Pats T-shirt that hit her knees.

"What about the others?" she said.

I ran into the first bedroom and motioned for the Russian girls to come with me. They looked so much alike they could've been twins. Their bodies shook and chins quivered as Carly tried to explain she was following me, pointing to the back door. When they started to pack the clothes, Carly grabbed their arms and shook them. "There's no time," she said.

Through the glass, I saw a bank of hibiscus plants rocking in the wind and rain. I slid open the door and motioned to the girls.

We could make our way north and down the hill from the big house. I looked at my watch. Rex would be there in ten minutes.

Hawk knew when and where to meet. All I had to do was get the girls to the landing. Like my uncle Bob used to say, all was going according to Hoyle.

The Russians whispered to themselves as they followed me and Carly. At one point, Carly lost her footing and nearly toppled down the hill. I caught her, and she kicked off her slippery flip-flops, scurrying behind, careful with each step.

I stopped and looked down to the illuminated pier, yet to see Rex. Five minutes.

Then there was shouting and shooting. Quick pistol shots up on the hill. The lights in the big domed house went dark. One of the Russians, blond hair plastered to her head, makeup streaming down her face, started to cry.

I winked at her. I tried to think of any Russian words but could only come up with *borscht* and *Bolshevik*.

I pointed down to the pier. One girl nodded and said something to the other. It was hard to tell which was which.

"They said if we made trouble, they'd kill us," Carly said.

"Not tonight."

Carly nodded.

We found a series of steps made of stone and coral with a terrace every ten feet or so, landscaped with neat rows of blooming flowers and tropical plants and what appeared to be Roman statues.

We made it down three terraces before we heard footsteps and heavy breathing. I lifted the Browning and pointed it over the hedgerows. Hawk and Godfrey broke through the brush, both out of breath, Godfrey placing his hands on his thighs like a sprinter after a long race.

"How many?" I said.

"Three guards," Godfrey said.

"And the others?"

"Left two in the dirt," Hawk said.

"Ruger?" I said.

Hawk shook his head. Godfrey looked at his watch and motioned us away from the garden terrace and down onto the next series of steps. Only three more minutes and we'd hop on board and head straight for Cat Island.

We let the girls go first down to the pier. I motioned for Godfrey and Hawk to follow while I covered them.

At the top of the stone steps near the big house, a man in dark clothing appeared.

I fired at him. He disappeared as someone shot back.

I moved downward from rocky terrace to rocky terrace, off the steps, cutting my face and arms on the broken vines and limbs until I reached the landing. Hawk was speaking French to the blond girls. They seemed to understand him.

"Rex?" I said.

"He'll be here," Godfrey said.

Thirty seconds. All I saw was blackness and more rain beyond the dock.

Rain dripped over Godfrey's lean black face and twisted down his graying beard. Bright lights clicked on all over the island while a high-pitched alarm pulsed from up the hill. He looked to Hawk and nodded.

Godfrey moved toward the staircase and started shooting. Hawk and the girls ran out onto the pier.

"Go," Godfrey said.

I didn't need to be asked twice.

I ran. Godfrey fired more.

We waited. We waited more. A minute passed.

No Rex. No Godfrey.

The shooting had stopped, and all I could hear was the

creaking of the dock and the strong wind coming off the ocean. A moment later, Hawk lifted his chin at the Roman steps.

A muscled guard marched Godfrey down to the edge of the pier. He had his gun against the back of Godfrey's head.

The sea churned and lashed at the edge of the pier. Rex wasn't coming.

"You told me everything is better in the Bahamas?" I said.

"It is," Hawk said, raising his massive gun fast, and shot the guard.

The guard caught the large round in the chest and fell onto a heap. I heard another shot, and Godfrey tumbled down into the sand like a marionette with cut strings.

I pulled the girls down to the pier and shielded them with my body.

Out of the darkness, Ruger appeared and stepped over Godfrey, picking up his gun.

Two more men followed down from the terraced gardens. I recognized the black guard as one of the men who tried to snatch Mattie in Southie.

Everyone had guns trained on me and Hawk. The girls were facedown and crying on the wet dock. It wasn't a pretty situation.

"Spenser," Ruger said. "Time to talk."

58

AFTER DRAGGING OFF GODFREY and the girls, Ruger and the two men from Cerberus marched us up to the main house. The blue dome shone bright in the dark, all the windows glowing as if the house were a large glass lantern. It was frigid when we were brought inside to stand under the mosaic blue dome. Ruger held the gun on me, still and lifeless. Not even seeming to blink once.

Steiner sat nearby in a high-back bamboo chair, smoking a cigar. He had a white terry-cloth robe, open and exposing his body and the aforementioned banana hammock.

"Do you mind covering up," I said. "There's only so much I can take."

Steiner grinned, lashing his robe closed as Poppy Palmer walked in through the kitchen. She had on a similar robe, cut short to show off her thick, muscular legs. Her black hair wet and spiky like an eighties rock star's. As she wandered in, her finger traced the edge of a mahogany bar.

Poppy sang to herself and poured herself a big drink from a crystal decanter.

She took a sip and then poured out two more into crystal

glasses. She handed one to me and tried to hand one to Hawk. "Warms the heart, doll," she said.

Hawk just stared down at her. He was shirtless, having used his shirt to tie a tourniquet around Godfrey's leg.

Poppy held the drink and ran a hand over his bare pecs and raked his abs with her long nails.

"We could've had some fun," she said.

"Rather fuck a bucktoothed goat," Hawk said.

Poppy stopped smiling. The black man from Miami stood at her back, the other guard stood tall and alert beside Steiner. I was within five feet of them. If I could get to Ruger, Hawk could perhaps jump the other two. We might get shot in the process, but at least there was hope.

Ruger stared at me as he held a gun toward my midsection. It was a simple, slick .22 with a suppressor at the end. He could kill me and Hawk with less sound than clicking his tongue.

His gray eyes didn't move. Gray shirt under a soaked gray linen suit jacket. His skin looked like a corpse.

"A man without honor is worse than dead," I said.

"Cervantes."

"You're soulless," I said. "But literate."

Ruger shrugged. He tilted his head, staring at me. He appeared to be looking forward to me shuffling off this mortal coil.

I took the drink Poppy had poured us. Cognac. Only the best for Spenser before he gets shot. I tried to control my breathing. I was wet. I was tired. I was nauseated and concerned. I wasn't thrilled with how the night was going.

"What about the girls?" I said.

"There will always be more girls," Steiner said, his voice raspy and worn. His face lean and tan with white stubble. "Like there will always be more champagne and parties. As long as you have money and friends, you make your own rules."

"The police and Feds might feel different."

"They've tried before," he said. "And they'll try again. But how many cops do you know who are both stupid and corrupt?"

"Not these," I said. "Think of me when you drop the soap in jail."

"Yeah," Hawk said. "Heard them boys already lining up to take a shot at your narrow white ass. Man into kids get that special treatment."

Poppy wandered over to a very long leather couch. She sat on the arm, leaning back with her robe open, nearly exposing her breasts. She smiled at me and pulled on her cognac. Her eyes sleepy and relaxed as Steiner took a seat beside her. Steiner took Poppy's glass and took a sip, licking his lips and turning to Ruger.

"Take them outside and shoot them," Steiner said. "Weigh down the bodies and have them dropped off on the reef. The one with all the sharks."

"Damn," Hawk said. "This motherfucker thinks of everything."

I set down the glass. I looked Ruger right in the eye. I'd been thinking of him since I'd heard he was back in Boston. I remembered every second of the bridge, him walking to me in the snow, a hatted shadow raising a gun and firing three rounds. It would be like that, only without the comfort of an icy river to catch me.

I looked to Hawk. Hawk's whole body coiled, like a jaguar.

I waited for him to jump on the guards while I'd launch myself at Ruger. I suddenly felt like Butch and Sundance racing out to face the Bolivian Army. I swallowed and inhaled a deep breath through my nose.

Hawk nodded. I took a small step forward.

Ruger lifted his gun at me. A twinkle in his eye and a small twitch at the corner of his mouth. I waited and held my breath.

Ruger pivoted in a blur and shot Peter Steiner in the forehead.

Poppy Palmer screamed and rolled from the couch as Ruger immediately shot the other two guards. My ears rang, feet unsteady, not sure what I'd just seen.

"The girls and your friend are safe," Ruger said. "Come with me."

For once in my life, words escaped me. My mouth hung open. Hawk looked at the Gray Man and the Gray Man at him.

Hawk nodded.

"Why'd you shoot Godfrey?" Hawk said.

"The boat captain worked for Steiner," Ruger said. "He sold out both of you. I shot Godfrey to save him."

"Can't trust no one these days," Hawk said.

"What shall we do about the woman?" Ruger said.

Poppy Palmer straddled Peter Steiner's body, a hole in

the center of his forehead leaking lots of blood. His brown eyes stared at the ceiling, jaw slack. She was crying and stroking his face and whispering sweet nonsensical things into his ear.

"Leave her," I said.

I reached down and snatched Poppy Palmer to her feet. She clawed at my face with her long nails, drawing blood. Hawk backhanded her and grabbed her by the front of her robe, dragging her outside into the rain. A nervous young black woman in a maid's uniform appeared from the kitchen, and Hawk yelled for her to bring him some rope.

I followed Ruger to one of the cottages, where we found Godfrey lying on the couch and Carly with the two Russian girls. Ruger pulled a cell phone from his pocket and began to dial. He said something harsh and quick in Russian and looked back to me. The rain picked up, falling in a slanting silver sheet across an immaculate green lawn.

"Who are they?" I said.

"Daughters of a very important and very rich man in Moscow," Ruger said. "The man's enemy kidnapped them and sold them to Steiner."

"You cozied up to Steiner to find them," I said. "Waiting for the right time to make a move."

Ruger's mouth twitched a bit. "I set in motion a nice diversion."

Carly rushed out into the rain to round up the other three girls who'd been poolside with Steiner and Poppy. We followed her outside, where Ruger looked up into the sky.

"I guess an apology is in order," I said.

Ruger shrugged. He walked over to the Russian girls, wet and shaking, and fitted his linen jacket around one of them.

"Some other time," he said, disappearing.

A few minutes later, I heard the whoosh-whoosh of a helicopter and saw a spotlight rove over the property. A black military-style helicopter set down in the open land behind the main house.

Ruger emerged from the domed house with a heavy canvas travel bag slung over his shoulder, walking the two girls onto the helicopter.

He stopped for a moment to place a gray fedora on his head. Ruger looked to me and Hawk and tipped his hat before sliding up beside the copilot.

We watched the helicopter lift off Bonnet's Cut and fly north toward Nassau.

"Now we gonna owe his ass," Hawk said.

"The world is round."

59

WE STAYED ON BONNET'S CUT until late the next afternoon. Hawk helped Godfrey with his wounds and Godfrey helped explain the situation with his friends at the Bahamian police. There were kidnapped girls, dead men, and Poppy Palmer crying foul. The police took her anyway and I was relieved I didn't have to fit her in the overhead bin on the flight home. Her fate now in the hands of the Feds.

Three days and many phone calls, interviews, and meetings with the American consulate later, Hawk and I were back on Cat Island. I'd made arrangements for Carly to fly to Miami to both meet her sister and speak with the Feds. Another American girl, a sixteen-year-old from West Palm, was also headed home, while two teenage Cuban girls sought asylum in the Bahamas.

That morning, we decided to take a run up Como Hill, the tallest peak on the islands. We'd been running for a few miles already when Hawk pointed out our goal, and we dashed up the rocky path.

At the top of the hill was a medieval-style monastery fashioned of stone. Four buildings, a place of worship, a tall turret, a cookhouse, and a small room where the priest slept. It was tranquil and meditative. You could hear the click and whir of insects in the scrub around us. High above, we could see every corner of Cat Island.

I caught my breath. Hawk, hands on top of his head, studied my face.

"Damn," he said. "She got you good."

I touched the gouges from Poppy Palmer.

"Could've been worse."

"Captain Rex," Hawk said.

"I guess what happened between him and Godfrey is now between the devil and the deep blue sea."

"Better not ask."

I walked up the stone steps and peered into the place of worship. I tried to picture this monk priest hauling every stone up the hill as an act of humility and faith. A salty wind blew in from the open windows, fluttering the pages of a water-logged guest book.

"I believe I just might stay awhile," Hawk said.

Hawk pointed beyond a wooden cross and a tomb where the priest was buried to a spot along the west coast of the island.

"That's my beach," he said. "Maybe start building while I'm here."

"I built that cabin in Maine," I said. "Very therapeutic."

"Fuck that," Hawk said, grinning. "Getting me the best contractor on the island."

"Seems like you have your hands full," I said. "With Karena."

"Been thinking about sending a ticket to Grace Bennett," Hawk said. "Lots here to paint."

"Landscape?" I said. "Or portrait?"

"How much would you pay for a painting of Black Moses?"

"At least five bucks," I said.

I studied the rocky terrain through the scrub brush and scraggly trees. We'd take the road back to the beach and then head north to the cottage. There was time for a few beers, maybe some conch fritters, and then the flight back to Boston. I looked forward to seeing Susan and Pearl and explaining to Mattie about how extradition for Poppy might work.

"The Gray Man," Hawk said. "Damn."

"Getting that head through customs will be tricky," I said.

"Man like Ruger don't go through customs."

"I would've preferred seeing Steiner in court."

"Yeah?" Hawk said. "Not me. I liked to see what was left of him bleeding out on that nice rug."

"Glad we have Rita," I said. "Getting money for his victims might take years."

"And then some," Hawk said. "Man like Steiner knows every nook and cranny to hide his cash."

"Arrogance," I said. "All he had to do was hand over that backpack."

"Folks like that don't believe in the rules," Hawk said. "You white and have money and you can do whatever you want."

"What if you're black with money?"

"Don't always work like that."

I nodded. Hawk motioned down to the steep rocky path. We bumped fists.

"Race you back," Hawk said.

The hot wind swept across the stones and broken rocks by the monastery, whispering through the cracks and holes, jostling an old bell inside.

"With all you did," I said. "I might even let you win."

"Haw," Hawk said. "Never have. Never will."

"Bottle of Iron Horse?" I said.

"Two bottles of Iron Horse," he said.

Without a word, I sped down the hill, Hawk catching up fast. The path rocky and steep down to the beach road. Out of respect, I didn't let up in the least.

60

ON MY THIRD DAY back in Boston, Matthew Greebel, attorney at law, rapped on my office door.

I was less than delighted to see him. But I let him in anyway.

He wore a pinstripe suit, his black hair slicked back, and smelled of men's room cologne.

The knock had awoken Pearl from a slumber on the couch, and she jumped off in time to bark at his pant leg.

"Didn't realize this office allowed animals," Greebel said.

"They don't," I said. "Get to the point fast and maybe no one will notice."

Greebel smiled so big, I was pretty sure I could play "The Entertainer" across his upper teeth. I leaned back in my chair as Pearl jumped back onto the couch, ever vigilant to our less-than-distinguished visitor.

He took a seat without being asked.

"I guess you've heard the news."

"Poppy Palmer has disappeared."

"Bahamian authorities had nothing to hold her on," he

said. "Did you expect her to fly back to Boston and answer these ridiculous charges about Peter Steiner? The man was brutally murdered, for God's sake."

"What a complete and total loss for humanity," I said.

"These girls knew what they were getting into."

"Would you prefer leaving by door or window?"

Greebel smiled and held up his hands. "Spense," he said. "Spense. I came with a fair and just offer for your clients. For any type of hardships they think they endured."

"Talk to Rita Fiore."

"I can't talk to that nasty woman," he said. "The language she used is highly unprofessional."

I nodded behind him. "Door?" I said. "Or window?"

Greebel smiled. He quoted a figure for each of the girls named in the civil suit, which now included Carly Ly and a few others. It was a great deal of money.

"Not my decision to make."

"Or you can play tough guy and keep everything tied up in court until these girls are grandmas," Greebel said.

"I'll pass it on to Rita."

"Um," he said. "This is a limited-time offer. Better act now."

I took a breath, stood, and walked to the bay window. I looked down to the sidewalk along Berkeley Street and then back to Greebel. "Only three stories," I said. "You might even make it."

"Can you imagine the trauma and horror Poppy has gone through," he said. "She's been abused for years by Steiner and then has to witness his murder and decapitation. It will take a lot of money and therapy to deal with everything."

"Those girls suffered much more," I said. "No kid should go through that."

Greebel shrugged and was about to climb out of the client chair when Mattie Sullivan entered the room. Mattie had been running errands for Rita that morning and was dressed in a green skirt with a long-sleeved black top. I believe this was the first time I'd seen Mattie in a skirt.

She looked over at Greebel and then over at me.

"What the hell's this?"

"Apparently your clients have been offered a settlement from the great beyond by Poppy Palmer, via this dirtbag."

"Hey," Greebel said.

I shushed him and waited for Mattie.

"How much?" Mattie said.

I told her.

"That's less than a quarter of what's in the suit."

"I know."

"You tell this guy to go fuck himself?"

I smiled and leaned against the sill of the bay window. "You know," I said. "I was just getting to that."

"You'll never find her," Greebel said. "Poppy can go anywhere. And has the money to live as she's grown accustomed."

Greebel's good-natured grin had melted. He stood up, buttoned his coat, and turned to Mattie Sullivan. "Hope the goddamn backpack was worth the mess."

I looked to Mattie and winked.

"Front door it is," I said.

I walked up to Matthew Greebel as he winced and

covered his face. I reached under his suit jacket and grabbed hold of his belt, lifting him up off the floor and marching him through my office and anteroom, where I unceremoniously dumped him into the hallway. Pearl was behind me, barking through my legs.

I pretended to dust off my hands.

I closed the door and walked back inside.

"I've already found more girls," Mattie said.

"I heard."

"And Rita knows people who can find Steiner's stash," she said. "She said they'll find Poppy Palmer and stick a microscope up her ass."

"That sounds like Rita."

Mattie smoothed down the wrinkles in her long green skirt and smiled. She looked self-conscious and a bit awkward in her new clothes.

"I think you look very nice."

"But where will I carry the gun?" she said.

"In a nice and fancy handbag?"

"Screw that."

"Talk to Captain Glass," I said. "Maybe she can give you some fashion tips."

"Already have," Mattie said. "Can I buy you lunch and tell you about it?"

"How about we walk over to Davio's, sit at the bar, and I buy you lunch?"

"That works."

I slipped into a lightweight khaki blazer. "You put in an application for the police academy," I said.

Mattie smiled. "Ah."

"Quirk told me."

"Hope you're not disappointed," Mattie said.

"On you not following in the footsteps of your sleuthing mentor?"

"Yep."

"Do not go where the path may lead, go instead where there is no path and leave a trail."

"Pretty good advice," Mattie said. "You make that up just now?"

"Absolutely," I said.

Mattie sat down by Pearl and rubbed her ears and neck. Pearl found a nice bone to keep her occupied while we had lunch.

"Susan loves her," Mattie said. "But she made me promise not to tell you."

"I know."

"She wasn't even mad about the fancy shoes Pearl ate."

"Did she say anything at all about me?" I said.

Mattie shrugged. "She thinks you're pretty okay for a Boston thug."

"I knew it."

"But Susan ain't easy to live with."

"I'm no cakewalk myself," I said. "Glad we both celebrate being individuals who often like being alone."

We walked down the office steps and out onto Berkeley Street, turning left toward Davio's. People rushed past us, without notice, as we took our own sweet time. I enjoyed not being in a hurry.

"Susan says my mom would be proud of me," Mattie said. "That I don't have to push so hard all the time. I can just be."

"You know Susan did go to Harvard?"

"Which makes her smart?" Mattie said, pronouncing *smart* in the proper Boston fashion.

"As a whip."